T0147137

Abducted

Abducted

A Dangerous Distractions Novel

Samantha Keith

LYRICAL PRESS
Kensington Publishing Corp.
www.kensingtonbooks.com

LYRICAL PRESS BOOKS are published by

Kensington Publishing Corp.
119 West 40th Street
New York, NY 10018

All Kensington titles, imprints, and distributed lines are available at special quantity discounts for bulk purchases for sales promotion, premiums, fund-raising, educational, or institutional use.

Special book excerpts or customized printings can also be created to fit specific needs. For details, write or phone the office of the Kensington Sales Manager: Kensington Publishing Corp., 119 West 40th Street, New York, NY 10018. Attn. Sales Department. Phone: 1-800-221-2647.

Lyrical Press and Lyrical Press logo Reg. U.S. Pat. & TM Off.

First Electronic Edition: August 2018
eISBN-13: 978-15161-0673-8
eISBN-10: 1-5161-0673-3

First Print Edition: August 2018
ISBN-13: 978-1-5161-0670-7
ISBN-10: 1-5161-0670-9

Printed in the United States of America

Acknowledgments

I have so many amazing people to dedicate this book to and to thank for its success. My husband, Jesse, you have been beside me through every hurdle. You're the most driven, positive, and motivated person I know. Seeing those qualities in you have made me persevere. You've also been my inspiration for these strong, yet sensitive heroes. Thank you for always supporting me and sharing in every up and down.

Skylar, this book is for you, and for every moment of attention it has taken from you. There will never be a moment of failure in my life because I have you. If there's anything I want you to learn from this, it's to never give up on your dreams. I love you so much. You are my greatest teacher, and you hold my entire heart.

For my dad, who was never able to achieve his dreams. I'm eternally grateful that your creativity lives through me and that you passed on this gift, in a different form of art. For my mom and David, who have always supported me. Mom, you've always believed in me and have never doubted my passions. I've withheld my manuscripts from you for a reason. I want you to read my writing for the first time as a published work, so that I can truly earn the pride you so easily lavish on me. Now, you have good reason!

I'd like to say a big thank you to my agent, Liz. I appreciate your time and effort throughout this journey. Caralee, thank you for all you've taught me. You've been a solid resource of information and experience, and have been my number one cheerleader since day one. I wouldn't be where I am had we not crossed paths. You're a saint. And to my wonderful critique partner and soul sister, Danielle. I love working alongside you every day and our daily mom-struggle exchanges. This journey has been more fun than I could have imagined having you a part of my life.

I'd also like to say a very special thank you to my fantastic editor, Selena. I'm so grateful you and Rebecca saw something in my work and were willing to give me this opportunity and help make *Abducted* what it is now.

Lastly, thank you so very much to my readers! This has been a long journey, and it means the world to me to finally have *Abducted* published. This novel holds my blood, sweat, and many tears. I fell in love with this story the moment the idea came to me, and I've never given up on it. I only hope that you, my reader, will love it half as much as I do.

Chapter 1

A bead of sweat broke out on his brow, and he wiped it away with his sleeve. Despite the cool air, he was roasting in his black camouflage gear. She should be home and in bed by now. Last Saturday night she'd been home by midnight, and even earlier on other nights of the week that he'd conducted surveillance. His pulse beat steadily against his eardrums with impatience. It didn't matter. He'd be waiting for her when she decided to come home. There was no chance in hell he was backing out of this job now.

Headlights cut through the night as a car pulled up to the front gate. Determination tensed his muscles, and his lips curved.

It's about damn time.

The passenger door opened. He sunk lower in the shadows, pressing his back against the outside of the garage. He was out of sight, but still had a direct view of his target. Satisfaction brought his breath to a steady pace. Once she got inside, he'd give her some time to fall asleep, and then he'd make his move. Her delicious bare leg stepped out of the car, revealing a barely-there miniscule dress. She laughed hysterically and pitched forward, nearly doing a face-plant on the pavement. He closed his eyes and shook his head. Just great. She was wasted.

Chapter 2

"Shit." The spike of her five-inch pump caught on the foot well as she stepped out of the car. She grabbed the car door for support and righted herself.

"Go to bed. You're drunk," teased Carly from the driver's seat. Lana tugged the hem of her tight minidress and leaned back into the car.

"Am not." She stuck out her tongue, then grinned and shut the car door. She'd only had a glass or two of champagne the entire time they'd been at the nightclub, and was completely sober now. Well, mostly anyway.

The cool midnight air caressed her exposed skin. She waved good-bye as she approached the property gate, punched in the code, and waited as the wrought-iron hinges swung open. The stamped concrete drive split into two like the long tongue of a snake. One direction led off to the main house and wrapped itself around the mountainous stone fountain. The other path stretched to the guesthouse, where she lived. The isolation from the main house granted her the privacy she needed from her father and stepmother.

Her high heels scuffed against the slick concrete as she strode down the mouth of the one-hundred-foot drive. Patio stones dotted the grass off the drive to the guesthouse beyond the pool. A line of bushes and tall shrubs peppered the front of the guesthouse.

Thunder rumbled from the sky, and a raindrop plopped on her forehead. The fountain in the backyard gurgled as water rushed over the massive stones to collect at the pool beneath. In the daylight, the sounds from the fountain were calming, but tonight it was too loud. Too invasive. The smell of moisture hung in the air from the rain earlier. It was chilly, but a coat would have clashed with her outfit.

She opened up her rhinestone-encrusted clutch to fish out her house keys. A movement out of the corner of her eye made her feet hitch. She grasped her keys in her fist and scanned the yard around her. The breeze kicked up and rustled the leaves overhead.

Just the wind.

Large elm trees and strategically groomed shrubs decorated the grounds. Tonight, the brooding mosaic of shapes gave her the creeps. The Mediterranean-style monstrous house hovered behind her. One lone light on the main level switched off like a creature closing its eye. Anne, the maid, would be the only one home.

Once she disappeared into the back, Carly backed out of the drive. The headlights sliced through the night before vanishing. The sensor light above her head flickered before going out. Her spine stiffened. She stepped through the grass and onto the patio stones, the safety of the guesthouse only feet away. Soon she would be in her cozy warm bed.

Carly dropping her off was a sour reminder that she still lived under the household of her parents and her lack of independence. At least in the guesthouse, she was concealed from their scrutiny and could come and go as she pleased. Thankfully, this weekend they were away for one of her father's business meetings in Monaco. He wouldn't find out until later in the week that she'd gone out tonight.

A shiver raced up her spine as the chilly breeze disturbed the placidity of the night. It was darker than usual. A cloud crept over the moon, shielding it against its will. The obscurity of its glow rippled in warning. The hairs on the back of her neck stood on end.

Someone was watching her.

Her throat closed. Razor-sharp fear bit into her. Her eyes darted around the shadowed yard in search of a predator. Tall, freshly groomed shrubs swayed in the breeze. Goose bumps raced over her flesh. Paranoia bubbled up in her throat and threatened to strangle her.

She braced for the attack, but it didn't come.

Get a grip, Lana.

She stabbed her key into the lock and swung the door open. Inside the house, her hand sought the light switch and flicked it on. She slammed the door, her fingers fumbling as she snapped the lock shut.

She was too old to be getting spooked.

At least for tonight, the closeness of the main house was a slight comfort. She raced from room to room and flicked on every light.

Empty.

She exhaled a pent-up breath.

She dropped onto the edge of her bed and began to undo her shoes. Her fingers stilled on the clasp of the black leather strap. Her eyes fixed on the closet door. Had she left it closed? She couldn't remember. The room crackled with tension. Her heart beat triple time. Her breath came out in short, sharp puffs.

She rose to her feet. Sweat moistened her palms. Shoe gripped in her hand, the heel wielded like a spear, she advanced on the closet. Her hand closed around the smooth metal knob. Her pulse raged with the force of a fire hose.

She yanked the door open.

Rods and racks of clothes and shoes stared back at her like the blank eyes of the stuffed animals that crowded her dresser.

Nothing.

She released her held breath through tight, exasperated lips. The shoe dropped from her limp fingers and landed to the carpet with a soft *thud*.

She raked her tingling hand through her loose hair and squeezed her eyes shut. *What is the matter with me?*

She had been on edge for days. She needed to get her mind off of the nagging presence that plagued her. She'd call Gina. Gina always made her feel better, and it was never too late to call her. Gina would find it hilarious that she'd gone out tonight against her father's wishes. She didn't like lying to him, but there was a heck of a lot less drama when she abided by his rules. At least when he *thought* she abided by his rules.

Edward Vanderpoel had his squeaky-clean reputation and a pristine image to uphold. Every move she made played a part. She was a grown woman, for God's sake. At twenty-six years old, she was tired of living under his thumb and his ideals. She was single, but mostly because her father had never approved of her boyfriends. Besides, men sucked.

She worked hard; her father had never let her take their money for granted. She loved her dad dearly, and Grace, her stepmother, too, but it was past time she got her own place. With that thought firmly planted in her mind, she slipped out of her dress and pulled on a pair of light cotton pajamas. She reached for the phone and dialed. The nights were cool at this time of year, but her suite was always too warm. She stepped into her en suite bathroom and began to remove her makeup and get ready for bed.

"Hey, girl, how was your night?" Gina's cheery voice washed away the dark shadows.

Chapter 3

One locked door stood between him and his target. It wasn't the lock that had him concerned. It was the cameras. There was a rotating camera attached to the roof of the main house. He would have to time it perfectly. It shouldn't take him more than ten seconds to get in, but it would be tight.

He slithered across the lawn, his footsteps cushioned by the lush grass. Edging around the corner of the guesthouse, he waited and watched the camera make its rotation, timing it. *Twelve seconds.* Perfect. He had been close to snatching her in the yard, but a light had switched off in the main house. Had he moved then, she would have seen him and been able to scream loud enough to wake the neighborhood. He waited fifteen minutes after her bedroom light had turned off. Now it was time.

As soon as the camera turned toward the driveway, he made his move. He gripped a small penlight between his front teeth and pulled his lock pick set from his jacket. He inserted the two small tools. The tinkling sound of metal on metal made his movements slow and softer than they would have been.

Click.

He stepped into the dark foyer and closed the door, shutting out the eye of the camera.

If people only knew how easy it was to pick locks, even dead bolts, they wouldn't even bother. Fact of the matter, if someone wanted in and had the skills to do so, he or she was getting in. Case in point.

He pointed the penlight to illuminate the room, and his soft-soled shoes glided over the tiled floor. He had scoped the place out for the last week and knew the basic layout of her suite.

From the foyer, he would enter the kitchen. It was on the small side, but from what he had previously observed, she wasn't much of a cook. More of a soup-and-sandwich kind of girl. An eat-in breakfast bar separated the kitchen from the living room. Next to that was her bedroom with a large en suite bathroom.

He waited at the door. He trained his ears for any noises in case she'd gotten out of bed since he'd left his spot in the bushes. Her being drunk might pay off. She was probably passed out. He checked his watch. Nearly 1 a.m. He would have preferred to wait until he was certain she was asleep. But in less than two hours, he would be getting the call. By that time, he needed to check in at his location—with his captive.

He stood tense and rigid, his feet braced apart. He stepped into the dark kitchen. His mouth went dry as he put all of his tools back into the inside pocket of his jacket. He checked to make sure the next items that he would need were easily accessible. His right pocket held a soft white rag, his left a small vial of chloroform.

Feeling the rag in his pocket, his chest constricted. He was a criminal, a goddamn sicko. What in hell was he doing? He knew he was stuck, that if he decided to leave, someone else would come and finish the job. Only they would kill her.

He took a deep breath—he didn't have a choice.

The dark kitchen encouraged him to peer into the shadowed and uninhabited living room. The smell of toasted marshmallows—or was that vanilla?—wafted through the spic-and-span kitchen from some kind of decorative dish that was plugged in on the counter. His house usually smelled like floor cleaner after his housekeeper left. Other than that, it smelled like his gym bag or whatever food he had recently eaten. He crept across the kitchen and into the living room. He paused, only feet away from her bedroom door.

A giggle erupted.

What the hell?

He skirted the few feet across the room and threw himself behind the couch. Her bedroom door opened. Was someone else here? How in hell had he missed that?

Miss Lana Vanderpoel waltzed out of her bedroom, her cell phone glued to her ear. Jesus Christ. Only a woman would be sitting in her room, drunk and talking on the phone in the dark. He shook his head at the image and breathed a sigh of relief. Had she come out seconds earlier, she would have caught him. Not that he couldn't take her, but the chances of her screaming would have been high and, at the very least, would have alerted the person on the other end of the phone.

"Oh my God!" Her sudden shriek made him jump and freeze. Had she seen him?

"He didn't! What did you say?" He relaxed the tense muscles in his neck. Damn, he'd nearly gone into cardiac arrest. From here, he could peer around the side and see straight into the kitchen, and to his left, to her bedroom door.

He watched from around the side of the couch in time to see her stretch up onto her tiptoes to pull a glass out of the cupboard. Her legs were sleek and toned, her feet small and bare against the tile floor.

When she turned from the sink, the slight curve of her slim body made his throat tighten. His gaze dragged from the top of her luscious, shiny locks all the way down to her pretty little toes, savoring every inch in between. Her tiny white pajama shorts barely reached the tops of her supple thighs. Her breasts were full and high, the small outline of her nipples visible through the thin white pajama top she wore. He grew warm at the sight of her.

Her dark hair hung in loose waves nearly to her waist, and her skin was smooth, soft, and pale. Her hair was longer and softer in person. She was shorter than she looked in pictures. But then, she wasn't in her neck-breaking high heels. Even though she wasn't wearing a hint of makeup, he could see how beautiful she still was. Lana was a knockout. His throat constricted as she paced the kitchen with her back to him. All he could see was her ass. Not that he was complaining. His dick hardened at the image of having her panting beneath him, those delicious legs wrapped around his waist.

His mouth firmed. He shouldn't be having this reaction to her—didn't want it. But the sexy little thing in front of him made something unfamiliar twist in his gut. He needed to get this over with.

"My father is going to kill me when he gets back and sees I went out tonight. Damn those paparazzi." She listened for a minute. "Okay, Gina. Yeah, I'm heading to bed now too. We should get together for lunch this week. Text me. 'Night." She hung up and dropped the phone on the island counter. He watched, fascinated, as she brought the glass of water up to her delicate, full lips and sipped.

She carried the glass with her back through the living room. The light switched off, and she disappeared into her bedroom. She didn't close the door. Perfect. The fewer barriers between them the better.

With her parents out of town, this was almost too easy. He waited ten minutes, giving her the chance to drift off. As he waited, his tension grew. He didn't know whether he was capable of this. She would panic and freak out. Hell, who wouldn't? Maybe she would be asleep, and he would only have to place the rag over her mouth. God, he prayed it would be that simple.

The urge to sneak out as easily as he'd snuck in weighed on him. But he was her only chance. If he left, she was as good as dead.

He rose from his position and took a deep breath. He pulled his black knit cap over his eyebrows and gave his latex gloves a tug. He moved toward the bedroom. He stopped at the door frame. A sliver of moonlight poured through a slit in the curtains, illuminating the small mound in the center of the bed. He entered the room. Lana made no movement. She was curled on her side, her back to him. The thick carpet cushioned the weight of his feet as he lurked, closer and closer. His eye caught a lone high-heeled shoe, carelessly strewn in his path. He stepped over it, bringing him only a few feet from the edge of her bed. His pulse slowed, and his breath came out in a steady, silent rhythm. His hands hung loosely at his sides, and his eyes stayed trained on the gentle rise and fall of her breathing. He reached the side of her bed and hesitated. Jumping her from behind wasn't how he had planned it. If he put any weight on the bed, she would easily feel it and wake up. He would have to pounce on her or risk tiptoeing around to the other side of the bed.

The air changed in the room.

She stopped breathing.

She knew he was there.

Adrenaline surged through him. She bolted. He threw himself onto the bed and lunged for her. He snagged her waist with his arm and hauled her back down. She screamed, piercing his eardrums. His free hand clutched roughly over her mouth, choking the scream off almost as soon as it started.

He had to move fast.

"Don't move!" he whispered fiercely. She was panicked. Her fingernails pinched his skin through the latex glove as she clawed at the hand on her mouth. She tried to scream, her cries pitiful from behind his hand. He wouldn't be able to knock her out until she calmed down a bit.

"Stay still," he rasped against her ear. He held her tight against his chest, until her thrashes slowed.

"I'm going to move my hand now, and we're going to get off the bed. Don't scream." She jerked her head in response. He released his death grip on her jaw. He winced at the stiffness in his hand. Her fingers settled over her face to replace his. Shit. He had hurt her.

"I need you to stand up now," he instructed softly. She nodded again, and with his hand still around her waist they moved off the bed. The material of her shirt was even thinner than it had looked. The smooth, satiny texture of her skin made his fingers tingle through the wispy cotton and latex gloves. Her feet touched the ground first, because of how close she was to the edge.

He shifted over, his hand still firm on her waist. With a flutter of movement, her bony elbow clipped him square in the jaw. His teeth slammed together and left a sandy taste in his mouth, stunning him. She tore herself from his grip. "Help!" Her desperate shriek snapped him to his feet. He threw his full 225 pounds at her and tackled her to the floor. She landed on her back and he on top of her. She kicked and struggled. Her body bucked wildly in an attempt to throw him. Unfortunately for her, he was easily twice her size. She only succeeded at turning him on as her breasts jiggled beneath her shirt. It was hard for him not to notice how soft and lithe she was, how pert her breasts were and how smooth her legs. His jaw worked at the direction his mind was going. This was wrong—all of it.

"Let me go, you sonofabitch!" Her fists flew aimlessly. One after the other connected with his forearms. He caught both of her wrists in one hand and pinned them to her stomach, then lowered himself so he was lying on her chest. A sharp pain seized him in his back as her knee connected with his tailbone.

"You're making this a hell of a lot harder on yourself," he muttered. Until he had her fully restrained, he couldn't chance taking the chloroform out. She'd go even more ballistic. After she landed another blow to his back, he shifted his feet and pinned her legs in place. She was quick, but no match for his mixed martial arts training.

"What do you want?" Her words came out in gasps. Due to his weight on her, she couldn't get enough air in to yell. He didn't answer. With his free hand, he pulled out the rag and the vial. She stilled as she watched him. Her eyes grew huge. Hysteria assailed her. He numbed his mind to her panic. He had to do this. *He was her only chance.*

"No, help!" She thrashed and twisted, trying desperately to escape. With a steady hand, he opened the vial to pour the contents onto the rag.

"Please, stop." She was sobbing, her body jolting beneath him with each breath. He couldn't take it anymore; he needed to get her unconscious. He picked up the rag and brought it down on her mouth, smothering her pleas. Her head shook from side to side as she tried valiantly to breathe in fresh air.

"Shh…it's okay." He couldn't help himself. All he wanted to do was reassure her and stop her from crying. After only a minute, her head lolled to the side and she lay completely still. He waited an extra couple of seconds, then removed the rag. Her cheeks and chest were wet with tears. Acid burned the inside of his stomach at the sight. He had been here much longer than he'd anticipated. Lana Vanderpoel had put up a damn good fight. He hadn't wanted to hurt her. Had she been a man, she wouldn't have lasted two seconds.

He got to his feet and searched her room. He couldn't walk out with her slung over his shoulder. He grabbed a dark blanket off the bed and bundled it around her limp body. He had originally planned to buy her some clothes to wear, but hadn't gotten around to it. Spotting her dresser against the wall, he strode over to the drawers and pulled out a sweater and sweatpants. He knelt down and tucked the clothes into the blanket with her. He picked up his bundle and tossed her over his shoulder. Lana was small, probably no more than 110 pounds, but dead weight was difficult to manage.

He gripped her thighs tightly and weaved his way through the dark house, not daring to turn on a light. Although he had managed to cut off her screams, she had made some noise. He doubted anyone had heard, but nonetheless, he needed to get the hell out. Once he reached the door, he opened it a crack and waited for the camera. At the right moment, he slipped out and shut the door behind him. He was at the gate in less than thirty seconds. He punched in the code, the gate swung open dutifully, and he strode out as if he were no one other than the mailman.

Tomorrow would be Sunday. No one would suspect that she was missing until Monday, when she didn't show up for work. He climbed into the back of the utility van he had borrowed from a friend, which had the name of a popular plumbing company embossed on the side. He unwrapped her.

She was out. Her chest rose and fell in peaceful sleep. Due to the amount of chloroform he had given her, she would probably be out cold for a while and would wake disoriented and nauseous. He had rented a cabin that was nearly a two-hour drive away. It was in a secluded area on the beach. They wouldn't be able to stay there long, but he needed to buy them some time while he devised a plan. Before he headed to the cabin, though, he would stop, change vehicles, and ditch the plumber's van.

Lana moaned softly in her sleep, pulling him out of his trance. He reached into his bag, pulled out a roll of duct tape, and began to tape her wrists. He didn't waste time doing her ankles. If she woke up before they arrived, she would be so groggy that she wouldn't even be able to get to her feet. He covered her from head to toe in the blanket and climbed into the front seat.

After twenty minutes or so, he pulled up to his own truck and loaded her into the back seat. It was spacious, and with the seats folded back there was plenty of room. She was still blissfully asleep, but not for long. How was he going to explain to her why he'd taken her? Would she believe the truth? Leaving her to sleep, he slid into the driver's seat and began the commute to the cabin.

Chapter 4

A sick feeling in the pit of her stomach was the first thing that tugged her out of the deep sleep.

Cramps?

No. That wasn't it. What the heck was the matter with her? Her body rose and dropped involuntarily. Nausea bubbled in her throat. She wanted to sit up, but her head weighed a ton. Why was she so dizzy? She pulled her knees in closer to her chest. She reached for her stomach…but couldn't budge her hands. She tried again. Something tugged on her wrists. An alarm went off in her head. She dared to open one eye, just a slit.

This wasn't her bed. It wasn't even soft. What was this rough, scratchy blanket around her? She opened both eyes. Nausea hit her like a punch to the solar plexus. She closed her eyes on another wave. She was moving. No, she was in something that was moving—a vehicle.

Her heart beat rapidly against her breastbone. Terror sank its sharp teeth into her flesh. She was lying on the floor of a vehicle, her wrists bound, her body covered. She took a soundless deep breath and tried to calm herself. What was the last thing she remembered?

She had gone out, that's right. To a nightclub, and she had gone with friends. Carly had given her a ride home. She remembered the whole night—had she even been drunk? She had gone to bed, she was sure of it. She remembered washing up and curling up in her cozy, warm sheets… but nothing after that.

No, wait. Something had scared her.

The rest flooded back with the force of a tidal wave. She could still taste the sweet-smelling rag.

She had to stay calm. Had to stay calm and *think*. From where she lay, she couldn't see the driver, but she was able to see the front passenger seat, and it was empty. She glanced to her side, only to discover that there weren't any seats for any other passengers. She was in a pickup truck with the back seats folded up. Either this man was the one and only kidnapper, or he was the one doing the kidnap and delivery. If he wasn't the mastermind, he was surely bringing her to that person.

Her best—and maybe only—chance at escape would be when he came to remove her from the vehicle. He would expect her to be unconscious. If he was alone and not meeting anyone, she might just have a chance. Her mind was foggy, but she remembered one thing for sure: This guy was big. Not fat, but very fit and muscular. She couldn't say how tall he was because she hadn't been standing next to him, but judging by the length of his body against hers, he was tall as well. He had been strong. Even though he had overpowered her easily, she had sensed that he had been holding back.

The restraints at her wrists bit into her skin. Even if she found a weapon, she wouldn't be able to use it. The radio was on, but it was barely audible. If she moved at all, he would surely hear.

Why, oh why, had she been so darn stubborn about those self-defense classes her father had wanted her to take? He had been pushing them on her for as long as she could remember. She worked out regularly, and did yoga and Pilates, although she doubted any of that would help her. Unless she could throw him off with her three-legged-dog pose.

Her only option would be to attack him when he opened the door. The idea of putting herself into an upright position turned her stomach. There would only be one window of opportunity. How long had they been driving? She couldn't see anything except the dark night sky whizzing past the window. Her head spun. She closed her eyes to fight off the nausea. She needed more time, at least another hour or two. She noted the sound of the ocean crashing against the shore. They were somewhere along the coast. That could be anywhere, but at least she had an idea of her surroundings. She would do anything she had to do to get away. This pervert might think he had picked an easy target, but he was sorely mistaken. Anger surged through her. If she had to, she would gouge his eyes out with her fingers. There was no way she would let him touch her.

No way. She would die protecting herself.

She lay as still as she could and took soft, deep breaths in through her nose and out through her mouth. She had to stay calm and levelheaded. The more oxygen she could get in, the better, right?

They traveled for another half hour, without any signs of stopping. She was still struggling with calming her nerves when her body rolled forward and her nose went under the driver's seat. Were they slowing down? Her pulse kicked up and knocked against her throat so hard she was afraid he would hear it. He turned onto what sounded like a gravel road. The uneven terrain bounced her around. She bit her tongue and tried to keep her body from rolling. A few minutes later, the vehicle lurched to a halt. She had to stay calm. If he suspected that she was awake, she would have a snowball's chance in hell at escape. The soft click of his seat belt unfastening sounded like a gunshot to her ears.

Brrring, brrring!

She jumped out of her skin at the piercing ring of a cell phone.

"Hello?" he barked into the phone, his irritation at the caller apparent. She shuddered at the sound of his voice. He sounded rough, mean, and pissed. Well, he was going to be even more pissed in a minute.

"Things didn't go as smoothly as I'd hoped. She put up a good fight and made some noise." His tone was terse. She waited as he listened to the voice on the other end.

"Of course I have her. She's out cold right now. I'll finish the job as planned, but I needed to get the hell out before I got caught." She could hear a barely audible voice on the other end of the phone, but she couldn't make out what it was saying. The job? What did that mean? The bottom of her stomach dropped out.

He was going to kill her.

Her kidnapper muttered something that sounded derogatory, then disconnected. The driver's side door opened and closed.

She tensed. This was it. She only had one shot. The *crunch, crunch, crunch* of gravel alerted her that he was making his way to the other side of the vehicle. The door at her feet opened, and a *whoosh* of cold, salty air swarmed around her. She forced herself to relax her muscles, going limp.

His large, rough hands grabbed her ankles. Even through the blanket, she could feel the muscle behind his grip. In one swift motion, he dragged her toward the door. The blanket slid up and covered her face even more. Her legs dangled off the side of the vehicle. He reached in to grab her arms and haul her up.

Her eyes snapped open and she catapulted up. Her bound hands formed one large fist. Her attacker jumped. His hands poised to restrain her. It was too late. She swung and slammed him in the face with her balled-up fists. He staggered back, but not far enough. Her head swam as the world tilted on its axis. She lost her balance and collapsed against the passenger seat beside her.

"Sonofabitch!" he yelped as blood streamed from his mouth. She took a deep breath and summoned all of her strength. She locked her ankles together and kicked him like a kangaroo. Her bare feet collided with his manhood. He yelped in pain but didn't collapse as she'd hoped. He sagged against the vehicle, his hands clasping his jewels. A string of raging curse words spewed from his mouth.

She leapt out of the truck. Her gelatin-like legs hit the ground. The impact made her knees give out. She crumpled to the ground like a wet towel.

In a heartbeat, she staggered to her feet. Her breath was strangled and shallow as her knees threatened to buckle beneath her weight. The metallic taste of panic flooded her mouth. Her heartbeat roared in her ears as she ran. Her feet were unstable, her movements clumsy. The crisp night air whipped her in the face. Her hair flew in front of her eyes and blocked her vision. She slapped it away.

The night was black; the only illumination came from the moon shining over the ocean and cascading over the beach. Her feet carved up the soft sand. She struggled to stay upright as each step sucked her foot in. Sand flew around her, the grains sharp as they pelted her legs and face. There was nothing around her, nowhere to go for help. Only one lone house was on her left—the place he was taking her. A scream bubbled in her throat. The wind swallowed it up. He was close. Her chest constricted with every painful gulp of air she forced into her lungs.

Dammit, she had never been a runner! The hairs on the back of her neck prickled to attention. Her kidnapper was in pursuit, but she didn't dare waste a millisecond to look. She had gotten a head start, but her lack of concentration and balance, combined with his advanced physical prowess, assured her that he would be on her heels. There was nowhere for her to run. He was going to catch her. He would be angry that she had gotten away, and even angrier that she had gotten in those lucky shots.

If he caught her, he would kill her.

She wouldn't last more than a minute or two now. He was gaining on her, and her muscles were weakening like air deflating from a tire. In her white clothes, she would be as bright as a spotlight running across the sand, a perfect target as the moonlight gleamed off of her pale coloring. Her only chance was the ocean. She wasn't a strong swimmer, never had been. Add in the fact that her wrists were tied, and she was likely to sink like a stone.

She had to try. She would rather die drowning than let him catch her. Using all her strength, she pushed herself the last hundred feet to the shore. Her feet cut through the water. Her splashes shattered the silence of the night. She gasped as she struggled through the waves. Her sharp breaths were the only sound that penetrated her consciousness, drowning out the fear and panic that echoed through her ears like white noise.

It was freezing cold. She sucked in her breath. Her body resisted the frigid temperature. His feet thundered through the wet sand behind her. She trudged deeper. He was close. His gaze burned through the back of her head like the laser of a sniper.

The water reached her upper thighs and she dove under. The icy cold waves washed over her head. Her vision blurred. She kicked downward with all her might, trying to disappear in the shroud of the water. The water was deeper now and getting colder. She kicked harder. Her lungs tightened. Her bound hands made it impossible to paddle or swim. All she could do was kick. The duct tape dug into her wrists. Without the use of her hands, she was a sitting duck if she surfaced.

Her chest ached, and threatened to explode. She needed air. She surged to the surface and gulped in air greedily as she came up. A wave of salty water smashed into her. The salt burned her eyes, and whipped her hair in front of her face like a wet mop. She could hear his splashes behind her. *Oh God, he was close!*

She forced herself to take in another gulp of air, and went under again. He was going to catch her. Her heart beat violently. She kicked and wiggled her body, every inch putting more distance between her and the madman.

Her lungs and chest screamed. Her arms and legs burned with exhaustion and prickled with the cold. She needed air again, but she needed to get farther. A little more …

A big, strong hand grabbed her calf and yanked her backward. The pinch of his hand made her gasp. Salt water poured into her mouth and nose as another wave hit. She stomped her feet back against him, kicking him anywhere she could reach. She might as well have been kicking a wall, for all the good it did. He had her harnessed. One arm locked around her waist, his other snagged her hair and yanked her head out of the water.

Her body betrayed her. Grateful for the breath of air, she sucked in frantically, only to have water sputter out simultaneously.

"Are you crazy?" he bellowed at her as he treaded water, holding her weight as well as his.

"Let me go!" she screamed. It came out in a croak. He turned them both around and paddled back in the direction of the shore. Reality hit her like a lightning bolt: She'd been caught. She splashed wildly.

"Hold still, dammit! You'll drown us both!" he snarled as he readjusted his arm across her chest; his palm now gripped the underside of her ribs. She tossed herself back against him and slammed the back of her head into his. The blow made her ears ring and stars flash in front of her eyes.

"Goddammit! This is your last warning. Hold still or I'll knock you out!" His threat didn't affect her. Once they reached land, she was a goner. She took a brief moment to take in another breath before she went for what could be her last shot.

Ducking her head down, she bit as hard as she could on his forearm. The tinny taste of blood touched her tongue. He thrashed his arm, releasing his hold. She shot her legs back and kicked herself away. Before she could kick again and swim, his hand sank into her hair and snapped her back painfully. A sharp blow to her head caused her muscles to go lax. Her eyes rolled back. She swallowed up the dark, inky waves.

Chapter 5

Jesus Christ, the woman was insane. His insides twisted with guilt as his palm slammed into her head, snapping it sharply to the side.

He'd had to knock her out to keep her from drowning them both. Before he could pull her limp body to his, a large wave hit him in the face and forced him under. He lost his hold on her. Water rushed into his mouth. His eyes screamed as he forced them open.

No!

He willed away all discomfort and dove under the waves. His arms stretched out painfully as he searched the inky darkness for any part of her he could grab. Dammit, he should have tied her feet too. He never should have let this happen. His lungs protested and demanded air. But if his lungs hurt, Lana's were filling with water. He dove deeper and searched. His eyes strained to see beyond the black that surrounded him.

He'd lost her.

His chest tightened. His heart rate skidded to a stop. His nose burned as water forced its way in.

What have I done?

From the moment he'd taken this job, he'd only wanted to protect her, and he was doing a real shitty job. Something brushed him—a light, feathery feeling across his hand. Knowing it could be seaweed, he reached and snagged a handful…*her hair*. Relief spread through his ice-cold veins. He pulled her close, clutched her to his chest, and kicked as if his legs were on fire. They propelled to the surface. He gasped, his lungs hungrily sucking in air as he paddled. She remained motionless, her body weightless in his arms as he kept them both above the rough waves.

Half-carrying, half-dragging her, he got her to the shore. Her body was heavy and limp. He collapsed on the sand beside her, examining her. Her lips were soft and parted, unbreathing. He tilted her head back gently, swept the hair away from her face, and began mouth-to-mouth. Her lips were salty and wet as his sealed over hers. He breathed into her mouth a couple of times and pulled away. Her face showed no sign of response. Goddammit. He began chest compressions. Her body jerked with the force of his pumps. Her pale, oval face was slack and expressionless. His heart clutched as he continued to work on her.

Nothing.

His stomach turned to lead.

Please don't let her die.

He was on autopilot, his brain focused on the task. He couldn't give up. She had to live. His flesh burned beneath his cool skin. Despite the cold water and chilled air, sweat mixed with water on his forehead.

He counted the next thirty compressions, then pinched her nose and molded his mouth over hers again.

One breath…two…

Her body gave a responsive jerk, and water rushed out of her mouth. His shoulders sagged. His eyes closed. Hope soared through him, but she wasn't out of the woods yet. He rolled her to her side as she fought a coughing fit. She desperately gasped for air at the same time that her body rejected the water.

"Shh…it's okay, relax. Try to breathe." He placed his palm on her cold, thin back to calm her. Sharp gasps seized her, and her whole body shook. He closed his eyes on a sigh.

He stared at the soft lines of her profile. The moonlight touched her face, and even now, he could see how pretty she was. Soft, fine-boned… She brought the back of her hand up to her lips as she struggled on a ragged breath… His fingers tingled with the need to touch her cheek. He curled his fingers in the sand, resisting the urge.

After a couple of minutes, the gasps subsided, and she took slow, shallow breaths.

He wasn't an expert, but she had swallowed a lot of seawater that she needed to get out.

"Do you know how to make yourself throw up?" he asked. He gently grasped her shoulders and helped her to a sitting position. Big, dumbfounded blue eyes landed on his face.

"What?" Her brow furrowed at him. Her voice was barely more than a hoarse whisper.

"You've swallowed a lot of seawater, and it could make you sick. I'm going to help you throw up, okay? Can you handle that?"

"No. Leave me alone." Her plea was weak and lacked venom as she shrugged him off.

"Look, I know you have no reason to trust me, but I'm not going to hurt you." She said nothing. He slid his body behind hers and let her rest against his arm. "I'm going to put my fingers in your mouth and make you throw up. Don't bite them off if you can help it." His attempt at humor was lost on her as she sagged against his left arm, her body boneless.

He pulled her mass of hair back and tucked it between them. He leaned them both forward and inserted two of his fingers into her mouth. She panicked, as he had expected her to, and grabbed for his hand.

"It's okay, hold on to my wrist if you need to." She relaxed only slightly. He eased his fingers down again. She gagged, and her body shook. Saliva swarmed around his hand, but he delved deeper.

She retched, purging the salty water. She coughed and sputtered. He waited until she was done, then patted her back until her body crumpled against his. He brought her wrists to his teeth and tore off the duct tape. She was shaking now, from the cold and the effects of the night. He scooped her up and got to his feet, gathered the clothes he had managed to shuck off before his dive on top of her, and carried her across the beach to the cabin he had rented.

She lay spent in his arms, her body cold and lax against his. She didn't struggle or open her eyes. His stomach muscles clenched. Not a good sign. Her breath came out in soft puffs, and her eyes moved beneath her lids, as if she was asleep. He struggled at the doorstep but managed to wrestle the keys out of his pants pocket and kick open the door.

The house was tiny. It consisted of one main room that served as bedroom, kitchen, and living room. The bathroom was at the back of the cabin.

He had come here a couple of days ago to prepare. There were blankets on his bed, which was situated near the fireplace. Close to the kitchen area was a futon pushed up against the window, which was where Lana was to sleep. His bed stood between hers and the door. He carried her to the futon and laid her down gently. She was sopping wet, and in seconds the bedding was drenched. He got some towels from the bathroom, threw one over her, and began to dry her body. At his touch, she stirred. Her tired, untrusting eyes narrowed at him.

"What are you doing?" she demanded as she coiled away.

"You need to dry off and get out of those wet clothes."

"Get away from me." Her voice was rough and sore sounding. A tremor laced her words. Fear? Or from the cold? He strived for a reassuring, patient tone.

"I'll leave you alone as soon as you're in some warm clothes. I have some I took from your house. I need to get them from the car." She struggled into a fetal position, and pulled her knees to her chest. Her stony gaze stayed trained to the floor. He got to his feet and went to the duffel bag he had brought to the cabin earlier in the week. He pulled out a pair of handcuffs. Her eyes grew wide. She leapt up from the bed. Her exhaustion made her movements awkward. She pitched forward off the edge, and dove headfirst into the hardwood floor. A squeak split the air as she landed with a thud. He rolled his eyes. God, he needed a drink.

"You really need to stop getting so worked up. This is exhausting," he mumbled, as he hoisted her up by her arms and deposited her back on the bed.

"You need to get a life and not kidnap young women, you pervert." Despite her breathlessness, her face was hard, daring him.

"I need to handcuff you while I run out to the car. After that I will uncuff you and you can get dressed." He snapped one cuff to her wrist and the other to the bed frame. She glared at him.

He grabbed his car keys and ran out to the truck to get her clothes. A cool breeze blasted him reminding him that he, too, needed to change. The air was cold. January in Seattle was damn near freezing. Lana was going to be a handful. For some reason he had expected her to be quiet and compliant. He hadn't considered that she would try to escape. Kidnapping was a new concept for him, something he would never do again.

He returned to the house to find Lana how he had left her, with a scowl still etched on her face. He unlocked the handcuffs and set the clothes down beside her.

"You should wash off the salt water and get dressed." He mustered his best no-nonsense tone. It had the opposite effect from what he'd intended.

"No." She tossed the clothes to the floor and folded her arms across her chest. The stance showed off her slight frame and tightened the thin white pajama top against her breasts. Her pebble-hard nipples put delicate tents in the material. Heat swirled in his gut.

"I get that you want to be defiant, but don't be stupid. You're likely to catch pneumonia."

"If you're so worried, take me to a hospital." Her lips pursed.

His temper ratcheted up a notch. He clenched his teeth.

"Change your clothes or I'll do it for you." He might not be able to force her, but he could damn well scare her.

"Over my dead body." Her shrill voice rang in his ears. Her foot jutted out to catch him in the kneecap. It took all of his willpower not to bend her over and slap her ass. He counted to ten. His breath came out slow and even. He'd had a hell of a night, and he wasn't going to stand here and fight with her another damn minute. He didn't have the energy for it. "That's fine. Sleep in wet clothes. I don't care." He cuffed her back to the bed, grabbed his own clothes, and went into the bathroom to wash off the salt water.

Good God, she was lucky he wasn't Stamos! The slimy bastard who had hired him would have relished stripping her naked. She was scared and beyond exhausted, and the fact that she was still putting up a fight was admirable—almost. He stepped out of the shower and dried off. His gaze landed on the bruising ring of teeth marks on his forearm. Blood spotted a few holes, and annoyance spiked his temper all over again. She was tough, he'd give her that, but there was no way in hell she'd get another lucky shot like that.

He was going to have to keep a close eye on her tonight. Aside from pneumonia, she faced many other risks. Within the first twenty-four hours after a near-drowning, the victim could still die. Her organs could have been flooded with water, causing her kidneys to shut down. He had made her vomit as much as he could, but he had no idea how much seawater she had ingested. Hopefully, she would come to her senses as she lay in a cold, wet bed.

Something told him she would shiver all night.

He emerged from the bathroom in dry clothes. His eyes automatically sought her out. She lay curled on her side, the wet blankets tucked around her. The light in the room was dim. A dingy glow shone from the lamp he'd turned on when they'd entered. Dark shadows cast over the room.

She watched him through heavy lids but made no other attempt at acknowledgment. The blanket was thin, with wet spots visible all over it—more wet than dry. He shook his head. If she froze all night, it would be her own damn fault. Her hair curled over the pillow, her cheek nestled into her palm. She was so soft and sweet. His hands ached to run over her body, to take her full mouth to his. Her lids fluttered, and her long eyelashes finally fell shut. He pulled a bottle of water from his duffel bag and left it on the floor beside her.

"Lana?" Her lids fluttered again until cerulean-blue eyes found him, her gaze unsteady and unfocused. "I left you a bottle of water here, okay?

Try to drink some. All that salt water will dehydrate you quickly." Her eyes closed in response.

Best to avoid provoking a snappy response from her. Her slumber was a welcome reprieve. He went over to the fireplace to toss in some logs. He had a fire started in minutes, the flames warm as they licked around the wood. He stretched out on his bed and stared at the ceiling. Her soft, even breathing sounded from across the room, and again he wondered what in the hell he was doing. A glance at his watch told him it was after three in the morning. Fatigue hummed through his muscles. The waves had been strong, and fighting against another person at the same time had been damn hard and mentally draining. In a few minutes, he drifted off to sleep.

When he woke, the air was freezing. A chill made him yank the covers up. A strange, rattling sound froze him. His senses prickled. He threw back his covers and got to his feet. As he got closer, he was able to identify the sound: chattering teeth.

Goddammit. She was probably on the verge of hypothermia. He dropped to sit on the bed beside her. His hands ran over the bundle of wet blankets.

"Lana, wake up." She stirred and pulled her body into a tighter ball. A whimper broke through her parted lips. A cold sweat broke out on his brow. He never should have let her fall asleep in wet clothes.

A cold draft blasted in from the old window beside her. He freed her from the handcuffs and wet blanket she clung to and sat her up on the edge of the bed.

"Go away." She shoved at him.

Her fingers were as cold as icicles.

"Enough of this. We need to get you warm." She didn't lift her head to look at him, but he took her silence for as much of an agreement as he was going to get. Grasping the hem of her shirt, he lifted it over her head.

He didn't want to look—tried not to—but the moonlight beamed in through the window, illuminating her creamy naked skin. Her delicate pink nipples were taut, her hair wild around her porcelain face. God, she gave him a hard-on like nothing he'd ever experienced.

Her hands clasped to her chest, her chin tilted up to see his face.

"Sorry." He grasped the back of his own shirt behind his neck and pulled it over his head. It was warm from his body heat, and long-sleeved. He tugged it over her head, covering her nakedness. She fit her arms through the sleeves. "Stand up, please."

She rose to her feet. Her knees wobbled beneath her. He rested her hands on his shoulders to steady her as he leaned forward, grabbed the waistband of her sopping wet pajama shorts, and pulled them down her legs. His shirt covered her to mid-thigh, shielding his view. Her fingernails gripped into his shoulders, either to balance herself or from unease, he wasn't sure. Her knees knocked, and her breath sucked in sharply around the clattering of her teeth. He cursed.

"C'mon, you can't sleep in this bed now, it's soaked." Not waiting for her to move, he scooped her up in his arms and deposited her in the center of the warm bed he had vacated minutes before. He went to the fireplace to restart the fire. He set the logs up to ensure longer burning time. When he finished, he turned back toward the bed. His insides clenched at the sight of her in his bed. Lana lay curled tightly, her cheek cushioned next to her slim hand. She hadn't even pulled the covers up before she passed out. Her sexy legs were bent at the knees, her feet kicked out onto his side of the bed. He rubbed the back of his neck. There was no help for it. She was far too cold, and he wasn't going to let her freeze to death alone in the bed. The fire wouldn't last all night.

Not bothering to find another shirt, he climbed into the bed beside her and tucked the blankets up to her chin. He inched his body closer until they were touching. She moaned and curled closer to his heat.

Not in his wildest imagination had he imagined "cuddling" with a woman he hadn't just banged—one he had kidnapped, as a matter of fact. Gradually her shivers subsided and she slipped into a peaceful sleep. The orange glow from the fire danced shadows over her face, and her soft lips parted. Her cheeks were slightly rosy from warmth, and her hair was strewn across the pillow.

His heart constricted. This might be his most difficult mission yet.

Chapter 6

Her body sank into a soft mattress, surrounded by blankets and warmth. A lead weight pressed down on her eyelids. She struggled to open them. A yawn escaped her lips as she stretched her legs out. Her body ached.

Why am I so sore?

The blankets piled in front of her face, blocking her view of the room. She stretched out her arm, and the sheets fell away. A large, brawny hand lay splayed near her face.

She gasped. Her blood pumped wildly through her veins. She looked around in search of the owner. The hand was attached to a long, equally brawny, muscular arm, which was draped lazily around her. Her back was curled into someone, his legs drawn up so her bottom was against his thighs. She scooted out of his grasp.

The kidnapper!

She let out a scream that reverberated off the walls. He jumped up as if he'd been shot, and his head came inches away from bashing into hers. She shrieked again as his eyes found hers, and she kicked him as hard as she could between the legs. He yelped and keeled forward, his hand clasping his injured member. She dove for the edge of the bed. His hand snatched her leg. He had her trapped.

"Let go!" Her fists came down to batter him anywhere she could reach: head, shoulders, back.

"Dammit, stop!" he bellowed, and rose from his bent position to grab her arms. Panic strangled her throat. She swallowed another scream. Had he raped her? She couldn't remember! Had she willingly slept with him?

No. No way...

"Let me go, let me go!" She threw her body backward to try to break his hold. He held tighter. She ended up on her back with him on his knees above her, her wrists tethered together by his fingers. His eyes were stormy, his face clenched. His fierce scowl darkened the sheath of stubble on his jaw. He had her pinned. Images of the things he could do to her with sickening ease whizzed through her mind. No. She wouldn't let him. She kicked him in the stomach like a madwoman. Her efforts were futile.

"I would quit kicking like that if I were you. You aren't wearing any underwear." The corner of his mouth turned up at her smugly, revealing even white teeth. Amusement laced his voice. The shirt she wore was bunched around her hips. Her feet rested against the hard wall of his stomach, giving him a clear view. His eyes never left her face. She froze. His hands still held her wrists together between them.

She inhaled sharply.

"*You*," she said. The events of last night hit her with the force of a tornado. His grin waned and his hold loosened. She scrambled to her knees to face him, tugging the shirt as far down as it would go.

The bastard had taken her from her bed last night. The sick sonofabitch…

"What about me?" He slid off the bed and picked a shirt out from the duffel bag on the floor, his back to her, a back that was thick and layered with muscles that flexed when he pulled the shirt over his head and down his body. She swallowed over a lump in her throat. Light gray sweatpants hung loosely at his hips. Good God, he was hot.

He turned to face her as he rounded the bed, a mischievous grin still slanting his mouth. That telltale smirk churned her stomach into knots.

"Y–You kidnapped me." Oh God. What did he want with her? "For what? Your sick pleasure?" Her breath expelled from her lungs on a hiss. "You disgusting sonofa—" She leapt off the bed.

Fire coursed through her. He'd picked the wrong target.

"Hold up, you're jumping to a shitload of conclusions." He held his hands out as if he was calming a damn horse. Her fingers curled into a tight fist. She raised her hands as she closed the distance between them.

He caught her arm before she swung. "Would you calm down? Jesus."

"What did you do to me in that bed?"

His face contorted. "*What?*"

"Did you…did you touch me?"

Something flashed in his eyes. His jaw worked. "No, dammit."

"Oh, I should just take your word for it?" Her body shook with anger, and her brain worked like a hamster wheel, trying to remember. The soft flutter of his shirt falling over her skin and the warm scent of him flashed through her mind.

"Don't you think if you'd had sex you'd be able to tell? You'd feel a bit sore or—"

"Don't talk to me like I'm stupid." Her words came out rapidly.

"Look, I know you're pissed, but you were awake when I put you in bed. Your teeth were chattering from sleeping in the wet clothes. I helped you get changed into my shirt, but that was all." His temper had settled. His tone was calm, almost placating.

Her teeth bit into her tongue.

She remembered sitting on the edge of the bed, him in front of her, taking the shirt off his back. He hadn't touched her then. But he had gathered her in his arms and put her in the warm bed. She didn't remember anything after that, other than waking up.

"Would you stop looking at me like I'm a rapist? I didn't touch you, and you know it."

"Sorry if I don't believe a kidnapper right off the bat. I'm a little judgmental that way."

His lips spread into a smile. "You're one feisty cookie, you know that?"

She eyed him carefully. She wanted to believe him. God, he was good-looking. Her gaze lingered on his smile, and her stomach flipped over. Being attractive didn't make him nice…but oh, how she wished he was. He kept his dirty brown hair clipped close to his scalp. His eyes were a sharp, intelligent green; his nose perfectly straight; and his skin a warm olive tone. His fingers clamped loosely to her wrist. A glance down at his hand, which still held her arm, revealed a big tattoo up his forearm.

"I'll make us some coffee, okay? Then you can ask all the questions you want." She salivated.

"You have coffee?"

His mouth twitched with amusement. "Put some pants on and I'll make it."

The scent of brewing coffee beans filled the air as she found the sweatpants that he'd brought her last night underneath the futon. She sat on the bed to tug them on, keeping one eye on the hunk in the kitchen.

She didn't even know his name. Her temples throbbed as she watched him fix their coffee. Hours ago, she'd thought she was going to die. He'd torn her out of her bed, and dammit, somehow it didn't fit. He was too at ease, too calm and confident. If he'd wanted to kill her, he could have done so without breaking a sweat. But he hadn't hurt her yet—and—that gnawed at her. Why the hell was she here, and what did he want with her?

She pulled her hair over her shoulder. The strands were thick and gritty with sand and salt water. She needed a shower badly. The linoleum floor was cold on her bare feet as she crossed the kitchen and sat at the table. She pulled her feet up so she sat cross-legged just as he deposited a mug of steaming coffee in front of her. Questions lingered on her tongue, but she needed coffee first.

Her hands circled the mug, and she inhaled the warm aroma, letting it waken her bones.

"Hits the spot, doesn't it?" He sat across from her and scooped three teaspoons of sugar into his coffee, then added milk. She took half a teaspoon of the sweet substance and stirred it in with a splash of milk.

"Mmm..." She eyed him carefully over her mug as she sipped. "Are you going to tell me why you kidnapped me? Did someone hire you? Or are you the mastermind?"

He took another big gulp of his coffee, then filled his mug again from the carafe he had set on the table. He reached over to a plastic container that sat in the middle of the table and opened it. "Danish?"

She wrinkled her nose. "No, I don't eat that crap. Especially in the morning." She watched as he took a huge bite. "And you shouldn't, either." He swallowed, his brows raised.

"It's a pastry. Pretty sure it's a breakfast one too."

"It's full of sugar." Her stomach rolled over at the thought of eating so much sweetness.

"Don't tell me you're worried about getting fat." His eyes slid over her. She wet her lips. Goose bumps raced over her skin under his intent gaze.

"No, that has nothing to do with it." She shifted in her seat. He took another bite and finished making his coffee. "Do you realize that you've had twenty-four grams of sugar just in those two cups of coffee? Look at all that icing...and the filling."

He chuckled. "Health-conscious much?"

"You say it like it's a bad thing."

He shook his head, but the grin remained. "Not at all. I'll have you know, I eat very well. Do I look like I sit on my ass eating shit all day?" His bulging biceps flexed as he brought the mug to his lips. The porcelain looked frail and dainty in his oversized fist.

No, he definitely didn't look like a couch potato. He looked like he spent all hours of the day working out or throwing cars. "Coffee is my big indulgence. This"—he gestured to the last bite of pastry in his hand—"was just for convenience. You should eat. I don't have much food here."

Her stomach rumbled. She plucked the smallest pastry out of the container and squinted at him. "You never did answer my question."

"About why I took you?" He wiped some icing off his lips with a napkin. She waited. His eyes met hers, all humor gone. A hard glare glinted in them, his jaw locked. He balled the napkin tightly and tossed it onto the table.

"I wasn't hired to kidnap you, Lana. I was hired to kill you."

Chapter 7

She sputtered on the sweet pastry, spit it out in a napkin, then washed down a gulp of coffee. Guilt flooded through him. She wiped her mouth, and her gaze found his. Sharp, real, and raw fear took the shine from her iridescent eyes.

Goddammit. He hated that she was scared. He'd rather her throw a million of those sharp little punches to his face than see the terror and uncertainty scrawled on her delicate features.

"Kill me?" Her voice was rough and uneven. He rose from his chair and paced the tiny kitchen. His hands laced together behind his neck, his gaze down. He couldn't look at her. Not when there wasn't anything he could do to take that look on her face away. What was he going to tell her?

The truth. He had no choice. Maybe, just maybe, she had an idea of who wanted her dead.

"Last week, I received a call from a guy I used to know. He's a sick bastard and I normally stay clear of him, but he convinced me to meet him. He said he had a job that I might be interested in. When he showed me your picture, I knew you weren't a usual target. I figured it had something do with your dad. But there's no way I'd hurt an innocent person." He looked up at her. Her face was white; her hands gripped the edge of the table as if it was anchoring her. He forced himself to sit again.

"You took the job? You told him you would kill me?" Her voice trembled. Her tongue came out to wet her lips. His insides twisted.

Shit. That sounded bad.

"I had to. If I'd refused, he would have just hired someone else. Someone who would have done it without a second thought." Stamos had been ready and eager to take on the job himself, but he'd said the source wouldn't hire him. Not that Cal was surprised. Stamos was too damn sloppy and inexperienced. He shuddered at the thought of what would have become of Lana had Stamos been hired instead of him. She would have died last night.

"And why kidnap me? How is that an acceptable solution? You could have gone to the cops—or alerted me." Her cheeks darkened, revealing the flash of her temper.

He closed his eyes. Her naïveté would be refreshing in any other situation. "I had very little time to decide how to handle this, and I didn't want to risk someone getting wind of my hesitancy to do the job. People like this... like the guy who hired me...they're scum. But they have contacts within the police force," he said softly. And it was true. The cops had never been a reliable source of help in his experience. Lana's lips parted, and her breath sucked in.

"And what would alerting you have done?" he continued. "You'd have gone to the police yourself, and it would have been the same scenario. I did the best thing I could think of: to get you the hell out before someone else beat me to it."

"Oh my God." She stood from the table, and her hands tunneled through her hair. "Oh my God." He stood and caught her arms before she could turn away.

"Hey, c'mon. You're safe, okay? No one is going to hurt you." She yanked her face up to his.

"Why did he come to you in the first place?" She searched his face. *"Who are you?"*

She stepped out of his hold. His mind went blank. What could he tell her? That he'd infiltrated drug rings? Hunted people? Killed them? Not people like her, though. And definitely not a woman.

"Oh my God... *You're an assassin,*" she hissed. Her hands covered her mouth, and she backed away.

"No." He slashed his hand through the air. "No, I'm not."

She shook her head, her eyes wild. "You're lying. Why would someone hire you to kill me if you weren't?"

His chest constricted. "Would you listen, please?"

She stared at him, her fist pressed against her full mouth. His hands ached to touch her, to ease her doubt. She needed space, and he would give it to her if it killed him.

"I'm a freelance security contractor." Her lashes lifted. Round, hesitant eyes met his. He stepped closer to her. She didn't back away.

"Do you kill people?"

"Yes, I've killed people. Bad people. People who hurt innocent people or who've done bad things. If you want me to elaborate, I will. I'll tell you anything about me you want to know." He wanted her to trust him. Her lips rolled in, and small white teeth nipped at her bottom lip. "Stamos is the name of the man who hired me. I'm the only contract hire that he knows. He wanted the finder's fee they had offered him, so he asked me to take the job."

"You associate with people like him? You must, if he came to you without hesitation."

Jesus, she was sharp. He didn't want to delve into his past. Didn't want to share that he'd been raised in poverty, that as a teenager he'd befriended kids like Stamos. Kids like him, who needed money and would do whatever was necessary to eat and not live in shit. He'd gotten away from that life when he'd left and joined the military. He'd grown up. Stamos hadn't. He shouldn't have had any contact with him since coming home, but he'd run into Stamos one night and out of pity, had exchanged phone numbers with him. Stamos tried to befriend him. Due to his workload, Cal had managed to keep a good distance, but in the beginning, he'd allowed his old acquaintance to get a little too close.

"I grew up with him. He's not a friend—far from it. But he's tried to get close to me."

She rested her hands on her hips. "Why would he do that? And why didn't you just avoid him?"

He let out a sigh through his nostrils. Damn, she was persistent. "Because he wants to be like me. But he's not cut out for my line of work. And I have kept my distance. It had been more than six months since I'd talked to him last before he called me and presented this job."

Her eyebrows bounced. "The job to kill me?"

"That's the one." His tone was dry.

"You're not going to hurt me?" Her arms folded across her chest. She spoke slowly, her words deliberate. His spine stiffened. Was that what she feared? Him?

"Hell, no."

She chewed her lip harder. He dared to reach out his index finger to tap beneath her lip. "Stop that, you're going to chew a hole right through."

Her lips pressed together, but she didn't pull away. "Don't you think I've had enough opportunity to hurt you by now?"

Her gaze shifted to her feet, then back up to his face. "Yes, I suppose."

"And have I?"

Her weight shifted from one foot to the other. "No."

The vise that had been gripping his heart released. "I want to help you, and I'm going to protect you. No one will hurt you, but you need to trust me." He held his hand out to her, palm open. "Deal?"

"I don't even know your name." Her slight shoulder raised in question.

Shit, how had he not told her that?

"Cal Hart. I didn't tell you that?"

She shook her head. "No."

She was right. He hadn't. His career had forced him to live a solitary life, to be cautious and private. Out of habit, he kept details to himself. But if telling her his name made her feel more at ease, it was a small price to pay.

"So, do we have a deal?"

She took a deep, shuddering breath and placed her hand in his. "Deal."

He squeezed her hand. The temptation to bring her soft palm to his lips arced through him. She was so dainty. The feminine curve of her slight frame just showed in the oversized shirt she wore. His shirt. His dick twitched at the thought of stripping it off her, his hands free to roam her delicious body.

Her hand dropped away.

"Do you have towels and soap here? I really need a shower."

"Sure." He led her to the bathroom and showed her where everything was, then left her to clean up. He was going to need another coffee.

Chapter 8

Someone wanted to kill her.

Badly enough to hire a professional to do it. She cranked the hot water up and inhaled the steam. Last night, she could have been murdered…in cold blood. Her stomach flipped over. A wave of nausea made her clutch the handrail on the wall.

She would not pass out. She was stronger than that. Tears stung her eyes. It had taken all of her control to keep her emotions at bay in front of Cal. Cal… She finally had a name to pair with his chiseled face and strong, capable hands.

Cal had said the man who'd hired him was named Stamos…but she didn't know anyone by that name. She had never heard it before, either. There was always the possibility that Cal was lying. What grounds did she have to believe him?

She filled her palm with shampoo and scrubbed the salt and sand from her hair. He was dark, dangerous, and mysterious…but the same traits that made him so sexy were also the makeup of a bad guy. A shiver rippled through her. She had to stay on guard. He was a smooth talker, and his wish for her to trust him weighed on her. Why did he care? Was he playing her? Did he have a bigger scheme in mind? She turned the hot water up again and finished washing her hair. She let the hard pressure of the water beat into the tension of her shoulders. Her mind churned. If he was telling the truth, then she was lucky to be alive. She pressed her fingers into the taut muscles in her neck and let out a groan. Dammit, she'd always been such a good judge of character. Why was her brain so muddled about Cal? After her shower, she'd try to feel him out and ask more questions.

She turned the water off, and towel-dried, her skin now pink from the heat. Cal was dangerous. He hadn't outright threatened her, but the pieces of the puzzle didn't fit. What did he have to gain by protecting her? If that's what he was doing. Was she to believe he cared about her safety out of just the goodness of his heart? And the way his eyes raked over her... He looked at her as if he was savoring a rich liquor. God, it was hot.

She stepped out of the shower and onto the woven bath mat on the floor. Shit. She didn't have any clean clothes. Why hadn't she thought to ask him for something to wear? Oh yeah, she was too busy thinking about why someone wanted to kill her.

The towel covered more of her body than her thin pajamas had last night. She took a deep, steadying breath and opened the bathroom door. Cal stood in the kitchen, a coffee mug halfway to his lips. His eyes found her and widened. His hand jerked, sending a stream of hot coffee down the front of his shirt.

"Shit." He slammed the mug down on the counter and brushed at the wet brown stain with a paper towel.

"Sorry, I didn't mean to startle you." She hid her smirk behind her hand.

"You think getting burnt with hot coffee is funny?" The corner of his mouth lifted and slowly worked to a grin. Her toes curled. She gripped the towel knotted between her breasts tighter and stepped farther into the room.

"You shouldn't be drinking more coffee. That's what, thirty-six grams of sugar now?"

"Glad you're keeping count."

"My pleasure." He gave up on the stain and pulled his shirt over his head. Her breath sucked in. Holy hell. His stomach rippled with...what was that, a six-pack? Good Lord, that much muscle looked like it would hurt her if she touched his stomach. She pressed her lips together as her eyes lingered over his wide shoulders and stacked chest. "I, uh...came out because I don't have any clean clothes." *Don't look at his abs, don't look at his abs...* "Do you have something I could wear?" The steadiness of her voice should have won her an Academy Award.

"Yeah, why don't you grab me the clothes you had on this morning and I'll put some laundry in the washing machine." He waved the balled-up shirt he'd just removed in his hand. "I need to wash this anyway."

"Okay." She backed up and reentered the bathroom. Sweatpants and long-sleeved shirt gathered from the floor, she straightened and turned to the door—and slammed into his chest.

His hands snagged her shoulders, preventing her from reeling backward. The clean clothes he'd brought her scattered to the floor.

"Sorry, I didn't mean to scare you." His voice was thick and husky. His hands never left her shoulders. His gaze traced her face. Dammit, she wished she had makeup on. This close, she could see the vibrant striations in his eyes, and the stubble on his jaw was thick and darker than the hair on his head. Her palm itched to reach up and feel the scruff of his beard. She could smell a hint of coffee on his breath, and his musky scent.

God, he was so masculine. She couldn't step out of his hold. Her nose hovered inches from his sternum. He towered over her, dwarfing her. He had to be six-foot-two at least, maybe taller. She let her eyes roam over the wall of muscle in front of her. A silvery scar beneath his collarbone caught her eye.

Gunshot wound?

Her throat tightened. She didn't want to think about the types of things that would warrant a shot to his chest. His hot breath spiraled in the air between them. She lifted her eyes and met his face. A dark stain tinted his cheekbones, and his gaze lingered on her throat before trailing down. She swallowed. She was in a damn towel, half-naked. Her skin tingled under his stare, and her instincts screamed at her to back up, but her feet remained rooted to the floor.

He was like a solid brick wall blocking her exit. His thumbs smoothed over her shoulders as if reveling in the feel of her skin. Her lungs screamed for air, but for the life of her, she couldn't take a breath for fear it would break his trance. He'd said he wouldn't hurt her. But he could if he wanted to. She'd fight to the death, but he was much bigger than her. His eyes finally found hers, and the burning intensity in them slammed into her solar plexus. As much as her body screamed at her to stay still, not to alert the wild beast in front of her, she wet her lips.

Like a spell being broken, his face softened and the heat ebbed out of his eyes, but the embers still burned. He took a step back and dropped his hands. She sucked a shallow breath in through her nose, releasing the tension in her chest.

She inched closer. A small part of her grieved at his distance.

"Get dressed." His voice was low and gruff. "We need to get a plan together."

Chapter 9

His muscles ached from the effort it took to hold himself back from capturing her stunned, moist lips. When her eyes had trailed over him and her breath had sucked in harshly, he had known. She wanted him as bad as he wanted her.

Any other day, any other woman, he'd have been all over that. Today, he had to keep his head in the game and devise a plan before whoever the hell had hired Stamos came looking for them. Any other woman besides Lana Vanderpoel was fair game.

She was not.

His only purpose now was to keep her safe and expose who wanted her dead. He rubbed his hand over his face. He would kill the sonofabitch with his bare hands when he caught him.

She was smart, witty, sexy as all hell...and that temper. Damn, he loved the way her eyebrows snapped; he loved her quick tongue, and her fists—slim but not in the least bit frail. His pulse quickened at all the ways he could tame that temper. But as much as his body craved hers, he could never get involved. Sure, relationships were great. Among people with normal lives. Men who came home to their wives every night. Men who hadn't murdered a hundred people, men who hadn't had a hundred people try to murder them. She'd seen the scar on his chest. He'd watched the horrific possibilities that had flashed across her face. That had been the clincher. The cold bucket of water that was his reality.

He went over to his gym bag and yanked on the last clean long-sleeved shirt he had. If she came out of the bathroom and looked at him with those large, wary eyes one more time, he wouldn't have the willpower to stop himself from kissing her. Dammit, he hated that she feared him. Not that he could blame her. He scooped their wet clothes from last night off the hearth and went to the small laundry room at the back of the house.

He started the washer and exited the laundry room just as she opened the bathroom door. His oversized Michigan State sweatshirt hung nearly to her knees, while an old pair of sweatpants, the only pair with a drawstring, pooled around her legs. Her hands gripped the material on either side of her hips so she could walk without tripping.

The baggy clothes should have hidden her frame and dimmed his lust. Nope.

Her face was pale other than the flush that still stained her cheeks from their encounter. She might have been scared when she'd bumped into him, but beneath her unease, he'd caught a flicker of awareness in her eyes.

"They're a little big." She shifted in the doorway, her gaze down at the clothes.

"Sorry, I don't normally carry women's clothes around. I save my cross-dressing attire for home." She flashed him a smile, some of the caution leaving her eyes. "Come have a seat, we need to discuss some things."

She gathered up more of the sweatpants material and shuffled to the chair he held out. She took it, folded her knees up, and turned her face to look at him. Indecision warred through him. It had taken all of his control not to pull her into his arms moments before. She was a smart woman, and she had to have sensed his attraction. She had nothing to worry about though. Their worlds were very different, and he had no desire to bring her into his. Even if it was for just sex. He needed to settle her mind. If he wanted her to let him help her, she couldn't be scared of him.

"What about?" She squinted at him, not taking her eyes off his face.

He cleared his throat. "About what just happened in the bathroom."

Her lips rolled in and then moved into a small pout. Need surged through him. God, she had the most kissable mouth. "I just want to clear the air. You don't have to worry about me coming on to you."

Her eyebrows rose and pinched together. A cute line creased her brow. "Uh…okay."

"I mean it. You can trust me. I wouldn't get involved with someone like you anyway."

That brought a deep scowl to her sapphire eyes. "What's that supposed to mean?"

Jesus. He rubbed the back of his hand over his beard, stifling a groan. This wasn't the direction he'd wanted the conversation to go. Just a quick "don't worry" was all he'd wanted to say.

"You don't belong in my world, that's all. No insult intended. Just do me a favor and avoid prancing around in towels from now on, okay?"

Heat rushed up her neck to coat her cheeks in crimson. Her mouth opened, then snapped shut. He'd made her speechless? Interesting.

He let loose the smile he'd been holding back. He had smiled more in the last few hours than he had all week. "Let's set aside your attraction to me—"

She reached out and gave his bicep a pinch. "You're so full of yourself. I'm not attracted to you." Her voice raised an octave. "Besides, you kidnapped me, you ass." Her pincerlike fingers fluttered for his bicep again.

He laughed and pulled out of her reach. "Hey, I saved your ass."

She stuck her tongue out at him, and the corners of his mouth twitched. She was funny when she was mad and adorable when she was trying to take a chunk out of his skin.

"Let's get to the important stuff. First of all, do you have any enemies?"

"Anyone who would want to kill me? No, I can't say that I do." She combed her still-damp hair back and secured it in a bun at the top of her head, exposing the soft lines of her profile.

He sat back in his chair. "It's very easy to dismiss people when you think in terms of them wanting to kill you. But we need to look at every single person in your life who doesn't like you. Does that make sense?"

She sighed. "Yes, but I really can't imagine anyone I know doing something like that. It's hard to picture."

"Someone did, though."

Her eyes somber, she nodded.

"What about any ex-boyfriends? Did you have a relationship end sourly?"

"I haven't had a boyfriend since college." Her arms crossed over her chest.

He frowned. "You haven't been involved with anyone since then?"

"No." Her knees shifted in the chair.

"I remember seeing a picture of you recently with a guy at a charity ball. He was leading you to the podium."

"That was Tanner, my stepbrother." Her eyes met his. "Not my boyfriend."

Huh. "He seemed pretty possessive of you for a stepbrother." Tanner's hand had rested on her back as he'd ushered her to the podium, and his gaze had been pointed off toward someone in the crowd, with a sharp look in his eyes that Cal had read as: *Back the fuck off.*

Lana wet her lips, and her eyes darted around the room before landing back on him. Huh.

"I wouldn't say he's possessive." She lifted her shoulder, but her blue eyes had darkened. She was hiding something.

"What would you say, then?"

She toyed with a tendril of hair that had fallen from the bun. Anxiety left faint creases under her eyes. She opened her mouth and then shut it, her gaze lowered to the top of her knee.

"Something happened, didn't it?"

Her eyes lifted and rounded on his. She'd learn soon enough that nothing got past him.

She pressed her lips together and nodded. "He, uh, came on to me a few months ago. It didn't end well."

Anger burned his skin. He kept his face passive, not taking his eyes from hers. "What happened?"

"I just told you."

"No, you told me something happened. You didn't tell me what."

She blew air through her lips. "You want the details? Fine." She straightened in her chair. "It was the night of the fall charity ball. I was home, and had just gotten ready for bed. It was after two in the morning when he showed up at my door."

His body tensed. He didn't like where this was heading. "Go on."

"He–he came on to me. I pushed him away and told him that I wasn't interested. He snapped. He broke some things, I kicked him out, and that was the end of it." The story tumbled out of her lips, like bile purging.

The muscles in his legs ached, demanding he get up and pace the floor, but he couldn't. He needed every last detail. "That was the end of it?" His tone was hard, distant.

She nodded.

"How did he come on to you? What did he do?" He crossed his arms over his chest. Her cheeks flared pink, and he tried not to stare at her mouth.

"He kissed me."

His brows snapped together. "That's it?"

She sighed. "Alright, fine. He pushed me up against the wall, shoved his tongue in my mouth, and groped me. I slapped him across the face. He hit me back, then put his fist through the wall and flipped over my coffee table. I told him if he didn't leave I would call the police." Her arms circled her waist. She pursed her lips, waiting.

He rubbed his hand over his beard and leaned closer to her. "Don't you think that's important?"

"I'm telling you about it, aren't I? But to think he could have something to do with wanting me killed…that's a stretch."

"Bullshit," he breathed. "Your stepbrother physically and sexually assaulted you and you brushed it off? A few months later, someone arranges to have you killed? That looks pretty damn significant."

The smooth lines of her face hardened, and she lifted her chin. Before she could tear into him, he added, "I'm sorry. Why were you protecting him?"

"I *wasn't* protecting him, dammit. I went to Grace and told her the whole story. Tanner came to me and apologized. He'd been drunk and had barely remembered, which was true because I had smelled the alcohol on him." She met his gaze. "I said I forgave him, but I also kept my distance. Never in a million years do I think he'd have anything to do with this."

Something nagged at him to drop it. She'd been through enough, and he didn't need to give her hell. But Tanner sat as a suspect in the forefront of his mind. He'd look into him later.

"He's your stepbrother on your father's side?"

She picked at the material covering her leg. Some of the fire had left her face, and her shoulders relaxed. "Mmm-hmm. He's Grace's son." Grace Vanderpoel. He didn't know much about her other than that she owned her own jewelry line and was a descendant of the Normand family. That was a very old, wealthy, and prominent name, and she had her own money and status.

"What's your relationship like with her?"

"Grace? I like her very much. She takes very good care of my dad, forces him to work out, eat healthy, and make more family time. We don't have an overly close relationship, mostly because she's very busy and so am I."

"Well, that rules out the evil stepmother." He crossed his arms over his chest. "What about your mother? Where does she live?"

"New York, with her husband. I fly out there a couple of times a year, or she comes here. I miss her terribly, but she's happy and so that makes me happy."

"Why don't you live with her?"

She lifted a shoulder and looked down at her mug. "She met Luke when I was in high school. She asked me to move with them, but all my friends were here, so I chose to stay. It worked out for the best, because they travel all the time and I would have been alone a lot."

He couldn't see any motive from her mother and stepfather's end. They needed to go deeper. "What kind of business dealings does your father have?"

Her eyes went wide. "Oh my. I don't even know where to begin."

He raised his eyebrows. Edward Vanderpoel was a self-made billionaire and one of the wealthiest men in the country. "That much?"

She sighed. "He started out years ago in e-commerce, he's written several books, and he's a partner in Hathway Suites, the hotel chain. They just expanded across Europe." Her lips tucked in as she thought. "Then there's Vanderpoel Homes and Realty. I've gotten really involved in that division recently. Outside the businesses, he has his stocks and investments, which I don't know much about. I'm sure I'm probably forgetting some smaller things."

Holy hell. He'd known Edward was a rich man, but he never knew the depth of his business dealings.

"That's a hell of a lot of businesses."

She shrugged. "I've never known him not to work. He's always coming up with new ideas, but he knows what he's doing, obviously."

"Is Tanner involved in his businesses at all?"

She nodded. "He has an office at Dad's building. Like me, he's interested in the construction side of things. I prefer the residential aspect and have started helping with home and interior design. He and my father have gotten close, and I think Tanner wants to expand into other areas of the business."

"With such an empire, your dad must have a lot of colleagues and associates. How many people does he employ?"

She snorted. Coming from her, the sound brought a laugh to his lips.

"In total, like around the world? My God, I wouldn't even begin to guess. He has a plant in China for the importing of goods, plus the hotels." Her eyes lifted to the ceiling. "Tens of thousands, at least…"

Jesus. "So, a disgruntled employee could be a possibility," he mused aloud. She wrinkled her nose at that.

"I can't see it. Other than in his building, the vast majority of workers wouldn't ever see his face. He doesn't have anything to do with hiring or firing—he has managers and people to oversee all of that. The last few years, he's spent most of his hours in the office. He's able to communicate easily with Skype and FaceTime."

"So, if there's a pressing matter in China or Europe, does he go or does he have someone else he would send?"

"He has Shawn and Vanessa. They do a lot of the legwork and act in place of him whenever possible."

"Has he ever had any projects fall through? Pissed anyone off?"

"All the time." She shrugged. "He's very straightforward, and people don't always like that. But to my knowledge there hasn't been anything huge."

Pinpointing a suspect was looking less and less likely. Anyone could have hired Stamos to hurt Lana to get back at Edward. Not just anyone in the city, but anyone in the world.

"I know he's received death threats against me before. That's just part and parcel of being the wealthy man he is. He doesn't always tell me for fear of scaring me, but all of a sudden he'll hire a bodyguard and check in a million times a day." She twirled a lock of her hair that had come free from the bun as if such a thing was normal. "It's always been brief, though. The FBI would get involved, track down the person, and that would be it."

"When was the last time that happened?"

She waved her hand in the air. "Years ago."

He was going to need help. Lana's life was an intricate web of people and scenarios. He couldn't make the wrong move.

"What's your plan?" Her eyes searched his face, hesitant and uneasy. He could see fear in her eyes.

He laced his fingers together on the table in front of him. "We need to tread carefully. I want to compile a list of as many suspects as we can." He slid a pad of paper and a pen across the table to her.

"Whoever your last boyfriends were—no matter how long ago—write their names down. As well as any men who have shown interest in you lately, or if someone sticks out in your mind. Also write down Tanner's full name and anyone else you can think of."

She reached for the pen and began writing. "Are you taking this list to the police?" She kept her eyes on the paper as she wrote.

"Hell, no," he said. Her eyes snapped up to his. "We can't go parading this around. If whoever is behind it gets wind that you're safe, they could bolt or do something drastic."

"But how are we going to find out who did this if we don't talk to the police?"

He leaned forward. Ah, such a fresh, naïve perspective. If she only knew how flawed the justice system was. Police, judges, politicians, almost anyone could be bought. He had no idea the lengths to which whoever was behind this had gone.

"I have connections with the FBI. A friend of mine knows what has been going on and is expecting a call from me today. Other than him and another colleague, I don't trust anyone. Police included."

Her eyes grew wide. The tip of her small pink tongue jutted out to lick her lips. A groan lodged in his throat. Fuck, she was torturing him, and she had no idea.

"What did you mean by 'if whoever is behind it gets wind that I'm safe'? Once my family knows I'm gone, they'll report me missing," Her brow furrowed.

"Yes, but the person who hired me wants you dead, not missing. It was supposed to be a clean kill." Her lips parted, and her breath sucked in. He cleared his throat. Shit, his words were pretty insensitive.

"Last night, I told Stamos you put up a fight and I thought it was best to complete the job elsewhere." He left out that Stamos had been pissed that he'd deviated from the plan. Stamos would have to wait to be paid until her body was found and his contact had confirmation of her death.

A low, grumbling sound made him frown at her. "Was that your stomach?"

Her shoulders shrugged. "Yeah, I guess I'm hungry. What time is it?"

He flipped his wrist to check his watch. "It's after one in the afternoon, so you must be starving. Want me to make you a sandwich?"

She shook her head and unfolded her legs from the chair. "No, I can do it myself." She got to her feet. The large sweatpants she wore slid down her hips. Not far, but far enough for her to gasp and yank them back up.

He chuckled. "You can lose the pants if you want. I'm pretty sure this sweatshirt"—he tugged at the excess material—"covers more of you than the towel."

She slapped his hand away. Her brow creased with annoyance. "Bite me."

His insides warmed. The image of her laid out, naked, for him to bite wherever he wanted, seared into his brain. "Be careful what you ask for."

Her eyes flew to his. The heat had changed. Her temper had vanished, but desire, hot and ready, flashed across her face and then disappeared.

He was going to need a vow of celibacy to get through the next few days. Better yet, a cold shower. His voice was gruff and a little more clipped than he intended, when he said, "Everything is in the fridge. I'm going to shower and then make a call."

Chapter 10

She didn't belong in his world.

What kind of lame rejection was that?

Okay, so his reasoning wasn't lame. It was realistic. Lana's hands shook as she searched the cupboards for plates. He shouldn't have this effect on her. All it took was one suggestive look from him and her stomach tied up in knots. He'd seen her attraction, read her like a damn open book. And he had a lot of nerve pointing it out.

Her stir of interest in him unnerved her. But it wasn't attraction, just hormones and adrenaline. He would be out of her life in a day or two when all this was over, and she would never hear from him again.

Besides, men sucked. Her last boyfriend had been back in college. And although now, at twenty-six, there had been many other possible suitors, none had sparked her interest.

Except Cal.

What was wrong with her? Was she craving a walk on the wild side or something? Intrigued and allured by his dangerous and sexy disposition? Probably. It had been almost three years since she'd last had sex. That would muddle anyone's judgment. The fact that someone wanted to kill her was messing with her mind too. Dread bubbled in her stomach like bile. Fixing food kept her hands and mind busy. Not busy enough, though. Her mind raced, trying to piece together something—anything. A reason, a motive, an enemy…but she had nothing.

Being in the spotlight had its curse. People were envious of the rich and famous, sometimes enough to do drastic things. She stayed active in the community and raised money for numerous causes. Her platform, ironically, was battered women and children.

Aside from that, she worked. She wasn't just a socialite who shopped all day and dressed like a Barbie doll. She put in full-time hours and then some at her dad's office. He'd always insisted she be well educated and work hard. It didn't have to be in his business, but that was where she'd found her fit.

It was challenging, being a billionaire's daughter. People treated her differently everywhere she went—at work and in her personal life. How in the world was she supposed to single out one individual who would have a reason to want to kill her?

She pulled open the refrigerator. Avocado, alfalfa sprouts, spinach, tomato, cheese, and lettuce.

Huh.

Not what she had expected. The sugar fiend did eat well. She took everything out, including the package of lunch meat and condiments, and began to fix a sandwich. The water still ran in the bathroom. Surely he was just as hungry. She took out another plate and a couple extra pieces of bread to fix him one too.

The pipes rattled in the wall. He'd shut off the water. A lump lodged in her throat.

Lord, please don't let him come out in a towel...

The mental image of those rock-hard muscles moist and wet made her mouth salivate.

The door opened, and he emerged in a T-shirt and a pair of jeans. He went to the dining room table and picked his phone up. Her eyes fell to his tattoos. She couldn't make out the words written across his skin in thick Gothic writing.

"Nate, what's up, bro?" He paced around the small cabin as he spoke.

Lana busied herself finishing the sandwiches, then remembered the clothes Cal had put in the wash. She set the plates on the table, then switched the clothes to the dryer. It would be a relief to get her own pants on. Pulling out a chair, she sat and began to eat. She wished she had a bra to wear. The oversized sweatshirt covered her well, but it was unnerving that beneath it she was naked. Cal crossed the room again and sat at the table.

"When does his flight get in?" He paused. "No, that's fine. It's late in the day now, anyway. I wouldn't mind resting before making the drive back in. We'll meet up tomorrow." He disconnected. His eyes landed on her just as her mouth closed around a large bite. A smile touched his mouth, making small crinkles around his eyes.

"You didn't have to make me one, but thank you."

She tried to swallow the lump of food, but spoke over the mouthful. "No problem." She swallowed and chased the bite with a drink of water.

"Was that the FBI agent you know?"

"Nate? Yeah." He took a bite of the sandwich. "Ethan is another friend. You'll meet him soon. He's flying in from Vegas. His flight was delayed, so he won't land until late tonight."

"What's your big plan?" She watched him carefully as she took another bite.

He shrugged. "I plan on paying Stamos a visit with some backup, beating the shit out of him until he tells me who hired him. Pretty simple."

She swallowed hard. He spoke so casually, as if such a thing didn't bother him in the least. Cal's thick, massive fists could do a lot of damage.

"Great sandwich." He stood, went to the kitchen, and started making another one.

She patted her mouth with a napkin. "Will that work? Beating him up?"

Cal grinned at her. "I can be very persuading." His arm flexed as he piled on his toppings.

She shifted in her chair. She had never witnessed a fight, and violence didn't sit well with her. "I don't think I'd be able to watch that."

"Don't worry, you'll be right here."

She swung around to face him. "Here? You mean at the cabin?"

"'Course. There's no way I would bring you along. You never know what could happen." He came back to the table and dove into his food.

"You can't leave me here. I'm coming with you."

"Not happening, babe." He wiped his mouth while he chewed. "Ethan is driving here in the morning and staying with you. I'm driving in to meet Nate and get to the bottom of this."

Her heart thumped at the endearment that fell so easily from his lips. But who did he think he was? He couldn't just leave her with a damn babysitter. She had every right to know who was behind this. She glared at him through squinted eyes. "Don't call me that."

He winked at her. Her blood simmered.

"I'm coming with you, whether you like it or not. I'm not a child, and I won't be left here twiddling my thumbs with a babysitter."

"Lana, it's dangerous. I'm trying to keep you safe, that's the whole objective to this. If you're with me, it will be that much harder for me to protect you. Trust me, okay?" His voice was gentle, pleading.

"I won't be breathing down your neck or glued to your side, but I am *not* staying here."

He crossed his arms on a long sigh. "Does everything have to be so difficult with you?" His tone was irritated, but his eyes sparked with amusement.

She'd won.

She smiled and cleared the table.

"I sing in the car, just so you know."

* * * *

"It doesn't make sense for you to sleep in the La-Z-Boy. I'm a lot smaller than you. You take the bed." Lana hovered by Cal as he arranged the logs in the fireplace.

The expansive view of his shoulders crowded her vision as he crouched down. He straightened and turned to snag one of the pillows off of the bed. They had discovered that the futon mattress was still damp, and the chair was the only other option besides the bed.

"I can sleep anywhere," he said as he pushed the La-Z-Boy closer to the fire. "This is perfect."

She crossed her arms tightly over her chest. He acted as if she had cooties or that she would sexually assault him if he came near her.

"Fine." He could toss and turn in the chair if he wanted. She had a king-sized bed all to herself. Only she wouldn't have the warmth and comfort that she'd had last night from Cal's body.

She climbed into bed and pulled the covers up to her chin. Cal had found a blanket in one of the closets and settled in the chair. He looked ridiculous. His feet hung off the edge, and no matter which way he shifted, his body folded in an awkward position.

He would be sore tomorrow. She closed her eyes and let the gentle roar of the ocean lull her to sleep.

An hour passed and she was still wide awake. Her thoughts churned like the brewing ocean outside. She wasn't safe anymore. That was obvious, but after this, how could she possibly go back to her "normal" life? Okay, her life was far from normal, but it was hers, and at the very least, she hadn't been worried that someone was going to jump out and kill her at any moment. Now she was. Did her family even know she was missing yet? Her father and Grace wouldn't return for another couple of days. No one would miss her until she didn't show up for work tomorrow. Even then, she doubted anyone would be concerned enough to bother her father about her absence while he was on a business trip.

Cal's flirtatious smile filled her mind's eye. What was the matter with her? He'd kidnapped her, for God's sake, and yet her stomach did flip-flops with every glance from him.

The chair squeaked for the thousandth time as he tried to get comfortable. She huffed. "Would you just get in the bed? I can't sleep with all the moving around you're doing over there. I won't bite, I promise. This bed is big enough for the both of us to have some distance."

He was silent.

Shit. Did she sound that desperate? Her pulse thumped in her throat. *Stupid, stupid, stupid.*

"Sorry, I'll be quieter." His voice was gruff and sleepy.

Tears stung her eyes. She shouldn't be upset. She didn't even know him. He was a stranger to her—a dangerous one. His distance was for the best.

* * * *

The warm, tantalizing scent of coffee drew her out of her sleepy haze. She had tossed and turned all night, her mind spinning over who could want her dead. And on top of that, a tingling sensation demanded release. A release she wouldn't get until she was far away from Cal and alone.

"We've had a change of plans." Cal's voice made her eyes pop open. He was on the phone in the kitchen, freshly showered, shaved, and dressed.

"We'll both be coming back to the city. Lana will stay with Ethan at my house, while you and I do some investigating." He paused, listening to the speaker, whom she assumed to be Nate. "Yeah, I know. We'll just roll with it, though."

She threw back the covers, sat, and stretched her arms above her head as she rested on the edge of the bed. Cal's eyes found her as he sipped his coffee, the phone pressed to his ear. His Adam's apple bobbed, and he turned his back when the toaster popped. She'd removed the bulky sweater in the night when the fire had gotten the room toasty. The air in the room was brisk now that the fire was out, and the sun was just coming up, its rays streaming into the window. She wore only a thin white T-shirt of Cal's, and the cool air chilled her skin. She snagged the sweater off the end of the bed and tugged it on.

Her toes touched the floor first, turning them to ice.

"Coffee is ready," he called from the kitchen. "I made some toast and we have fruit. We can grab something more substantial on the way."

"How far are we from the city?" It hadn't even occurred to her to ask where they were.

"Under two hours. We're just outside of Mount Vernon." He turned to face her again. "We'll meet Nate and Ethan at my house, and Ethan will stay there with you." She shuffled across the room and met him at the table. He handed her a mug while she sat. She'd grown up in Seattle her whole life, but had only been to Mount Vernon a handful of times.

"That's the best compromise you'll get, so don't push it." His eyes were warm and not as distant as last night. She smiled as she accepted the cup.

"Fine, but I can't wear your clothes anymore. I need something else."

He placed a plate with half a dozen pieces of toast and a plastic container of precut fruit on the table.

"No problem, we can stop somewhere on the way." He polished off a piece of toast in three bites. She nibbled on the crust of one.

"We can't risk going to the mall. It's Monday, and by now, someone could have discovered you're missing. It won't be long before your face is plastered all over the news."

She swallowed hard. A wave of nausea roiled in her stomach. The harsh reality slowed her breath.

"You okay?" Cal watched her closely, his eyes heavy with concern.

"I'm fine. I'll take anything that will fit."

He nodded. "If you want to shower before we go, hurry up. I want to get on the road before people are out looking for you."

"If it's okay, I'll just shower at your house once I have fresh clothes."

"Fine with me. We can leave after we get packed up."

They packed up the food that was left over and the rest of their belongings. Cal knelt on the floor in front of his duffel bag. He pulled a black object from it and slipped it into the waistband at the small of his back.

A gun.

Her breath sucked in.

"Sorry, you're probably not used to seeing these." He stood and lifted the bag to his shoulder. "I always have one on me. But don't worry, the safety is on, okay?"

Of course, he would have a gun. It made sense, but the fact that he needed one sent a tremor down her spine.

She nodded.

They stopped at a boutique on the way back to the city. Cal had thought it would be best if they avoided shopping where someone could spot her. She picked out some leggings and long-sleeved shirts, and when Cal wasn't looking, a couple of bras and panties. Cal insisted she buy a few extra outfits in case it took longer than planned to get her life back on track. Her feet were bare, but thankfully the store was empty. She grabbed a simple pair of black flats and met him at the line of registers.

Without hesitation, he pulled out cash and paid for her purchases.

"I'll pay you back as soon as I have access to money." He took the bags from her fingers as they left the store.

"Don't be ridiculous. I'm not hurting for money." He tossed her bags in the back seat, then opened the passenger door for her. The gesture came without hesitation. Her eyes landed on his. "Hop in."

"I didn't expect chivalry from you." She hadn't meant it as an insult, but it sounded that way. His eyes clouded, but his smile didn't fade. Separate worlds. They were from separate worlds.

"Glad I could surprise you." He waved at her again. "Let's go."

He closed the door and came around to the driver's side as she buckled up.

"What led you to become a freelance security contractor?" she asked as he started the truck and pulled out onto the street. The words rolled over her tongue, unfamiliar to her idea of careers. The title itself was complicated and gave nothing away to indicate what he claimed to do. His hand held loosely to the top of the steering wheel, his right hand resting on the console.

"I was in the military, and then I advanced to recon. I was good, and when I learned I could contract myself out, that seemed like the right fit for me."

He made it sound so simple. "What do you do, exactly?"

"I take jobs and assignments that are sometimes organized by the government, sometimes private requests. In some cases, it has me out of the country and in very dangerous situations."

She couldn't imagine that kind of life. His life was so strange, almost like an alien's. Her hands fumbled in her lap. She wanted to keep the conversation moving and she needed the distraction. No matter how hard she tried not to think about it, it surged from her subconscious. Someone wanted to kill her. Two nights ago, she could have been dead.

His fingers went to the cruise control. He eased his foot off the pedal and stretched out his long, jeans-clad legs. She let her eyes trail down his body, and her gaze stopped on the bulge at the front of his pants. Her pulse hitched.

Cal cleared his throat, loud and deliberate.

Her eyes shot to his face.

He was grinning.

She bit her lip and turned to look out the front window. Her cheeks burned. But not nearly as bad as the fire that had started in her belly.

"I've tried to be selective about the jobs I take. I'm getting older and don't have the same mind-set I used to have."

She turned back to look at him. "How old are you?" He didn't look older. His skin was nicely tanned, his body beyond fit and toned.

"Thirty-two. Don't get me wrong, I love what I do, but I don't want to die doing it."

"Don't you want to have kids? Get married someday?"

He kept his eyes on the road, but his mouth twitched fondly. "I'd love a couple of kids, but I would never subject a wife and a family to my lifestyle. It wouldn't be fair."

"You just said you wanted to slow down."

"Slow down, not retire."

"You're giving up so much of your life for your career." She bit her lip after the words left her mouth. "I'm sorry, it's really none of my business." She folded her legs in the seat, getting comfortable. He pulled onto the highway.

"Don't be. Maybe one day I'll retire, buy a farm or start my own business. For now, I like the bachelor life."

Aha. He was single. A thrill raced through her. Hope expanded in her chest.

"How have you stayed single since college? I find that hard to believe." She twisted in her seat. Her hands locked in her lap. "It's simple. I haven't found anyone that I wanted to date seriously. I, too, enjoy being single."

Cal laughed.

She narrowed her eyes at him. "What's funny about that?"

He shook his head, his lips tight. "Nothing—nothing at all."

She pinched his forearm. "Tell me, don't back down." He caught her hand as he twisted out of her reach. His hand covered hers, those long, strong fingers dark against her pale ones.

He let go.

"It's just that your idea of a single life is very different from mine." She folded her arms in front of her chest. "How so?"

"I still have sex. A lot of sex."

She pursed her lips. Yeah, big difference. No wonder he'd thought it so funny. "Oh. Well, that's nice for you, I guess."

He laughed again. "I'd like to think I'm not the only one who enjoys it." He slanted a salacious grin at her. Her toes curled. "You're turning red." He reached over and tugged a lock of her hair. She leaned out of his reach.

"Just keep your eyes on the road."

He pinched her knee between his thumb and forefinger, then moved his hand back to the console. She couldn't talk about sex with him. It made her picture it. In her experience, sex hadn't been phenomenal. But with Cal...the fantasy made her nerve endings tingle.

They were quiet the rest of the drive. It was early afternoon by the time they made it through traffic and to the west end of Seattle. The sun set low over the mountains, its golden rays scattered across the sky, beyond the heavy clouds. He turned into an older neighborhood along the coast of Elliott Bay. She loved this area. But she hadn't envisioned Cal living here. A lot of the homes were old, historical even.

He turned down a long driveway that led to a sprawling rancher. He'd done a nice job with the landscaping, though it was a little overgrown in some areas. Likely a by-product of his busy career.

"This is beautiful. How long have you lived here?"

He pulled into the first bay of the three-car garage and turned off the engine. "I bought the house about five years ago. It was built in the seventies."

She got out of the truck while he got her shopping bags from the back seat. He paused to insert a key into the access door to the house and swung it open.

"I did a complete remodel," he continued. "Just finished it last year." He switched on the hall light that brought them to a walk-through butler's pantry, and exited in the kitchen. She trailed behind him, admiring the cool travertine tile that transitioned to hardwood once they reached the kitchen. He flipped on more lights.

"Sonofabitch," he growled.

She looked up. "Oh my God." A gasp sounded from her throat. She covered her mouth with her hand. The house was trashed. Kitchen cupboards hung off their hinges, and shattered dishes littered the counter and floors. The fridge and freezer doors were wide open. Water lay in puddles on the gorgeous hardwoods. The open-concept living room was in shambles. The stuffing from the couch cushion looked like popcorn had exploded around the room. Holes littered the walls like the end of a baseball bat had been shoved through them.

He stormed through the main area, taking in the damage.

"W–who would do this?" Her fingers trailed along the crisp white quartz counters. Before the intruders, the home would have been gorgeous. Cal rubbed a hand over his head. The muscles in his jaw worked.

"They must have found out I never completed the job." A vein bulged and pulsated in his throat. He didn't say it specifically, but they had come here and destroyed his home because she was still alive. Had they been looking for him? Or her? He dropped her shopping bag on the floor next to the couch. "Come here. I want to look around, and they could come back."

She came to his side and rested her hand on his arm. His bicep flexed beneath her touch.

"I'm so sorry, Cal."

He shook his head. "It's not your fault." His hand fell to the back of her neck. "Come on, stay close." His fingers closed around hers as he led her down the extra-wide hallway. Artwork that hung on the walls had thick slash marks through them, broken pieces of glass from a tall mirror at the end of the hall scattered the floor. The only thing that hadn't been destroyed was the hardwood floors.

He stopped in his tracks. Her nose bumped into his shoulder blade. "There's glass everywhere." He turned and scooped her up in his arms.

"I can step around it," she protested. He ignored her and skirted around the glass. When they were safely in the master bedroom—his room—he set her back on her feet. The intruders hadn't spared his personal space. Clothes scattered the floor, a dresser lay on its side on the floor, and a large chunk had been taken out of the wall. The massive California-king mattress lay flipped over against the far wall.

"*Why would they do this?*"

He paced around the room, into the master bath and out. His hands balled into tight fists at his sides. "They were looking for the money."

"Money? What money?"

Thump, thump, thump!

Cal jerked his head up. "Someone's here." He pulled her farther into the room, his hands firm on her shoulders. "Stay here and don't come out until I come and get you."

Her breath sucked in. She nodded.

"Lock the door."

He shut the door behind him. Her hands shook as she clicked the lock. She backed away from the door, her eyes riveted to the solid steel device.

He had a dead bolt on his bedroom door.

Chapter 11

Cal pulled his Glock out of the waistband of his pants and advanced on the front door.

Thump, thump, thump!

If they had come back hoping to find him, they'd be really fucking sorry. A quick look out the side window revealed Nate and Ethan's tall forms. He exhaled and swung the door open. "Dammit, I thought you guys were going to call."

Nate entered first, his height almost equivalent to Cal's. Ethan was about an inch taller. The three of them had served in recon together, before each had branched out into different careers. Nate preferred the intensity of putting drug dealers and sex traffickers behind bars with the FBI. Ethan, on the other hand, was still figuring out his career choice. He'd been the last of the three of them to leave recon, and had just left the FBI.

"I sent you a text. You didn't get it? Lana's face is all over the news." Dammit. He hadn't checked his phone since their last bathroom break.

"No, I didn't. Sonofabitch."

Ethan whistled. "What the hell happened here? You get in a tussle?"

"No." Cal shut the door behind them. "We just got here. This was waiting for me." He spread his arms wide as he led them through the foyer and into the common area.

"Motherfucker," Nate breathed.

Cal grimaced. He didn't want to estimate the damage, but the smashed seventy-inch TV screen made him cringe.

"Only possessions, right? It can all be replaced." Ethan clapped him on the back. Had Cal been a smaller man, the force would have jarred his shoulder. It didn't. "Good thing you've got lots of dough. Don't worry, bro.

I know a great team that can come in and get this place back in order. You won't even know it happened."

"Thanks, appreciate it."

"Don't mention it."

"Where is she?" Nate circled around the living room before meeting them back in the kitchen.

"In the bedroom. I was on edge when I heard the door, so I left her back there. Didn't even occur to me it would be you guys already."

Ethan grinned. "Have you forgotten how fast we're used to moving?"

The mention of their military days brought a wave of nostalgia. Despite the shitstorm around him, he didn't miss that life. He saluted Ethan, and headed down the hall to retrieve Lana.

He tapped lightly on the bedroom door, "Lana, you can come out. It's just Nate and Ethan." He heard the dead bolt turn, and the door slowly opened.

She stood in the doorway, her hair tumbling around her shoulders, her big blue eyes wide and cautious. Her hands fidgeted in front of her. His insides twisted with guilt. He hadn't meant to scare her.

"It's okay, honey. I doubt whoever broke in will be back. But still, we're going to leave soon and check into a hotel." He reached for her. She inched closer. Her face was pale, and she trembled beneath his hands. Guilt tightened his gut. God, he wished he could erase that flash of fear on her face. His arms ached to wrap around her, to slow her rapid breathing. But doing so would be playing with fire. She nodded slowly, and her throat bobbed on a swallow. He cursed under his breath. Screw it. He pulled her to his chest, tucking her head beneath his chin.

A soft sigh escaped her lips. Her body relaxed against his. He smoothed his hands gently down the slim curve of her back. He dipped his head, inhaling the soft scent of her hair. She smelled like coconuts, the same shampoo he'd used. Only it was different on her. Her own sweet smell mixed with it and tickled his nostrils. Her hands gripped the material of his shirt.

Unbelievable. He was getting hard just from the smell of her. God, he couldn't take it anymore. Being around her was torture. It was affecting his health and his sanity. If he didn't find a release soon, he'd explode.

"Let's go." He eased her away and led her down the hall.

By the time they reached the common area, all signs of fear had vanished from her porcelain face. She wore not a hint of makeup, her hair fell in wild waves around her shoulders, and she still wore his large sweatshirt and the sweatpants from this morning. Her spine straightened, her chin lifted, and she smiled warmly.

Ethan and Nate each reached for one of her hands for introductions.

"It's so nice to meet the both of you."

"Pleasure is mine." Ethan winked at her.

"You're even more beautiful in person." This came from Nate. Lana smiled demurely. The bastard was hitting on her. Cal cracked his neck from left to right and shot Nate a look to kill. Nate ribbed him in the side with his elbow and leaned in to whisper, "Got your panties in a bunch, did I?"

"Go fuck yourself."

Nate chuckled and fell back into step behind Lana and Ethan as they moved around the living room. They were surveying the damage, and their constant pacing put Cal on edge.

While the three of them chatted, Cal pulled out his phone. He would need to get a hotel room for at least a couple of nights. He made reservations, making sure to book a large one-bedroom suite so Lana would have her own bed. He would take the pullout. The room price had been staggering, but he'd chosen one of the city's finest hotels. Tight security was of the utmost importance. He hoped they could get through the lobby without anyone recognizing her.

"Alright, the room is booked," he announced. "I'm going to pack a few more things, and then we can get going."

Everyone nodded, but they still continued to talk. Nate said something to Lana that made her cover her mouth as she let out a delicate laugh. When she wasn't looking, Cal pointed a warning finger at Nate. He raised his hands in an *"I'm innocent"* gesture. Fucking prick.

Nate wouldn't swoop in on Lana. That he was sure of. Nate was a loyal friend, and he'd had Cal's back for more than a decade now. He just enjoyed getting a rise out of him, and dammit, it was working.

In his room, he emptied his duffel bag from the last couple of days, and replenished it with fresh clothes. He grabbed some extra shirts for Lana. The boutique hadn't sold pajamas, and he didn't want her to have to sleep in her new clothes. Besides, she looked sexy as hell in his T-shirts.

On the way out, he stopped in the kitchen and grabbed a couple of protein bars. His stomach growled. The second they were settled, he was ordering a feast from room service.

They loaded up and pulled out of the garage. "They seem like really sweet guys," Lana commented as she buckled her seat belt. Nate and Ethan would meet them at the hotel.

"Don't be fooled, they're asses."

She waved that off. "I can tell you guys are close. It's adorable."

Adorable? Ha. That was a laugh. If she only knew the shit they'd all done. She was right on one point, though. "They're like brothers to me."

A soft smile touched her lips. "I wish I had siblings."

* * * *

When they got on the road, he reached into the back seat and pulled out a black baseball cap. "Put this on and keep your head low. Nate told me your disappearance has made the news."

She accepted the hat and fit it over her head. "My dad must be so worried. I should call him." Pain, heavy and raw, wavered her voice. His heart wrenched. He flitted a glance her way. With her head down, he couldn't see her whole face, but her mouth thinned. Edward was surely going through hell. He couldn't imagine being a father and finding out his daughter was missing. Nausea made his stomach lurch.

"I'm sorry, babe. I know how much that must upset you." He placed a hand on her thigh and smoothed the cotton material with his thumb. "But you can't call him. Not yet, okay? It's too dangerous. Not only for you, but for him. I'll do my best to find out who is behind this tonight. Then all this will be over."

And she would never have a reason to see or speak to him again. The minute this situation was resolved, she would be gone. Back to her life, her other world—and far away from the darkness of his—right where she belonged.

She nodded and kept her gaze down.

When they pulled up to the hotel, he parked out front and turned to face her. "We can't bring you in through the lobby. Someone will recognize you. I'm going to go check in. Then we can self-park in the Parkade and we'll take the stairs up to our room, okay?"

"Okay."

"I'll have the guys come wait with you." Almost on cue, Nate and Ethan pulled up and parked a few spots down. "Wait here."

Nate and Ethan got out of the vehicle, and Cal told them his plan. They agreed to wait with Lana, and once they'd slid into the back seat of his truck, he went to the front entrance to check in.

There weren't many people checking in, probably because it was Monday. He asked for extra room keys—just in case—and declined the valet parking.

Lana, Nate, and Ethan were talking amiably when he got back to the truck.

"All set." He passed a room key to each of them. "Hang on to those in case of emergencies." He pulled out of the parking spot and drove to the underground parking lot.

When they got out and headed toward the entrance, Cal instructed Lana to keep her head down and out of view of the cameras. He, Nate, and Ethan formed a human shield around her; Cal walked in front, Ethan to her left, and Nate to her right. They made it up to the room without encountering anyone.

"Whoa, honeymoon suite, or what?" Nate whistled when they walked in. Cal glowered at him.

"Cal, you didn't have to do all of this," Lana said in a hushed voice. The room was more opulent than even he'd expected.

"It was the only room besides the penthouse with a separate bedroom, alright? Lana, the room is yours. You need your privacy."

The shine in her eyes faded. Had he said something wrong?

"Thank you," she said. "If you boys don't mind, I'm dying for a shower and clean clothes."

"Go right ahead, honey."

"'Honey'?" Nate and Ethan echoed when Lana shut the bedroom door and was out of earshot. The endearment had been meant to soften the blow of whatever he'd said that had put that look in her eyes.

"Shut it." He went to the bar and poured himself a drink. He didn't normally indulge before a job, but after being cooped up with Lana for two days, he needed some form of release.

"You're calling her 'honey' and banishing yourself out of the bedroom? Tell me you're tapping that." This, of course, came from Nate. Ethan smacked him on the back of the head.

"Go to hell," Cal warned. His tone was lethal. Lana wasn't one to 'tap,' plain and simple.

"Hey, I'm looking out for you, bro. I saw that look in her eyes. She likes you. Like, a lot. Tell him, E."

Ethan accepted the drink he'd made him. Nate could damn well make his own. A pit formed in his stomach. Shit, were they right? He hadn't meant to push her away. He was only trying to protect her. Ethan's mouth lifted into a knowing smirk. Whatever. It was none of their damn business anyway. And he sure wasn't going to discuss his thoughts about Lana when he'd barely had a chance to analyze them himself. Emotions were always high in situations like this. So, if Nate claimed to have seen something in her eyes, it sure as hell didn't mean it was really interest in *him*. Fear was the more likely source of her wide eyes and sultry lips. Nate would interpret anything as sexual.

He met Nate's stupid grin. "Let's just stay on track, all right?" He didn't need the damn distraction of their input in his personal life.

Ethan chuckled, and Nate lifted a hand in surrender. "Fine. You always liked to figure shit out the hard way." He took a sip of his drink, and Cal suppressed the burning comment that singed his tongue. "Who do you think trashed your place?"

"Stamos, without a doubt. His fee depends on the job being complete, so when Lana's death wasn't reported, he would have known I deviated."

"Why the hell are you still in contact with that guy, anyway?" Ethan settled into a chair and shook his head in disgust. Yeah, Cal was pretty disgusted about it too.

"He's hard to shake. He never got so annoying that I had to tell him off, just some harmless phone calls a couple times a year."

"He knows where you live?"

Cal sighed. The nosy bastard had a way of weaseling himself into people's lives. Looking back at Stamos's questions into Cal's career and his fascination with his life, it was obvious now that he'd wanted information.

"Yeah, I let him come over when he presented me the job to kill Lana. You know I never bring random people to my house, but in all the years I've known him, he's never crossed me. He claimed the job was top secret and had to be discussed in a secure location. I should have known better."

Nate's lip lifted into a snarl. "Why the hell would he think you'd kill an innocent woman, anyway?"

Cal shrugged. "I've never given him too many details about what I do. But I *have* told him that it's dangerous and takes me to the darkest places of hell on earth. I let him gather his own assumptions. When he told me the job, though, there was no way in hell I could walk away."

Ethan nodded slowly, and Nate's eyes darkened. "We'd have done the same thing," Ethan said. "It's a damn good thing he came to you and no one else."

Cal took a long sip of his drink.

That was what kept creeping up into his head from the back of his mind, tormenting his thoughts.

Had it been anyone else but him, she'd be dead.

* * * *

"Just be careful." Lana bit her lip as she pleaded. He rubbed his hands up and down her arms. Ethan pretended to change the channels on the TV, and Nate waited by the door, looking around the room. Both doing a shitty job of pretending they weren't listening to every bloody word.

Damn, she looked sexy. She was freshly showered, her hair still damp. She wore light gray leggings and a deep V-neck long-sleeved shirt, with her pert cleavage just visible.

It was a good thing he trusted Ethan with his life.

"I'll be fine. I'll be back late, so don't wait up."

She nodded. Her teeth nipped at her bottom lip. It took every ounce of his resolve not to take that wounded lip into his mouth and kiss her. He chucked her under her chin with his knuckle and winked. That earned him a shy smile.

Ethan and Nate might be right, but he sure as hell wasn't going to kiss her for the first time with their watchful amusement.

He closed the hotel room door tightly after Lana sat in the living room with Ethan. They'd had a huge dinner, and he'd insisted she order anything she needed from the concierge. He and Nate took the elevator to the main floor and exited the lobby to where Nate's truck was parked. It was too risky to be driving around in his own. Although the police wouldn't have identified him as a suspect, whoever had trashed his house would, and they would be on the hunt.

They got in and drove to Capitol Hill.

"You think he'll be there?"

Cal looked at the time; it was going on 7 p.m. "I don't know. I suspect he spends more time there than he does at home."

Nate parked in front of the strip club that Stamos had said he frequented. "Well, we can't exactly bust in there, guns blazing."

"You wait here. I'll go in and see if I can spot him. If he's there, we'll wait until he comes out. He smokes, so it won't be long."

He fit the baseball cap Lana had worn onto his head, then exited the truck. The club was quiet. A few old men sat at the bar, and the other few scumbags were peppered around the stage. A thin, leggy blonde gyrated on the stage; her gold-sequined thong reflected the strobe lights, sending a flurry of golden light into his eyes. And there, front and center, was Stamos, tossing singles.

"Woo-hoo. Come over this way, sexy." Stamos's immature catcall sounded through the half-empty room.

Cal groaned under his breath and adjusted his cap. He quietly left the bar and crossed the street. A gaggle of young women passed him on the way out. A cloud of their cheap perfume swarmed his face. Their skimpy outfits led him to believe they would be starting their own shifts soon. Their wandering eyes raked over him.

"Mmm…yummy." One of the girls traced her leopard-print fingernail over his shoulder. He stepped out of her reach.

"Sorry, I'm done for the night."

She pouted her red painted lips. "Too bad."

He smiled and sidled through them. "Good night, ladies." At one point, a spark of interest would have shot through him. Not enough interest for him to sleep with a stripper, but a stir of sexual attraction would have warmed inside him.

Not now. Not the slightest hint of reaction raced through him. All he could think about was Lana.

"He's there." Cal slid into the passenger seat and shut the door. "Looked as though he had a few buddies with him. We'll need to take them all."

Nate snorted. "Easy peasy." He pushed his seat back and got comfortable. Cal, on the other hand, kept his gaze trained on the club entrance.

"Have you had any word on that list of people I gave you?" Tanner kept popping up in his mind. He couldn't shake the possessive glint he'd seen in the photo taken at the gala. If there was one thing he could easily read, it was a guy staking his claim. But Tanner's damn attack left acid churning in his stomach. If the bastard had anything to do with wanting her killed, Cal would find out.

"No, I should have something late morning or early afternoon tomorrow. You have a hunch?"

Nate knew him well. "Sort of." He didn't want to get too deep in conversation, though, and miss Stamos if he came out.

"Trust your gut, man. It hasn't misled you yet."

Fifteen minutes later, Stamos strode out, two friends in tow behind him. They laughed and shoved each other around, then stopped in a tight circle on the sidewalk and sparked their cigarettes.

Nate rubbed his hands together. "Let's roll."

Cal pulled his cap down low again. They stepped out of the truck and moved swiftly down the sidewalk toward the small group.

"S'cuse me, you got a light?" Nate asked as they approached the group. All three swiveled to look at them. Stamos had his short, curly hair gelled close to his scalp. Idiot Number One had long black hair fastened in a ponytail at his nape. Idiot Number Two had a poor bleach-blond dye job.

"Sure—"

Nate's booted foot connected with the back of Idiot Number One's knee. He folded like a cheap lawn chair.

"What the fu—" Stamos and Idiot Number Two tossed their cigarettes and charged them. Cal threw a sucker punch to Idiot Number Two's nose.

It crunched beneath his knuckles. He howled and staggered back. Blood squirted through his fingers.

"Here's your chance, Ponytail. Run while you can," Nate warned. Ponytail staggered to his feet and advanced on Nate. He stopped him with a swift kick to his solar plexus. Stamos's eyes connected with Cal's.

"Motherfucker," he breathed. His hand dove for the gun at his waist, but Cal aimed his Glock at his head. Stamos froze as his body vibrated with rage and his eyes turned beady. Cal reached for Stamos's gun and shoved it into the waistband of his own pants. He snagged him by the collar of his jacket with his free hand, then shifted him to a chokehold. Stamos struggled and bounced against Cal's chest. Stamos's heels connected with his shins.

"Hold the fuck still, you punk. We just want to talk."

Nate turned as Ponytail hobbled away. "Cal, look out!"

The hairs on the back of his neck stiffened. He turned with Stamos still in his grip. Idiot Number Two slashed a knife through the air, then it sliced through his deltoid like a hot knife through butter. Fire shot through his shoulder, but it numbed in a heartbeat. His adrenaline stifled the pain.

"You're going to pay for that," he growled.

"I got it, dude." Nate charged. Idiot Number Two went down like a ton of bricks after a deadly dropkick to the face. "He'll feel that later."

Cal backed up toward Nate's parked car. "Hop in the back and get the duct tape ready," he barked to Nate.

He opened the truck door. Stamos hung in the crook of his right arm. "Someone's probably called the cops," he moaned.

"Not to worry, we aren't sticking around." He heaved Stamos's 170-pound frame into the back seat, where Nate was.

"'Sup, buddy? We're goin' for a ride." He peeled a strip of duct tape and worked at securing Stamos. Cal climbed in the front passenger seat.

"Be sure to seal his mouth. If I have to hear that dumbass pubescent voice again, I'm going to thump him."

Nate tore another strip of duct tape. "Done." Nate got out and climbed in the driver's seat. "Where we heading?"

"Let's take him back to my place, so he can pay for every broken thing in my house."

Nate nodded, started the ignition, and peeled away from the curb.

* * * *

"What do you think, Cal, an eye for an eye?" Nate balanced his hands on his hips. "I guess it would be more like a couch for an eye, wouldn't it?" he mused.

"Sounds about right."

"I didn't do it, man. I was at the club last night—all night." He wrestled against the duct tape that secured him to the chair in the center of the destroyed kitchen. A red strip outlined his mouth where Nate had removed the duct tape.

"That so?" Cal uncrossed his arms over his chest and pulled his phone out of his back pocket. "Luckily I have security cameras. One sec while I log in to my account," he said politely.

Stamos cursed.

"How much was that couch?" Nate lifted himself to sit on the edge of Cal's quartz island.

"Ten grand."

Nate coughed. "Seriously, dude?"

"It was custom-made." He shrugged. A couple more clicks, and he had his surveillance video for the last twenty-four hours pulled up. He fast-forwarded until he saw three thugs break in through the back entrance. The hairs on the back of his neck prickled as he watched his home—his stuff—being vandalized, contaminated. He exhaled a hot breath through his nose. Pausing the video on a good view of Stamos, he turned the screen to Nate.

"Who's that look like to you?"

Nate gasped. "My goodness, Stamos, I think you have a doppelganger." He took the phone from Cal's fingers, hopped off the counter, and held it an inch from Stamos's nose. "Tell me, douche. Who is that?"

Stamos gulped. A bead of sweat rolled down his forehead and over the outside of his eye. He whimpered. "They made me."

"Oh." Nate straightened. "Well, *that* changes everything."

Cal's rage threatened to bubble over. He was glad Nate was here to intervene. His hands itched to break every bone in Stamos's body. Not because he'd trashed his house, but because he would have gladly killed Lana two nights ago. He pulled his Glock from the waistband of his pants and strode dutifully to Stamos.

"I'm sorry, man! I'll replace it."

He shoved the barrel of the gun under his chin. "I don't give a shit about my house or the couch—"

"Super-sharp couch, though. Didn't you say you used an interior designer?"

Cal unlocked the safety. Stamos whimpered.

"Yeah, *Stephanie*. Why do you think I paid ten grand for it?" Cal grinned at Nate. Stamos looked from Nate to Cal and back again. Nate was having fun screwing with Stamos. It was the only thing keeping him calm—and it beat killing him.

He dropped the gun to Stamos's shoulder. The man's eyes widened and his lips trembled.

"What was that game we used to play? You remember, when we caught that sex trafficker?" Cal asked Nate absently.

"Ah, yes. Eenie, meenie, miney, mo."

Cal pointed his Glock from one shoulder to the other. "Eenie, meenie, miney, mo."

"Please, man. I said I was sorry."

"Sorry for what? For planning a young woman's murder?" He spat the words out. Stamos shook in the chair.

Nate clapped a hand on Cal's shoulder.

"I'm going to take your shoulder out, Ian." Cal spoke calmly, using Stamos's first name. "You tell me who hired you, and I won't take out the other one."

Nate moaned. "That's a bitch injury. You're going to need surgery and physio after that."

"Fuck, man." Stamos sobbed.

"One." Cal's voice echoed through the room. "Two."

"Will. His name is Will Anderson. That's all I know, I swear." Cal looked at Nate. He shrugged in response.

"Where does he live?"

Sweat dripped over his eyebrow and into the corner of his eye.

"Don't make me repeat myself," Cal ground out.

"I don't know, honest." He blinked the sweat away. "Please don't do it." Stamos's voice broke.

Cal stood from his crouched position, keeping his Glock trained on Stamos's right shoulder. Ice filled his veins, numbing him to Stamos's pleas. This man would have killed Lana without blinking. For that, Cal couldn't be forgiving. He moved his forefinger over the trigger.

"No!" Stamos lurched forward, but Cal's finger was quicker. He turned his face away to avoid the blood splatter and pulled the trigger. A gush of blood landed at his feet, just missing his shoes.

Stamos screamed, his face contorted in pain. Sweat collected at the collar of his shirt as he heaved shuddering gasps through clenched teeth.

"Man, that's gross." Nate tugged on Cal's elbow. Cal shook off his hold and tucked his Glock back in his pants. He wasn't done yet. He grabbed the arms of Stamos's chair, his knuckles turning white on the smooth plastic. He jerked it backward, balancing it on its back legs.

"If I catch you sniffing around her again, I'll kill you in the most painful way you can imagine. Got it?"

Stamos kept his hold on his shoulder, blood oozing around his fingers. Not a shred of guilt touched him. Stamos's wild eyes met Cal's, and a flash of rage dilated his pupils. He gave one sharp nod.

"I fucking mean it. The only reason you're alive right now is because I haven't found out yet who's really behind this. Unless you want me to come back and finish what I started here tonight, stay the hell away." He let go and the chair toppled over. Stamos spilled onto the floor in the pool of his own blood.

"C'mon, Cal. Let's get out of here."

It took both of them to drag Stamos to the vehicle. They dropped him off outside the strip club where they'd collected him.

"Think you can find everything we need on Will Anderson?"

Nate nodded. "Should be easy enough. I'll let Ethan know, too. Won't hurt to have us both working on it."

"Good call," Cal said. As he settled back in his seat, his mind returned to Stamos. He should have killed the bastard. It had taken every ounce of his control not to. But until this was over, Stamos needed to stay alive.

Will Anderson was next.

Chapter 12

Lana threw the covers back and inched on tiptoes to the closed bedroom door.

Cal was back. The men spoke softly. A laugh erupted from Ethan, then all went quiet. Little did they know that she'd been lying awake, watching the hours on the clock tick by, waiting for Cal to return.

It was after midnight. She had excused herself from the sitting room and Ethan's company hours ago, with no intention of sleeping. How could she, when he was out hunting the streets? She'd been terrified that something would happen to him. She had no clue what they were getting into or what he would find out. Her mind kept circling around people she'd met, her father's business associates... Still she came up blank. It was very likely her father had enemies, but would they set out to kill her over a business dealing? It felt like a stretch. Cal had said her disappearance had been on the news. It had taken every ounce of control not to pick up the phone and call her mom or dad. They would be devastated. Her throat tightened. It wasn't fair—none of this was. But she couldn't risk ruining all the hard work Cal was doing. She had promised to trust him, and she did. Maybe after tonight everything would be solved.

She tangled her hand in her hair and squeezed her eyes shut. Had he found Stamos? Did he know who was behind this? God, she wished this entire nightmare would be over with.

The hotel room door closed. The *clink* of metal on metal told her he'd chained the door. Ethan and Nate were gone for the night.

The en suite bathroom to the large bedroom also connected to the hall. After a minute or so, the bathroom light clicked on and the hall door shut.

Wearing only one of his T-shirts that reached mid-thigh and a pair of panties, she tapped lightly on the door with her knuckle. She held her breath. Her pulse raced.

The door opened. Cal stood in the doorway, wearing only the pair of dark jeans he'd had on when he'd left. A black T-shirt lay strewn on the bathroom floor. Blood trickled down his arm from a gash near his shoulder.

Her hand flew to her mouth. She gasped.

"You're hurt," she hissed and stepped onto her tiptoes to inspect the deep cut. His hand covered hers when she grabbed his arm.

"You should be sleeping," he chastised. His eyes were dark and brooding, a crease settled deep into his forehead. She dropped down to flat feet. He wasn't happy to see her.

Well, tough.

"I couldn't." She turned from him and wet a washcloth to clean the wound. He took the cloth from her and placed it against the cut before she could mop up the trickle of blood.

"I'm fine, babe. I got caught with a knife. That's it." A small smile touched his mouth.

She glared at him. How could he take this lightly? Anger made her lips thin. "A knife?" Her voice shook. This was all because of her. He could have been killed... Her stomach dropped at the thought.

His fingers brushed her hair behind her ear. His palm settled on the crook of her neck. The contact turned her feet to lead. His eyes locked with hers. Pure lust sparked from his eyes, electricity arced through the air. His lips parted, his breath came out in short puffs. Slowly his gaze dropped over her body. Her muscles firmed, her nipples turning to pebbles under his scrutiny. Her pulse thundered against her throat. She wet her lips, afraid to breathe.

He leaned in, pressed his lips to the sensitive spot on her neck above his fingers.

Her breath sucked in.

His tongue came out to lick and tease her skin. Her knees wobbled. She grabbed his shoulders for support. His mouth moved from her throat and over her jaw, and then hovered, a breath away from her lips.

"I missed you," he whispered.

Her heart leapt into her throat. His eyes opened and found hers. Their green depths surrounded her, consuming her in their fire. She knotted her fingers together behind his neck and pulled his mouth down to hers.

He didn't pull away.

His lips, soft and moist, sealed over hers. His hands glided down her back until they closed on her butt, grasping her. He lifted her against him and settled her onto the bathroom counter. She pulled him closer, wanting more. His tongue licked softly into her mouth, tasting her. She moaned when he settled himself between her legs, the stiff denim of his jeans rubbing against the delicate insides of her thighs.

His mouth pulled away to place soft kisses on her parted lips. He rested his forehead against hers.

"Christ, Lana. I can't do this anymore." His voice was heavy, pained.

No. He couldn't do that. He couldn't start this fire in her and walk away. She wouldn't let him. Her hands came to either side of his face, forcing him to look at her. Her brain searched for words…she came up with nothing. When he spoke, her heart stalled.

"I need you, baby. I can't fight it anymore."

Her chest expanded. Tears stung the backs of her eyes, but she wouldn't shed them. Not now. "Cal, I need you too. I want you."

His thumb smoothed over her cheek, then traced the line of her jaw. "I can't promise forever, honey."

She nodded. She didn't care. Having Cal once was better than not at all. "It's okay. I understand."

His mouth firmed as if he didn't like her easy agreement. Had he hoped she would refuse? Would it have made it easier for him? He kissed her again. His hands came down to settle on the outside of her thighs, beneath his T-shirt. A shiver rippled through her at the touch of his hands in such an intimate place.

Slowly, he inched the shirt to her waist. His hands tensed on her skin. "Are you sure you're ready?" His voice was low, gravelly.

She sank her teeth into her bottom lip. She was more than ready. There was no turning back. The pulsations that plagued her needed relief.

Her eyes locked on his, without wavering. "Yes."

Fire lit his eyes. A deep hue stained his cheeks. He picked her up off the counter, her legs wrapped around his waist, one arm holding her across her backside. He stepped into the bedroom and kicked the bathroom door. It stayed ajar, sending a sliver of yellow light into the room. He set her on her feet.

In one motion, he lifted the shirt over her head. A low growl sounded in his throat. "Goddamn."

Heat crept from her toes to her forehead, tingling under his gaze. Her hands twisted in front of her, fighting the urge to cover her chest. He grasped her wrists and opened her arms. "You're gorgeous." He dropped to his knees in front of her, his mouth closed on her belly. She rose on her tiptoes as he branded her with his lips. Resting a hand on his head, he kissed and sucked, down, down, down, until he found the waistband of her black lace panties. His fingertip trailed along the top.

Her nerve endings hummed. She needed to feel him, to touch him, to have him inside her. Her fingers dug into his scalp. He smiled, his mouth scant inches from her hip bone. He pressed his lips against the thin material. She gasped when he moved over her, dropping down to where her thighs met.

"Cal—" Her voice broke.

He laughed softly, pressed a kiss to her, and stood. "You need to lose these, babe." His thumbs hooked into her panties, and he pulled them down for her to step out.

Her hands found the snap of his jeans. "Your turn."

"You don't have to tell me," he said with a soft chuckle. "One minute." He pressed a kiss to her mouth and went to his duffel bag. The metallic sound of foil tearing reached her ears. A condom.

Her heart beat like a caged wild animal. She stood there, in the center of the room, several feet from the bed. But she couldn't move, couldn't breathe. She was afraid to shatter the moment, as if the wrong movement would bring him to a halt. He came back to her, shedding his jeans and boxers on the way.

Her eyes dropped to below his waist.

She gulped. His manhood jutted out, hard, huge, and ready. He rolled the condom on. She opened her arms for him. He lifted her again, her legs around his waist. She waited for him to settle her down on the mattress. Instead, he pressed her back against the wall, his weight supporting her, his hands splayed wide on her butt.

Her nipples tightened with excitement. Never had she had sex anywhere other than on a bed. His tongue urged her lips open, coaxing her. Her hands dug into his shoulders, loving the feel of the hard contours of his muscle. He shifted her so her knees spread wide; his mouth left hers and closed on her collarbone. He nibbled down to her nipple until he caught the small hard bud in his mouth.

"Oh God." Her body shook as he sucked and licked. She felt her wetness, her body ready and open for him. His mouth came back to hers at the same moment that he sank deep into her. She cried out. Her teeth bit into his bottom lip.

He smiled, slow and sexy, against her mouth. "Damn, you feel so good, Lana," he ground out. He lifted her higher. His rhythm was urgent, filling a need they'd both been suffering from. With every withdrawal, she grasped him frantically, begging for more, for him to come back.

He plunged in deep, long strokes, stretching her, completing her. Her climax was building, her head spinning. Everything fell away around them. She locked her ankles at the small of his back. His mouth came down on her throat; her head fell back against the wall. At the touch of his slick tongue against the column of her neck, she came. She cried out on every hard, jolting spasm. Her body tightened against his shaft. Her own throbbing ebbed away until she lay limp against his chest.

His hands caressed her backside, where he supported her weight. The tickle of his touch was rough on her sensitive flesh. A giggle caught in her throat and she squirmed.

She'd just had sex with Cal.

Mind-blowing, rough, against-the-wall sex. Her cheeks were on fire. She pressed her face into the safety of the crook of his neck, afraid to look at him.

He peeled her away from the wall, still joined with her. Cradling her body against his, he walked to the bed and laid her down on the sheets, the covers still thrown back from when she had gotten out.

"That was amazing." His voice was mischievous, teasing. He came down on top of her, one hand on either side of her face, staring her down, not letting her hide. A gleam of light through the window bathed them in light, revealing his face. He was still inside her, his weight pressing him deeper and deeper. His thumbs brushed her temples, waiting for her response.

She nodded. A small, shy smile tightened her lips.

He laughed. "Shy all of a sudden? I never thought I'd see you speechless."

She pinched him. "I'm not speechless—I'm stunned." She chuckled. One hand lay lax against her chest, the other on Cal's shoulder. Her heart beat steadily against her palm. She hadn't done much, but then she hadn't needed to.

Cal laughed. "I like stunning you. But I'm nowhere near done."

"I thought you…"

"Came?" He finished easily. She bit her lip. He was so vocal and unashamed. "No way. I want this nice and slow. That against the wall was because you needed it like that. Now I want to enjoy every minute of watching you come."

He rocked gently against her. She gasped. Her legs fell open, welcoming more of him. His mouth pressed softly to hers, not the insistent need that had been there only moments before, but patient, leisurely. Her tongue mingled with his, the feel of his wetness in her mouth and her own wetness as he moved steadily in and out intoxicating her. He left her mouth to trail kisses down her face, to her throat. Her insides coiled, the burning sensation surged through her body. She matched his thrusts, needing another release, but he slowed. She panted, her mouth dry.

"Not yet, honey. Slow down." He took her nipple into his mouth, his teeth nipping at the sensitive flesh. Her hips convulsed, her insides tightening like a guitar string.

"Cal, I need you." Her voice trembled. A curse fell from his lips, as if her begging had undone him. He slid into her, long, even strokes until she clutched him, suspended over the abyss of pleasure. She shook from the constant friction of him rocking into her, giving her what she so desperately needed. Her release didn't come as fast and hard as the last. This time she spiraled higher and higher until her voice broke, until her body vibrated as she fell down to earth. His shoulders bunched beneath her hands, his body rigid as his orgasm grew. She clung to him, hanging on as he groaned her name against her ear, his body going lax in her arms.

His breath was warm and shallow against her ear. She inhaled deep, breathing in his musky scent. She could stay like this forever, her arms around him, his face pressed into her, their bodies joined as one. He stirred and pushed himself up to look down at her.

"I didn't hurt you, did I?" The rough pad of his thumb spread over her bottom lip. She kissed the tip of it.

"God, no. That was…perfect." His free hand toyed with the skin on her shoulder.

"Mmm…perfect, huh?" His smile revealed his even, white teeth. She nipped his thumb with her own teeth. Pulling it away, he replaced it with a soft kiss to her mouth. He pushed himself off her, separating them, and went to the bathroom to clean up. She met him on his way back into the bedroom. His hand squeezed her naked backside as she walked by.

"If you choose to walk around naked, I can't promise to keep my hands to myself," he cautioned.

She slipped into the bathroom, and behind the safety of the partially shut door, a giggle erupted. Keep his hands to himself? He could touch her anywhere, anyhow, in any way, and she would never refuse. She took a cloth from the counter and cleaned up from their lovemaking. It had been sex. Just sex. Casual sex was a part of Cal's life. He had said he couldn't promise forever. Did that mean he promised for now? She would take it. Would he be waiting in the bed, or had he collected his clothes so he could sleep on the couch as planned?

When she finished, she entered the dark bedroom and inched toward the bed. A big, solid lump rested smack-dab in the middle.

Cal.

Carefully, in case he was sleeping, she lifted the covers and slid under them, facing him on her side. He lay on his back, his broad, muscled chest just visible above the top of the blanket, his arm drawn over his head.

Fatigue settled into her bones, her eyes got heavy and her body tired. Cal shifted, and his arm slid under her shoulders and pulled her to his side. She settled her cheek on his chest, her leg thrown over his thighs, her hand rested over his heart. His hand came down to cover hers.

Satisfaction tugged at her lips. She hadn't known this had been missing from her life, hadn't realized the vast hole that had left her incomplete, until Cal had come along and filled it. It might not be forever, but for now, he was hers.

Sleep tugged at her until she gave in, surrounded by Cal's warmth.

Brrring, brrring, brrring!

Cal bolted out of bed. Lana shot to a sitting position and rubbed her eyes. A glance at the clock showed they had only been asleep for twenty minutes. The shrill alarm continued. Cal was yanking on his jeans.

"What's going on?" She clasped the covers to her chest and stood.

Speakers crackled overhead. *"This is not a drill, please exit the building. Repeat, this is not a drill."*

"Fire alarm." Cal yanked a long-sleeved shirt on. "Get dressed—and stay here." He came to her then, pressed a hot, firm kiss to her lips, and turned away. She reached for him, but her hand closed around air.

"Wait"—she scrambled to find her clothes—"I'm coming with you." The alarm echoed through the room, piercing her ears. She dropped the blanket and pulled her clothes on.

Cal opened the bedroom door. "I'll be right back, babe. Stay here." His voice was stern and unwavering.

He closed the bedroom door behind him.

Chapter 13

Cal believed in coincidences as much as he expected pigs to fly. A fire in the hotel they were staying at, hours after he had tracked down the name of the person who'd invested in Lana's murder, was not a coincidence.

He held the Glock at thigh level as he approached the door. He paused to look through the peephole. The bright lights showed nothing but the hallway. His fingers slid the cool metal chain, unlocking the door. He opened it and stepped out, keeping his gun drawn but out of sight. To his left, a few people were exiting their rooms; to his right, an older couple hovered in the doorway as he did. In the hall, the alarm was deafening.

They needed to get the hell out. When he shut the door and turned, his body slammed into Lana's much softer one. He hadn't heard her approach over the constant blare of noise through the speakers.

"I told you to wait," he said, as if reminding her would send her back. Whoever had started the fire could be on their floor now, looking for them. He could protect her a hell of a lot better if she wasn't right beside him.

Her lips pursed. "You left. I didn't know where you were going."

"You should know I wouldn't leave you. We have to move, now." He was glad to see she was fully dressed in the clothes she'd worn before he had left, plus one of his sweaters. He slipped his shoes on and passed her hers. "I need you to promise you'll do exactly as I say."

Her eyes rounded. "You don't think this has anything to do with me, do you?"

"There's no doubt in my mind." He shoved his Glock into the waistband of his pants. His mind shifted gears. He couldn't worry about anything right now except getting her out safely.

"Hold on to me, stay right behind me, and keep your face down." He pulled the hood of her sweatshirt over her hair. She nodded, her eyes dark with worry. He took her hand. Her soft, cool fingers jolted him. She wasn't trained like he was. She was vulnerable—and a fucking target.

He looked out the peephole again. This time he saw people racing hurriedly down the hall to the stairwell. He opened the door and stepped out, scanning the floor both ways before leading Lana after him.

"Whatever happens, don't let go of my hand." He raised his voice over the shriek of the alarm. Her fingers tightened in response. Once they reached the stairwell, people would be frantic, and a tight space filled with scared people was dangerous.

He ushered them down the hall, weaving around people with big eyes, shouting to their family members and children. Out of the corner of his eye he saw Lana hesitate, wanting to stop and help. He gave a light tug to her hand and shoved open the stairwell door.

People swarmed, herding down from the twenty stories above them. They were on the eighth floor. Lana's hand stiffened in his. Her other hand grasped his elbow. He led them into the crowd and down the stairs. The elevators would be shut down. The only way their pursuers would be able to reach them would be by stairs. There were two main stairwells on either side of the building. They would be searching both.

"Gun—he's got a gun!" A woman's terrified scream echoed throughout the stairwell, rivaling the alarm. He looked up at the flights of stairs. A few floors above, another woman screamed. People flocked, shoving each other out of the way. Cal's eyes landed on a bulky man dressed in black, a knitted black mask over his face.

Cal's pulse slowed.

The man's eyes found Cal, then zeroed in on Lana. Cal's brain moved into overdrive. He grabbed Lana, shoved her in front of him, and pushed people out of the way, barreling them down the stairs. Lana moved swiftly. Her hand gripped his like a vise. A glance upward showed that the predator was only a couple floors up.

Cal had to take him out.

At the next floor, Cal opened the door and shoved Lana into the hallway. He held tight to the metal handle blocking the jaws to the stairs, and faced her. Her face was pale, her blue eyes hauntingly sharp in contrast to her white skin. "You need to run."

Her breath sucked in, and she shook her head firmly. "No, you said to stay with you."

"Lana, don't argue. Run down the hall, stop at the ice machine, there will be an inlet. Wait for me there. I need to get rid of this guy."

She swallowed. Screams pierced the air. He was close.

"*Go!*"

She turned and ran. Her hair flew out around her like a parachute. The door yanked beneath his grasp. He gripped tighter. The person on the other end jerked on the door with determination. A fist slammed into it next. A look over his shoulder showed Lana slowing as she rounded the corner to the ice machine inlet.

This motherfucker was going down.

Fury burned in his stomach. He let go of the handle and the door opened. Cal stepped back and shot his foot out, catching the man in the chest. He flew back into the hall. People screamed and leaped over him. Cal grabbed him by the scruff of the neck and dragged him back onto the floor. The door slammed behind him. The man wheezed and struggled for breath. Cal seized his weapon and turned it on him. With his free hand, he pulled his mask off.

Dark, curly hair pasted to his forehead and scalp.

He shoved the gun into his neck. "Who hired you?" His voice was cold, void of emotion. Cal's pulse beat steadily in his throat.

The man stiffened but remained silent.

"I'll blow your head off without blinking an eye. Now, tell me."

He licked his lips. "His name is Will. I don't know his last name."

Good enough. Cal slammed the butt of the gun into the man's temple. His head snapped to the side and his lights went out.

"*Cal!*" Lana's scream spilt the air, cutting through him with the sharpness of a razor blade. He jerked his head up. A man had her back pressed to his chest, an arm locked across her throat. He held the barrel of a gun pressed to the delicate spot at her temple.

His heart slammed into his chest. His breath hung in the air. Lana's creamy face turned gray. Her hand clawed at the black-clothed arm that held her, her toes barely touched the ground. His blood turned to ice.

He charged.

The man's cold, dead eyes found Cal's through the cutout holes of his mask. "One more move and she's dead." He began stepping backward, heading for the other exit at the end of the hall. Cal froze. The man's eyes never left his face. If he so much as raised his gun, the man could get a shot off in a millisecond, putting a bullet in her head before he could even fire.

Lana's eyes flew to his. Her lips firmed. From here, he could see her temper flare. His stomach flipped over.

No, no, no.

In one swift movement, she threw herself back against the man, then forward. It was just enough to throw his step off with the need to reposition her. She wriggled her arm away and slammed her elbow into his stomach.

"Get down!" Cal bellowed. She threw herself to the floor. Cal fired. Two bullets ripped through the air. The first bullet took out the man's knee. The second hit him in the throat.

Cal tore down the hall. Lana lay unmoving against the wall, her head down. "Lana," he breathed as he dropped to her side. She pushed herself to her knees. He pulled her against him. His chest constricted. He could have lost her. In one moment, she could have been dead. One wrong move, had one thing gone differently, had she not fought back… Every scenario flashed through his mind. He dropped his face to her hair. His arms locked tighter around her.

"Cal." Her voice was small, strained.

He pulled her away to search her over. "Are you okay, baby?"

She nodded. "I'm fine."

He cupped her face. "You scared the hell out of me." He smothered the bite in his voice. How could he be mad when she was the one who'd given him the opportunity to shoot the sonofabitch? "Good job, honey." A small smile flitted through her glossy eyes. "Let's go. Don't look down at him, okay? He's dead."

Eyes huge and somber, she swallowed and let him pull her to her feet. He kept her tight against his side and moved past the dead body and the pools of blood that soaked into the oriental rug.

The other stairwell was clear other than the odd straggler. After three more flights, they made it to the basement. Cal kept Lana hidden in the safety of the stairwell while he opened the door to the Parkade. He scanned the parked cars, looking for signs of a threat. It was still.

His hand reached for hers and he pulled her after him, keeping her close. She hadn't said another word. His jaw worked. He hated that she'd been exposed to that. Now she'd seen him murder someone without batting an eye. For him, this was normal. For her, all sense of normalcy had been shattered. There was no weight on his conscience over the man's death. Those days of remorse had long since passed.

He hustled them through the parked cars, and stopped when he reached his truck. With Lana's hand still snug in his, he opened the passenger door and lifted her in.

"Cal, I can get in myself." She took the seat belt from his hand and secured it. Her chin lifted. Shadows lined her eyes, but she sharpened her gaze on him. "I'm fine."

She was tough. Her hands twisted in her lap, belying her words. Admiration swelled in his chest. "That's my girl." He pressed a kiss to her pouty lips, shut the door, and went around to the driver's side. He had to get them out of there. Although he hadn't smelt smoke, that didn't mean there hadn't been a fire. Will's men could have pulled the fire alarm, but Cal suspected they would more likely have started one as a distraction. One man was down, but Cal hadn't had the chance to take care of the other.

His hands gripped the steering wheel as he eased them out onto the street.

"Are you okay?" He turned to her. The hood still shielded her face, her legs now tucked beneath her.

"Yes." Her voice wavered. "Are you?" Her hand closed around his elbow.

Was he? No one had ever asked him that before. He took her fingers in his hand. God, she was so sweet. "Of course, honey. I'm used to this stuff. You're not, though."

"You might be used to it, but you seem different, rattled."

Rattled. That was a damn understatement. Yeah, he was used to violence. He was used to killing people without blinking an eye. He *wasn't* used to a gun being pressed to a woman's temple. And not just any woman... but Lana. The way her eyes had darkened in her white face was an image that would haunt him for the rest of his life. Stark fear had etched the fine lines of her face, the look of death at her door. He made a fierce vow that he would never allow her to be in that position again.

"I'm fine. It's just adrenaline. It will pass." Not that he would ever fully recover from almost losing her. A vise closed around his heart. In those moments, his world had crashed around him. The thundering of his blood had been deafening. All he could see was her face, and all he could think was that he couldn't live without her.

Her fingers squeezed his. She was reassuring him? "Where are we going to go now?"

Good question. He navigated the dark streets lazily, staying off the main avenues of travel. "We need to get off the road. I don't want to take any chances until I get my hands on Will." His fingers itched on the steering wheel. That sonofabitch would have a much worse fate than Stamos.

"Who's Will?"

"The man who hired Stamos. I'm suspecting he's just another middle person, but someone hired him and I'm going to find out who."

Lana shifted in her seat. "Where are we going to go? It's almost two a.m."

"Nate is an early riser. He'll be up in a few hours. But it wouldn't hurt for us to pull over somewhere and close our eyes until then." Nate wouldn't mind if they showed up at his door now, but if he started talking about everything that had gone down at the hotel, he would feel the need to track down Will immediately. And as much as he wanted to do that, they both needed some sleep. "I know a secluded place we can park near the beach. This time of year, we won't have to worry about the high school kids who like to party there."

Lana's hand covered her mouth on a yawn. "I am quite tired. I wouldn't mind resting."

"We're not far, about ten minutes. Why don't you recline and close your eyes?"

She fumbled for the lever and the seat stretched back. Her legs curled up tightly on the seat. Cal kept his eyes on the road. Who the hell was he kidding? He wouldn't be able to sleep. His mind kept turning, churning up possibilities and suspects. It was Tuesday now. In a few hours, Nate would be able to follow up with the background checks on the list of people Lana had given him. His gut told him he was missing something—a piece of the puzzle. The answer was right under his nose, he could smell it. Maybe he needed to question her more, but not now. Her breathing slowed. One glance at her made the tension in his shoulders ease. She looked so comfortable. He loved sleeping with her. More than he should.

A few minutes later, he pulled down a long gravel road and into the deserted beach's parking lot. A few lone streetlights scattered the parking lot. He parked at the far end, nearest the trees, where they were shrouded in darkness. When he turned the engine off, Lana stirred and sat up.

"Go back to sleep, babe. I'm just getting out to get some blankets from the back."

"You have blankets?"

"Yeah. I keep an emergency bag with food, water, blankets, and extra clothes. Do you need anything?"

"A blanket would be nice."

"Sure thing." He slid out and opened the rear driver's side door. From the bag he kept beneath the back seat, he took out a blanket and a couple of sweaters for pillows.

Lana turned to him when he climbed back in the driver's seat. "You can't sleep there. You won't have any room with the steering wheel and pedals. Switch seats with me."

She was right. Even with the seat fully reclined, he wouldn't be able to move his knees or stretch out his legs. "I have a better idea. How about I sleep in the passenger seat and you sleep on top of me?"

A small smile touched her lips and warmed her tired eyes. "Okay."

Once they moved around, she settled on his lap. A sweater pillowed under his head, and a blanket covered their bodies, keeping the heat in. It was tight with both of them in one seat, but her ass nestled on the side of his thigh, her side tucked between his arms, and her face rested on his chest. He exhaled a pent-up breath. Just the feel of her smaller, lithe body against his released his tension—most of it. His dick still throbbed, but only one kind of a release would cure that. The soft beating of her heart slowed his to a normal rate.

She was good for him.

Admitting that to himself put a hole in his gut. How had he let his guard down? He hadn't. Lana had wriggled her way into his heart, and there was no turning back.

"Cal?" Her voice, filled with trepidation, cut through the silence of the night.

Beneath the blanket, he stroked his hand over her hip. "Mmm?"

"Are you sleeping?"

He let out a breathy chuckle. "I'm not now, no."

Silence. Then, "Oh, sorry."

"I'm teasing, honey. What's on your mind?" His hand came up to smooth her hair back. She lifted her head to look down at him. Her teeth nipped into her bottom lip. On a deep breath, as if she'd been working up the courage, she straddled him.

His rock-hard dick grew another inch. Christ.

Her tongue, small and pink, wet her lips.

"I want you again." Her voice shook, but her face never wavered. Her eyes burned into him. She nestled comfortably on top of him, her apex lined up directly with his crotch. Her mouth crushed to his, her tongue licking his lips open, urging him. His hands found her ass and squeezed, then caressed.

She moaned, spread her knees wider, and rocked against him. Sonofabitch, he was going to blow any minute.

He pulled his lips away. "Sorry, babe." His body pulsed. Need sharpened every atom in his body. "I don't have a condom."

Her lips parted, then clamped shut with disappointment. "Oh." She groaned and dropped back to where she'd been cuddled. "I didn't even think of that."

"It's okay." He pressed a kiss to the top of her head. "Rest now." Why in the hell did he not carry condoms on him?

She nodded. Her cheek pillowed on her hand.

His hand drew lazy circles over her hip, then slid down to trace the gentle curves of her incredible ass. God, he loved how she'd just come on to him. How did he have everything else in his extra bag but fucking condoms? Because he'd never expected to be stranded like this with a woman, that's how.

When his fingers slid over the smooth cotton of her leggings to touch her delicate folds from behind, she stiffened.

He felt her heart rate hammering against his side. He continued to gently tease and play, stroking and rubbing against her.

She gulped, loudly. "I thought you didn't have a condom." Her voice shook on a tremor as his fingers moved over her clit. Her breath sucked in roughly.

"I don't. But I'm sure not letting you go to sleep horny."

The comment earned him a pinch on his hand that rested near hers. He stifled a laugh. He moved away from where she throbbed, and pushed his hand down the back of her pants, picking up where he left off—only this time pushing her panties aside. She jerked against him when he separated her folds and worked his fingertip inside her.

She moaned and curled tighter against him. She was hot and wet, and his finger pressed in and out slowly.

"Cal—" She panted against him, and her back arched. His body hummed, wanting inside her more than anything he'd wanted in his life. Later, when he had a condom, he would make up for it.

"Just relax, baby. I want you to come nice and slow this time." He loved how sexual she was. How she panted and grew wet right before she came with his name on her lips.

Her breath was rough and raspy. He delved deeper, filling her up and then pulling his finger out. She fisted her hand in his sweater, her nails biting into his chest. He spread her more, letting the very tip of his middle finger tease its entry.

She cried out when he joined it with the other one. She throbbed around him, coating his fingers in her orgasm. Her body turned boneless against him, her breathing still raspy and sharp, until slowly, it regulated. He pressed another kiss to her head and withdrew his hand.

"Go to sleep now."

He tightened his hold around her, trying to still the throb in his own body. Tomorrow, they would do this right.

Chapter 14

Lana woke to Cal's lips on her forehead. Her eyes snapped open. Sunlight blasted through the windshield, blinding her. Small white puffs dotted the air from their breaths. Frost and fog lined the windows. Cal's hand held hers on his chest; his other arm was drawn tightly around her hip. Beneath the blanket, she was toasty and warm against the heat of his body.

"Did you sleep at all?" His voice was gruff, his breath warm on the top of her head.

"Better than I did the other night." She stretched her knees out. Her hip locked, shooting pain down her leg. As much as she loved sleeping with Cal, staying in the cramped position for hours had left her body sore.

He shifted beneath her. "My arm is asleep."

"Oh, sorry." She sat up on his lap. His hand went to the shoulder, massaging it. He smiled at her, and his lips lifted lazily. His five o'clock shadow was thick and full. The sun caught his green eyes, the hazel flecks catching the rays. God, he was sexy. She smoothed her bedhead down and straightened her sweater.

"Why didn't you sleep the other night at the cabin?" His brow furrowed, his tone curious as his hand brushed her cheek.

She shrugged. "It's a little hard to sleep when you know someone was planning to murder you." She strived for humor, but her voice shook.

His eyes clouded over. "You don't need to be scared, honey."

"That's easier said than done."

"Wait a minute." The crease in his forehead deepened. "Is that why you wanted me to sleep with you?"

She pinched his shoulder. He yelped and rubbed the area. "What did I say?"

"You make it sound like I was begging you. You were horribly uncomfortable in that chair, yet you acted like I was going to bite you."

He chuckled.

"It's not funny."

"I wouldn't mind if you bit me, that's all." He winked at her.

She narrowed her eyes at him.

"You should know by now that I was in physical agony. Being around you and not being able to touch you is torture." Her heart fluttered softly in her chest. If only this was a profession of his actual feelings for her and not just lust. She wasn't complaining, though. Lust was better than nothing.

"I guess it was a losing battle, wasn't it?" His hand reached behind her, grabbing the lever to put the chair in a sitting position. "If I hadn't been so stubborn, I would have seen you were scared. That didn't even occur to me."

"Well, now you know." She rested her hand on his jaw, and the prickle of his beard scratched her skin. He turned his face to press a kiss to her palm.

"Duly noted." His voice was gruff and raspy. Coffee would fix that, as she had learned from the past two mornings. "We should get going. I'll give Nate a call and give him a heads-up that we're coming over."

His hand cupped the back of her neck, and his lips sealed softly against hers. She pulled away and slapped her hand against her mouth. Her other hand pressed against his chest, holding him at bay. He frowned at her.

"I haven't brushed my teeth." Her mouth was dry and gritty. He didn't need to smell her morning breath.

He laughed. The fine lines on his face multiplied, and his eyes sparked with amusement. "We can stop at the drugstore and buy some necessities if you want."

"Yes, after we get coffee."

"Keep sweet-talking me like that, and we'll be eloping." Her breath hitched, and her heart stuttered. He pinched her chin with his thumb and forefinger. He was kidding, undoubtedly. Nevertheless, pictures of what life with Cal could be like danced through her mind. Waking up to that bristly beard and thick voice every morning, his calm hands coasting over her body.

She could get used to that.

She was getting used to that.

They climbed out of the truck. The sun had crept into the sky, the winter air brisk and chilly. Lana stretched her hands high over her head and held on to the truck as she stretched her legs. Cal's stretch was much quicker. He grabbed his phone out of the center console and placed it to his ear. He paced around the empty parking lot as he spoke to Nate.

Her tongue stuck to the roof of her mouth. Needles prickled her throat when she swallowed. She needed a drink of water, bad. Cal had said he kept food in a bag in the back seat. Maybe he had a bottle of water. Not waiting for him to finish, she opened the back door. There, on the floor tucked under the seat, was a black duffel bag. She pulled it out and unzipped it. A thick pullover sweater and a change of men's clothes sat on top. She pulled it out and dropped it on the seat.

Her eyes went back to the contents.

She gasped. Her hands clasped over her mouth.

Bundles and bundles of cash crowded the bag. Water bottles and snack foods lay scattered beneath. She reached in and pulled out one of the bundles of hundred-dollar bills, her fingers spreading the edges. There had to be almost a hundred thousand dollars there.

Cal's footsteps scuffed across the pavement. She wheeled around as he rounded the open door. "What the hell is this?" She slapped the bundle against his chest, then yanked her hand away from the tainted money.

His eyes darkened. He tossed the money into the bag behind her. "It's money."

She crossed her arms over her chest. "I was looking for a bottle of water." Why was she explaining herself to him? "I found that. Why are you carrying so much money around?" Her throat tightened. Had he lied to her? Was there something he wasn't telling her?

He stood close, his shoulders so wide she couldn't see the parking lot beyond. Her breath sucked in. He reached behind her and pulled out two water bottles, then put everything back in the bag and zipped it up. "Here," he said, handing her one of the bottles. "Get in so we can leave." His tone was terse.

She folded her arms in front of her chest. "I'd rather you answer my question."

"I plan to. In the truck."

She accepted the water and climbed in the passenger's seat. He got in, started the engine, and turned to her instead of pulling away. "I had to accept the money, Lana. Otherwise, they would have suspected I wasn't going to complete the job. They were to pay me the remainder later."

Her stomach churned. Later, as in after he'd killed her. She believed him. It made perfect sense, yet nausea threatened to take hold. "Why didn't you tell me?"

One dark eyebrow rose. "I told you Stamos had hired me, remember? What do you think he was paying me with? Coupons?"

She squinted at him. Her lips pursed. "Of course not. But there's a big difference between telling me that and carting around a hundred grand in the vehicle with us."

He nodded. "You're right. I meant to tell you about it at my house, but everything got out of hand after that."

Realization dawned on her. "That's why you said that they had destroyed your house looking for the money."

"Yup."

She hadn't had the chance to ask him about it. It had never occurred to her that "the money" had anything to do with her. "How much did they pay you?"

"They offered to pay me one hundred fifty thousand. Half up front, half later."

She swallowed over the hard lump that had formed in her throat. The other half—after she was dead. That wasn't chump change. That was serious money. The air grew so thick in the vehicle that she couldn't draw any into her tight lungs. The seat belt rubbed against her neck, much too tight. She pulled it away.

Cal's hand grabbed her shoulder.

"Are you okay?" He gave her a shake.

She wouldn't fall apart. Not now. She nodded and concentrated on slowing her thumping heart. She brought her eyes to his. "I'm fine."

The corner of his mouth lifted. "It's okay to be upset."

Her hands twisted in her lap.

"It's damn scary. You've done a hell of a job holding up. I've seen grown men break down over less—men who are used to this shit." His hand found hers and squeezed. "I admire your strength, but it's just me here. You can trust me."

She squirmed under the scrutiny of his gaze. He was right. She was strong. She lived under constant judgment and scrutiny. She'd had no choice but to grow a thick skin.

"I do trust you, very much."

He smiled and brushed his lips over her knuckles. "You sure about that?" His breath caressed the back of her hand. "You looked pretty pissed off when you saw the money."

She tried to hide her smile, but couldn't. "I wasn't pissed. But it did raise some questions."

"Ah, the truth comes out."

She gripped his hand tight. "I do trust you, Cal. It's just hard to let certain guards down."

"Showing weakness?"

She took a deep, shuddering breath. "Apparently. I never realized it was a problem until now."

"It's not a problem. As long as you know you can trust me, I'm happy. I don't want you feeling like you have to bottle things up." He pressed a firm kiss to her mouth. This time, she didn't push him away. "Not with me, okay?"

She nodded.

"Alright. Now, let's go get some coffee before I start having withdrawals."

She laughed as they pulled out of the parking lot. They found a coffee shop first, and then stopped at a twenty-four-hour drugstore.

"Maybe just I should go in." Cal unbuckled his seat belt. It was just past 6 a.m. The store was quiet. The chances of anyone recognizing her at this hour were slim.

"I'll come, too. I need a few personal items."

He reached in the back and pulled out the baseball cap. "Let's be quick, okay. We can't chance anyone seeing you."

She nodded and followed him into the store. She made a beeline for the makeup department, and Cal headed to look for the other items. She was sick of not wearing makeup. After grabbing a few basic cosmetics, she hurried to the checkout counter where Cal waited. Toothpaste, toothbrushes, and condoms sat on the counter waiting for her. Her cheeks burned. She shot him a withering look, and dropped her makeup on the counter. He hid his chuckle on a cough. She elbowed him in the ribs.

"Excuse me, miss?" A hesitant voice spoke behind her.

Lana stiffened and turned. "Don't I know you from somewhere?" Her breath caught. She had Cal's baseball cap on, and she still wore his oversized sweatshirt, but dammit, she had been distracted by the condoms and hadn't kept her head down.

Cal circled his arm around her and brought her close. "I'm sorry, ma'am. She doesn't speak English."

"Oh, I'm sorry. She has such a familiar face." Cal smiled warmly at the older woman, but didn't continue the conversation. He was quick. Had Cal not been there, she wouldn't have known what to say.

Lana dropped her gaze to her feet, Cal paid, and together they left.

Cal opened her door and hustled her in, then circled around to the driver's side.

"You were right. I shouldn't have gone in."

"It's alright. She probably won't remember. But we need to get moving." He clicked his seat belt and pulled out of the parking lot.

She kept the hat on, and sat back in the seat, sipping her mocha latte. Cal had bought condoms. And not just a small convenience-sized pack. It had been a *value* pack. For her? She frowned down at her cup. Not likely. For all she knew, he'd run out and was just stocking up.

Fifteen minutes later, they pulled into Nate's driveway. He had a nice brick home on the west side. It wasn't as large as Cal's, but it was secluded and well-manicured. Cal took her hand when they got out and led her up the front steps. Nate opened the door before Cal knocked.

"Morning." Nate's light brown hair was tousled, his hazel eyes bright and cheery for the early hour. "Come on in."

They entered the tiled foyer and followed Nate to the kitchen at the back of the house. The aroma of frying eggs and bacon greeted them. Her mouth watered.

"I figured you'd be hungry. Have a seat." He gestured to the granite island in the center of the kitchen.

Her eyes widened at the food on the counter. "Oh my. You didn't have to cook for us."

Cal pulled out a chair for her and she sat.

"Of course I did. You guys had one hell of a night. And unlike my asshole friend over here, I never let a woman wake up hungry." Nate winked at her. "Toast?"

"Please."

He filled her plate and set it down in front of her. Her deeply ingrained manners told her to wait for them before she started eating. Her stomach rumbled. Screw it. She dug in.

"Nate is full of shit. He's never had a woman stay here before. He kicks them out long before breakfast."

Lana pinched her lips tight on a giggle. She took a bite of toast as Nate passed Cal a full plate and began fixing his own.

Nate laughed mischievously. "Go ahead, broadcast my commitment issues. Cal here is the king of those."

Lana's eyes rose to Cal's still-standing form. His jaw worked.

"He's going to kick my ass now. Let me reword that. He *was* the king, before he met you, honey."

"Don't call her honey," Cal ground out. "And you can shut up anytime now."

Click, click, click, click, click.

"What's that noise?" Lana looked around.

"That's Rufus. He likes to sleep in. He either heard you guys, or he finally smells the breakfast."

A big Doberman came barreling down the hall, straight for her. His tongue hung out and his tail wagged as he slapped his paws up on her lap. She laughed and reached to scratch his ears.

"Oh, he's such a sweetheart."

"Careful, he's a killer." Nate's tone was dry.

She laughed. "I can see that."

"Roof, lie down." The dog gave her hand a big lick, then settled at her feet. Nate grinned. "He's a ladies' man."

Nate stood at the island across from them and took a big bite of scrambled eggs. "I have the guest room all ready for you guys, it's just off the living room. You might want to grab a couple more hours of sleep." He took another bite. "Don't worry. My room is on the other side of the house. These walls are thick."

A piece of toast lodged in her throat. She coughed, dropping her fork to her plate to cover her mouth. Cal passed her a glass of water. At the moment, sleep sounded more heavenly than sex.

Cal shook his head at Nate. "You're such an ass."

When they finished eating, Cal got his bag from the vehicle and led her to the spare room. A nice king-sized bed took up the center of the room. Cal opened a door off the bedroom. "There's a bathroom in here. Feel free to take a shower and change into something else. I think I have an extra shirt in my bag." He dropped it on the floor.

A shower could wait. She shuffled over to the bed, pulled back the covers, and got in. A soft smile touched Cal's lips. He pulled the heavy brown curtains shut and approached the side of the bed. He lifted the covers to her chin and pressed a kiss to her mouth.

"I'm going to go pick our stuff up from the hotel. Get some rest, and I'll see you in a bit."

Her eyes closed before she could respond.

Chapter 15

"You did it, didn't you? You rascal." Nate stood in the kitchen with his arms folded across his chest, a stupid grin on his face.

Cal scowled at him. "What the hell are you rambling about?"

"You slept with her. I can see it on your face."

Cal shook his head and poured a cup of coffee from the pot on the counter. "None of your damn business."

Nate pumped his fist in the air. "Yes. I knew you had it in you, bud."

Cal took a swig of the strong brew as Nate slapped him on the shoulder. The hot liquid splashed his face. "I can tell you're happier, not as tightly wound. I'm proud of you."

"Would you can it? I'm too tired for your shit." He grabbed a napkin and wiped the coffee off his cheek. His brows pinched at Nate. He was getting on his last nerve.

Nate laughed. "Alright, alright. Go take a nap, Carol. Nothing is happening around here for a few hours at least."

Cal's lips tensed at the feminine nickname Nate had dubbed him with since they were in recon. "Go organize a circle jerk, you prick."

Nate laughed. "Can't. That's E's specialty." He dropped some bacon and egg scraps to a not-so-patiently-waiting Rufus. "Really, though, catch a couple of hours. I have a feeling it's going to be a long day."

Cal shook his head. "I can't sleep. You know how it is."

Nate nodded, his expression quiet and understanding. A rare moment. "Anything on Will Anderson?"

Nate blew air through his lips. "Not a damn thing. No record, no driver's license, no lease agreements. He's a ghost. But E's working on it. If anyone can find him, it's Ethan."

Cal pulled out a chair and sat. Will couldn't be a dead end. They didn't need that shit right now. He ran a hand over his jaw. He hadn't gotten the chance to dig deeper with Lana. His gut told him some answers lay with her, answers that she didn't even realize she had.

"Let's hope something turns up soon."

Nate nodded. "Where's your head at? You've gotta have a hunch on who's behind this."

"My gut tells me it's a personal matter. The obvious scenario is something to do with her fame or her father. But it just doesn't ring true." He took another swig of coffee.

Nate joined him at the table, propping his feet up on the chair beside him. "How come?"

He raised his shoulder. "They offered a big sum of money and even paid Stamos a finder's fee for locating me. That's a total of two hundred grand. Seems pretty damn personal to me."

Nate rubbed his jaw. "You going to tell me who your hunch is about?"

"Her stepbrother, Tanner. He came on to her and assaulted her. They had a big spat, but he apologized for it later. Still doesn't sit right with me."

"Could just have a mad crush on her. I mean, she's gorgeous. Can't say I'd blame him."

Cal bit his tongue. Nate wouldn't make a move on Lana, that he knew for certain. But with Nate's roster of women, Cal didn't like him commenting on her appeal.

"Man, don't look at me like that. I'd have to be blind and deaf not to notice. She's all yours—"

"You're so gracious. As if there was even a competition."

"—she has eyes only for you, dude. So calm your nerves."

Eyes only for him? Huh. His stomach knotted. It wasn't fair for her to think like that. Hell, it wasn't fair for him to let his mind explore what life could be like with her. Life would be pretty damn good. Better than what he deserved. Last night, cramped in the seat of the truck, he'd slept better than he had in years. She was good for him. He was getting used to having her around. She didn't belong in his world, and yet...she fit.

"Aw, you've got hearts in your eyes."

"Shut the fuck up." He shook his head and laughed.

"What's the plan for today?"

"To find Will Anderson." He set his coffee cup down and Nate nodded, his eyes small with doubt.

Ding, dong.

Rufus perked up under the table with a sharp *woof*. Cal stood. His muscles tensed as he focused on Nate. His hand went to the gun at the small of his back.

"It's just E. Relax."

Right. Ethan. He dropped his hand and sat back in the chair. Nate disappeared to the front of the house and returned with Ethan, Rufus in tow.

Ethan squeezed his shoulder as he passed, taking the seat next to him. "Nate told me about what happened last night. How's she holding up?" Leave it to Ethan to be concerned about Lana. Ethan was a big dude, but he was also the biggest softie. He wasn't afraid to show his sensitive side, and if anyone made a comment, as some had in the military, he'd put them in their place with one hard stare. He was respected and kind. Cal valued his friendship, and Nate's, as well, when he wasn't wanting to throttle him.

"Pretty damn good. She's resting right now, though."

"What's the plan?" Ethan crossed his ankle over his knee, his mouth set in a grim line.

Damn, he was lucky to have such good friends. "I want to see what Nate's buddies at the office come up with on some suspects. In the meantime, I need to pick our things up from the hotel."

"I can go with you," Ethan offered.

Cal watched Nate out of the corner of his eye. "Think it's safe to leave him here with Lana?"

"Dude, c'mon. You really need to ask that?" Nate held his hand out, waiting.

"Nah. I wouldn't be here if I didn't trust you."

"Good, because we have a slight problem." Nate pulled out a chair and sat.

Cal groaned. He had enough problems.

"Lana is going to be reported missing. I know her whereabouts, so that puts me in a tough spot as an agent. This is a delicate situation, but I need to be careful. Ethan will probably have to join you on future head hunting."

Ethan clapped his hands and rubbed them together. "Sweet. I need to blow off some steam."

Cal turned back to Nate. "I don't want to get you in any kind of trouble."

Nate shook his head. "Her safety is our main objective. I'll keep a low profile and help as much as I can."

Cal nodded and stood from his chair. "I'll arrange to get my house back together and increase the security so we can stay there."

"Already got a head start. There's a team there now fixing the damage," Ethan said before he stood and downed his coffee. "But you're not going back there, are you?"

Cal lifted a shoulder. "What else are we supposed to do? I'm not going to keep hiding. All I care about is keeping Lana safe, but at some point, this has to end. Let them come for me, I'm ready."

Nate made a *tsk*ing sound. "Man, that's not smart. You can stay here."

"No. I appreciate your hospitality, but—"

"I know where we can go." Lana's silky voice sounded from the hallway. Cal jerked his head up, and Ethan swiveled in his chair. Fatigue laced deep shadows beneath her eyes, and guilt spurred in his stomach. The last few days had been rough. He was used to it, but she wasn't. She crossed her arms over her chest and her lips pursed haughtily. Not that her demeanor showed her fatigue. If he hadn't been used to studying those unwavering eyes, he'd be convinced she'd been unaffected. He couldn't take his eyes off her. Her sassy grin spread warmth through his chest. It was all he could do not to cross the kitchen and pull her mouth to his.

"Where?" His gravelly voice belied his train of thought.

"I have a place." She stepped farther into the kitchen, pulled out one of the stools at the kitchen island, and sat. Ethan's eyebrows rose, and he looked from Cal to Lana. Cal downed the rest of his coffee and then set the mug on the table, waiting for her to continue.

One slender leg crossed over her knee, and she smiled easily. "My family owns a chalet in Glacier. No one's used it in years."

Cal grimaced. With all the arrows pointing to Tanner, using one of her family's properties was too close to the hornets' nest. He shook his head. Lana drummed her fingers on her thigh, waiting for his rebuttal.

"Do you have a better idea?"

He swirled the empty white mug in his hands and his mind worked. Dammit, he didn't. They could go to another hotel, but they had been found at the last one. He could always rent another cabin, but finding one available nearby would be a bitch.

"Well?"

"Sorry, babe. It doesn't make sense for us to go to a place your family owns. I still think Tanner is behind this. That would bring us right where he wants us."

Indecision weighed on his shoulders. He had the perfect place to go, but he didn't want to take Lana there. Not when it was an hour away and he had to keep leaving her behind to solve this shit. If something happened, and he was that far away...

Then again, no one except Ethan and Nate knew about it. Ethan's eyes met Cal's, his brow furrowed in consternation.

"Any other options, Cal?"

He let out a deep sigh. Screw it. It was a hell of a lot safer than Lana's chalet, and he could be certain not another soul knew about it.

"I have a place."

Lana's shoulders snapped back and her lips parted. "Why didn't you say something?"

He rested his elbows on the table and tented his fingers beneath his chin. "Because it's more than an hour away and I don't like you being that far. It's my safe house. No one outside of this room even knows it exists." He kept his gaze on Lana's. "What do you think?"

She lifted a shoulder. "It seems the best option to me."

"Alright, we'll leave tomorrow. But for now, we need to pay a visit to Stamos. I'll drop off our stuff from the hotel first. You should get some rest, babe."

On cue, her lips parted with a slight yawn. "You don't have to tell me twice." She slipped off the stool and sauntered toward him, and his arm reached out for her as if he were a magnet welcoming metal. His hand looped around her hips as she pressed her mouth to his cheek.

"Be careful." She squeezed his shoulder and waved to Ethan and Nate before leaving the kitchen. God, he couldn't wait to be alone with her again.

Tonight.

He turned to Ethan. "Thanks for arranging to have my place cleaned. I wasn't even thinking straight enough to call anyone today."

"Don't worry about it. You had enough on your plate. It should be done late tonight."

A warm, fuzzy feeling expanded in his chest.

"Shit, you're not going to kiss me, are you? Bro, don't make this awkward."

Cal elbowed him and laughed.

"He's getting soft. I kind of like this side of him, though." Nate stood and cleared the table.

"Shut the fuck up, you two." Cal followed Ethan out with a shake of his head.

They took Ethan's truck to the hotel, just in case anyone was looking for them—surely they were by now. Cal had left Nate his keys so he could move his vehicle into one of the garage bays. He climbed in the passenger seat and Ethan backed out.

"You're not worried about Nate coming on to Lana, are you?" Ethan asked, his tone concerned.

Cal shook his head. "Like I said, I trust him. Both of you. Nate can be an idiot, but I know he would never overstep like that."

"Aha." Ethan grinned at him.

"What?"

"You've staked your claim. You just admitted it."

Cal let out a long sigh. "What is it with you guys lately?"

Ethan shrugged, the ridiculous smile still on his face. "It's about time, that's all."

"Me? It's about time for me? Unbelievable." He rubbed his jaw. "You've been pining over Brittany for what? Three years? And Nate has a different woman in his bed every night."

"Two years. And I haven't been 'pining', you make me sound pathetic."

"Not pathetic. Sad, though," Cal said as Ethan's hands tightened on the steering wheel.

"Can we not talk about it?"

Cal nodded. Regret knotted his stomach. He'd hoped Ethan would have been ready for the friendly nudge, but it was something he would need to do on his own.

They pulled up to the hotel and parked. Ethan turned to him. "I think I should go in and get your things. They'll be looking for the person involved in the murder."

"Good thinking. They've probably pulled the tapes by now." Cal passed him the room key.

"They don't have your credit card on file, do they?"

"Don't worry. I didn't register under my real name."

Ethan disappeared. Cal kept his head low and waited. Ethan was a good man. He would give the shirt off his back for anyone. He hated seeing his friend suffer, but hell. It was a personal battle. Nate had tried getting him out and partying, hoping he would get laid and move on. Instead, he'd gotten drunk and cried. It had been fucking depressing as shit.

He shook his head. Why the hell was he worrying about Ethan's relationship status? Maybe Nate and Ethan were right and he was getting soft. Was that such a bad thing?

Christ. All he could think about was Lana. She'd monopolized his mind since the moment Stamos had showed him her picture, and now he was damn near obsessed. He scrubbed his hands over his face. It wasn't lust. The guys were right about that much. He'd been in lust a million times before. One good lay got that out of his system. Not this time.

The smell of her hair, the way she laughed, the feisty spark in her eyes, and her smoking-hot body—every damn thing about her drove him wild. He'd never get enough. But he didn't want anyone else, either.

He only wanted Lana.

The back door opened. "Got everything." Ethan dropped their bags in the back and got in the driver's side.

"Any luck tracking Will?" Cal asked as they eased out of the parking lot.

Ethan made a face, and disappointment burned in Cal's chest. No, they couldn't be wrong about this. If they were, they had jack shit.

"I might have a small lead, but I'm not too hopeful. I was actually hoping to have Lana have a look at something."

Cal nodded. "I'm sure she'll be eager to help."

When they arrived back at Nate's, they walked in without ringing the doorbell. Quietly, Cal tiptoed to the spare room and set their bag inside the door in case Lana woke and needed something. Rufus weaved in and out of Cal's legs on the way to the kitchen until he dropped down to greet him.

"She hasn't woken at all?"

Nate shook his head. "We need to talk." His tone was gravelly, his eyes hooded.

A fist curled in Cal's stomach.

"You said you had a hunch about the stepbrother? Tanner?" Nate and Ethan sat. Dread clouded his mind in dark shadows.

He'd been right.

Cal rose from his crouched position and took the chair nearest him. Rufus rested his head on his lap as if he sensed Cal's pulse ratcheting up.

"Yeah. I saw the two of them in a picture, and he looked territorial. Enough so that I assumed he was her boyfriend and not her brother. Aside from that, he attacked her. I told you about that."

Ethan made a fist on the table, matching Cal's. Nate tented his fingers under his jaw, nodding that he remembered.

Cal's patience thinned. "You going to tell me what you found out or what?"

Nate sighed. "I don't know where to start. When Tanner was a minor, he was a suspect in a rape case."

The bottom of Cal's stomach dropped out. His breath came out sharply. "Motherfucker." Blood thundered through him, making his head pound. He massaged his temples.

"He was charged. But he was a minor, so he got a slap on the wrist and it never affected him once he turned eighteen. But that's not all." Cal looked up at him, and Nate's mouth firmed a tight line. "He was questioned about a murder."

Cal dropped his hands to grip the table. "Questioned? What the hell does that mean?" He couldn't think straight. He needed to stand, to blow off some steam before he imploded.

"It means he wasn't a suspect, but a person of interest. It passed very quickly, before it even hit the papers, so no one knew about it publicly. My bet is his family had to pay a pretty penny to keep things quiet."

"Whose murder?"

"Andrea Reid. She was a college sophomore, and he was a senior."

Ethan swore. Cal rose to his feet and paced the kitchen.

"What has Lana said about Tanner? Do you think she knew about this?" Nate asked.

Cal locked his jaw. Knew about it and didn't tell him was what Nate was implying.

"Hold on," Ethan said, extending his hand to Nate. "Give her the benefit of the doubt." He turned to Cal. "And I'm sure she would have told you had she known, right?"

His neck muscles bunched. He couldn't see her lying to him to protect Tanner. That didn't make sense. He turned his attention to Nate to answer his previous question. "She didn't say much about him. Except that he's 'intense.' Whatever the hell that means."

"You didn't ask?" Ethan crossed his arms.

"We got to talking about her stepmother, and I made a mental note about Tanner. This is more than I had expected, though."

Ethan and Nate nodded somberly, their expressions hard. "Find out if she knows about his past. In the meantime"—Nate looked to Ethan—"start snooping around Tanner. Think you can hack into his social media? I'd ask the techs at work, but I don't want to alert anyone that he's being watched. We should tread carefully now that we have a lead."

Ethan nodded. "I'm sure I can." He reached into his pants pocket and pulled out his phone. "I've got something here. It's not much, just a social media account under the name Will Andy. I'd love for Lana to look at his picture, see if he looks familiar." He passed the phone to Cal.

Cal studied the blond-tipped young guy with a bottle of vodka in one hand and a cigarette in the other. His mouth hung open in a wide laugh, his pupils so dilated that it was hard to tell his eye color. He turned his attention to the man next to him, with his arm looped around Will's shoulders. They had the same wide nose and outrageous smile.

Not a single light of recognition struck him. Shit. He'd hoped to hell Will would look familiar. That at some point he'd have met him through Stamos, or at least seen them together. Cal rarely forgot a face.

"Doesn't ring a bell for me. But Lana should have a look too."

"Cal, you better wake her up. We need some answers."

"Answers about what?"

Cal whipped his head around to find Lana standing in the doorway. Dammit, she needed to quit doing that.

There she stood, hair damp and wavy around her shoulders, nearly touching her waist. She wore a snug, white long-sleeved shirt—definitely not one of his—and gray leggings. With her makeup immaculate, the sharp blue of her eyes popped, and her skin was smooth and pale. Whatever fatigue had been there this morning was long gone.

His cock grew an inch.

Cal got to his feet, approached Lana, and took her hand. "We have something for you to look at. We're not sure it's Will Anderson, but we found a social media account that could be his." She lowered herself into Cal's chair and he handed her the phone.

Her brow furrowed, studying the screen. Cal stared at her profile, praying for a sign of recognition. Her teeth came out to nip the corner of her lip, and she brought the phone an inch closer to her face.

"I know him," she said. Her finger tapped the screen, and Cal leaned forward. His eyebrows rose.

"Are you sure? Because, judging by the other pictures, this is Will Anderson." He pointed to the other man in the picture.

Lana adamantly shook her head and met Cal's gaze. Her eyes sparked with excitement. "No, I've never seen him before. But this is Shawn Lawson, my dad's manager." She brought her focus back to the screen. "It must be an older picture. His hair is shorter, and he has a beard now. But it's definitely him."

"Sonofabitch," Ethan hissed. "This has to be the connection."

Lana nodded wildly. She straightened in her seat. "I still don't see what Shawn could have to do with this, but if that's Will Anderson, it's too much of a coincidence."

Cal pinched his chin between his thumb and forefinger. "We need an address for one of them."

Silence hung in the air.

"I might be able to help with that," Lana said. Cal shifted his gaze to Ethan and Nate, who shrugged at him.

"How, babe?"

"Well, it would involve me calling a friend, Casey, my coworker. She's my dad's receptionist. She'd be able to get me that information."

Cal grunted. "No way. If you call, and Shawn or Will gets wind that—"

Lana wheeled on him. "That what? That I'm alive? I think they've figured that out. She's a good friend. She wouldn't breathe a word to anyone if I ask her not to."

Ethan folded his arms across his chest. "I can look into Shawn Lawson and see what I can find. It's hard to be certain, but my bet is that they're related. Let me research a bit, and if I can't find anything, Lana should make that call."

Cal closed his hands into fists at his sides. Dammit, he didn't want Lana sticking her neck out. But if it meant bringing all of this to an end, it might be worth it. He took Lana's hand in his again and pulled her from the chair. "Let's go talk in private."

"Yeah, but we don't have time for the kind of talking you have in mind," Nate called. Cal ushered Lana out of the kitchen and turned to shoot Nate the finger.

Ethan roared, "Take your time," then to Nate he said in a scolding tone, "Don't be a cock-blocker."

"What are they talking about?" Lana glanced at him over her shoulder as they passed through the living room to the guest room.

"Ignore those idiots," he said. Ethan and Nate were harmless, but it drove Cal nuts to have them notice her. Yet another reason he ached to be alone with her, to avoid their smart-ass remarks. His gaze traced the gentle curve of her back as they entered the room, and his fingers itched to run through the dark strands of her hair. He shut the door and pulled her into his arms. She circled her hands around his neck. A warm smile touched her lips, igniting a fire in the vibrant blues of her eyes. He took her mouth in his, savoring her sweet taste. She nipped his lip. Her hands curled at his nape. He lifted her in his arms, and her legs swung easily around his waist. Her mouth opened hungrily.

Every urge in his body told him to lay her down on the bed and get her naked. Not yet. And not with his bozo friends waiting on them.

He sat on the edge of the bed and eased his mouth from hers. "I like this." He trailed his fingertip over her cheek. Damn, he loved that she'd gotten done up. "Did you do this for me?" He smoothed his hands down her back and filled his palms with her perfectly round ass.

She giggled. "Maybe. It's nice to dress normal."

"Mmm. I liked your look at the cabin too."

She smiled, her fingers twisted in the material of his shirt. "What did you need to talk to me about?"

The excitement left his body. "Tanner."

Her eyebrows rose. "What about him?"

"When were you planning on telling me about the rape charges? Or the murder case?"

She gasped and her body stiffened in his arms. The color drained from her cheeks.

His jaw locked.

She knew.

Chapter 16

Her breath hitched. Icy fingers raced over her body. She tried to swallow, but her tongue turned to sandpaper. Rape? Murder? She leaned back in Cal's arms and narrowed her eyes at him. It couldn't be. "Tanner? Are you sure?"

He frowned. Doubt clouded his face. "You didn't know?"

"Of course not!" She scrambled off his lap and ran a hand through her hair. She zeroed in on him. "Tell me what you know."

He stayed seated on the edge of the bed, his face dark. "Nate got the information from his guys at the FBI. When Tanner was a minor, he was charged with rape. In college, a young woman was murdered, Andrea Reid—"

Her stomach leapt into her throat. "Andrea?" She croaked. No. Oh, God no.

Cal nodded, his eyes never leaving her face. "You knew her?"

The blood drained from her face the way water drained from a sink when the plug was pulled. She tried to regulate her thumping pulse.

"I didn't know her. But I heard what happened to her." She paced the bedroom. Her mind raced. All this time…how had she not known?

"What happened to her?"

Nausea coiled her stomach in knots. Andrea's death had shaken their community. Even though she didn't know her personally, the attack had hit close to home. Fear had struck her and her friends…everyone. "She was drugged at a frat party." It took every effort she had to speak over the lump in her chest. "She was raped and died of a drug overdose." Memories of the young woman flooded her mind. Her face, her eyes…a blow hit Lana to the solar plexus.

Her stomach lurched. She doubled over on a gag and raced for the bathroom.

Cal was right behind her. He scooped her hair out of the way, his hand on her back. She crouched down and struggled on a deep breath.

"Are you alright?" His voice was heavy with concern.

Her mouth swarmed with saliva. She swallowed once, twice. Her eyes closed. She wouldn't throw up in front of him. She wiped her eyes where tears had leaked out. She took another shuddering breath, nodded, and straightened away from the toilet. Her eyes locked on Cal's. "Did you happen to see her picture?"

His mouth dipped at the corner. "Andrea's? No, why?"

"Look it up."

He pulled his phone from his back pocket and sat on the edge of the tub. She sat on the floor against the wall. The room spun. She inhaled through her nose and blew out through her mouth.

"Holy fuck," he rasped. More curses fell from his lips. "She's your damn twin." He turned the phone for her to see. She squeezed her eyes shut and shook her head. "The comparison is unreal."

The resemblance had meant nothing to her before. And it had never dawned on her before that Andrea's attack could have been because of her.

Cal got to his feet and extended a hand. She placed her fingers in his palm, and he pulled her up. He guided her back to the bedroom and sat her on the bed.

"I'm going to get you some water. I'll be right back."

She closed her eyes and dropped her face into her hands. Could Tanner be behind all of this? Had he raped and murdered Andrea because she looked like her? A tremor rippled through her. Every touch, every snide or salacious smile from Tanner flashed through her mind. She'd been stupid to think the incident after the charity ball had been just an honest mistake.

Cal returned with a glass of water in hand and a hard glint to his green eyes. He passed her the glass and sat beside her. She took a long sip, letting the cool liquid coat the dryness in her throat. He took it from her when she finished and set it on the nightstand.

His fingers circled her arm, then trailed down to her hand, grasping it. "You okay?"

She swallowed. Her eyes met his. She wanted to say yes, to push everything away, and be tough. But she couldn't. A young woman was dead because of her. Tears burned her eyes and fell from her lashes.

"Christ." He pulled her against the wall of his chest and held her. His hand cupped the back of her head; the other stroked slowly up and down her back.

She inhaled his scent. A hint of woodsy cologne mixed with the faint smell of coffee tickled her nose. His five o'clock shadow was now twenty-four hours old. The thick bristles moved against her temple as he pressed a kiss to her hair.

She exhaled deeply, letting her body melt against his. Her cheek nestled against his chest, and his arms enveloped her. Never had she felt so protected, so cared for. She was falling for Cal. He was a solid presence in a world of turmoil. She couldn't bring herself to think about what would have happened had he not "kidnapped" her. Her hands clutched the material of his shirt at his waist, steadying her.

"You never knew about the rape charges and him being a person of interest in Andrea's murder?"

"God, no. I would have told you—"

He nodded. "I know, babe." He smoothed his hand up her arm. "I just can't let that attack go. It's too coincidental. I think he may be obsessed with you, or—"

She shook her head. "If he was so infatuated with me, why would he hire someone to kill me?"

"Why would he kill Andrea?"

"But did he?" She rubbed her forehead where a dull throb started. "I mean, if he was a person of interest, why did they not pursue him further? Maybe the evidence didn't add up—"

Cal shook his head. "The more likely scenario is that someone paid a lot of money to wipe his name clean."

Her mouth fell open. Her heart slowed.

"Did your dad know about Tanner's assault on you?"

She wet her lips and shook her head. "No. Grace handled it, and he apologized. My dad would have overreacted."

"Overreacted?" Cal's voice raised an octave.

"He would have made a big deal of it, and it would have been hard on everyone, including me. If Tanner hadn't apologized, I would have told Dad."

Cal's jaw worked. "Was Tanner living at the house when this happened?"

"No, he hasn't lived there in years."

"So, he drove there in search of you? That's serious intent."

Worded like that, it didn't sound good. Had Tanner just stumbled from the main house over to hers drunk, it would have been more conceivable that he'd gone there without the intention of sleeping with her. But driving to her house from where he lived downtown…that was a different story.

"How did Grace take it?"

Lana tucked her hair behind her ears and sat back on the bed. Cal remained standing. "She was angry. Not at me, at him."

"So she believed you?"

"Yes, she believed me."

"Doesn't that strike you as strange? I mean, most mothers would defend their children to hell and back."

Her hands twisted in her lap. "Grace is hard on Tanner. She keeps close tabs on him. I don't believe she thought he would hurt me, but he had upset me and she didn't like that."

Cal stroked his jaw with his thumb and forefinger. "Where's Tanner's dad?"

She frowned. "He lives in Paris. Tanner doesn't see him often."

"I'd like to look into him. What's his name?" His eyes sharpened on her.

She frowned at him. What in the world would Tanner's dad have to do with this? She'd never even met him. "Marcel Theroux."

He nodded. His face darkened, and his eyes were distant. G.I. Joe mode had kicked in. She was learning to notice the subtle ways he changed when he moved from military Cal to regular Cal. A shiver of excitement raced over her. Both sides of him intrigued her. He was dark and dangerous one moment, then teasing and charming the next.

His hand went to the small of her back. "Are you hungry?"

Her stomach rumbled. "Starving."

He grinned. "Let's go eat." He took her hand, and they left the room. Rufus met them in the kitchen with a stuffed toy. She stopped to greet him, welcoming his wet kisses. She missed having a dog. She'd had one growing up, but Lady had died when Lana was a teenager. One day when she had her own place, she would get another dog.

"That was quick. Dude, your reflexes must be slipping."

Cal grabbed Rufus's toy and chucked it at Nate. He tried to dodge it, but it hit him square in the face. Lana stifled a laugh, Ethan roared, and Rufus charged after the toy, tail wagging.

"What do you have for lunch?" Cal opened Nate's fridge and began rummaging.

"I just had a sandwich. There's some focaccia bread on the counter and turkey meat in the fridge." Ethan nodded to the plate in front of him.

Nate scowled at Ethan. "There goes my lunch for the week."

Cal was already taking everything out and fixing their food.

"Cal, maybe we should go pick up something. I don't want to eat Nate's lunch meat."

Cal shook his head in response at the same time Nate spoke, "Don't worry, there's plenty. I was messing with him."

Ethan offered her a seat at the table. "I keep running into dead ends for an address on either Will or Shawn. Think you can give your friend a call?"

Lana shifted her gaze to Cal. His shoulders stiffened, and he lifted his gaze from the sandwiches he was making. His eyes connected with hers, and a dark shadow crossed his green orbs, but he gave her one slight nod. He wasn't happy about it, but he was as eager as she was to put this behind them.

Lana smiled at Ethan. "Absolutely. Do you have a phone I can use?"

Cal crossed the room and set one on the table in front of her. "Use this one. It's encrypted. Be sure to tell her not to breathe a word of your contacting her to anyone. And avoid having her call you back. Stay on the line until you get the information."

She nodded, picked up the phone, and made her way to the bedroom. A tiny ball of unease wound deep inside her stomach. Everyone thought she was missing; it was a lot to ask Casey to keep quiet. She dialed her number and sat on the bed. The phone rang in her ear, and Lana chewed the tip of her thumb.

"Vanderpoel Homes, this is Casey speaking. How can I help you?"

Lana's pulse kicked up a notch. "Case, it's Lana—"

Casey's sharp intake of breath pierced her ear. Lana cringed. "Don't freak out, okay? I need your help, but I need you to promise you won't tell a soul that you've heard from me. Not even my father." A stab of pain shot through her chest. The words burned her tongue, and shame filled her heart. To imply that it wasn't safe for her father to know she was okay ate at her.

"My life depends on it, Case."

Casey cleared her throat. "You can trust me," she said softly. "I'll do whatever I can to help."

"Thanks. I'll explain more later, but I need you to get an address for me…an employee's. I know that's a breach of confidentiality, but—"

"What's the name?"

"Shawn Lawson." Her voice shook on the words. Silence vibrated through the phone, and Lana closed her eyes. As her dad's manager, Shawn was a very prominent employee. Under any other circumstances, giving out his information would be cause for an immediate dismissal.

The heavy tap of Casey's purposeful typing sounded in the background. "Do you have a pen?"

Lana leaned for the nightstand drawer and pulled out a pad of paper and pen. "Go," she said. Casey rattled off a phone number and an address. Lana jotted it down, thanked her, and hung up.

Yes!

It wasn't definitive, but it was a solid lead. Satisfaction rippled through her as she made her way back to the kitchen and slapped the paper on the table in front of Cal. He read the address and got to his feet.

"You're incredible." He caught the back of her neck and brushed his lips over her mouth. She laughed and let him pull her into his lap.

He waved the paper in the air. "Here's our next stop, boys."

Ethan and Nate applauded, and warmth spread through her.

"Did Cal tell you about last night?" Ethan asked.

Her eyebrows rose, and her stomach flipped over as she looked back and forth between the two men. "No, what happened?"

Cal chomped on a carrot stick from the plate in front of her, but tension creased the corners of his eyes. She picked up the sandwich and nibbled, keeping her face passive.

"Tell me. I can take it."

Cal lifted his shoulder and pressed his back into the chair, allowing her to read his face better. Her eyes lingered on the muscles that strained the material of his shirt.

Focus, Lana. "Well?"

"Let's just say that Stamos is going to need some physical therapy," Cal informed her, as a grin spread from ear to ear, crinkling his laugh lines.

Nate snorted. "He shot him in the shoulder."

Lana clapped her hand over her mouth. Her stomach coiled into knots at the image of such violence. But at the same time, she realized, this was a man who had helped plan her murder. She met Cal's steady gaze. He was watching her carefully, waiting for her reaction.

She lowered her trembling hand and took another bite of her sandwich. "Was that necessary?"

Ethan snorted. Cal's lips stretched into a sexy smile. A deep, throaty laugh rumbled through his lips.

"It was completely necessary, unfortunately. To be honest, I spared him what he really deserved. But it was a good enough warning for him to stay away from you." The amusement left his face, and his eyes darkened, reminding her of how dangerous and deadly he was. Her toes curled against the smooth tile floor at her feet. She should have been unnerved by his revelation, but she wasn't. He was hard, unapologetic, and fiercely protective of her.

She'd never been more attracted to anyone in her life.

Chapter 17

His phone buzzed in his pocket, snapping his attention away from the TV screen. It was after 6 p.m. and he didn't have the heart to wake Lana yet. He got to his feet, stretched his tense muscles, and pulled out his phone. Nate was in the kitchen refilling their drinks, and Ethan had gone to grab food. He glanced at the screen. Ethan.

"Yeah?"

"Get the hell out—now!"

Adrenaline spiked through his veins, and he made a dead run for the bedroom. "What's going on?"

"I just drove past Stamos's building because I was in the neighborhood, and I saw him load into a black SUV with a fucking assault rifle. He had two carloads of people with him, and his arm was in a sling and bandaged to shit. He's gotta be after you. Get the hell out as fast as you can."

"Sonofabitch. How the hell could he have found us here?"

"Who knows? He could have tailed one of us."

Anger rippled through him. He wasn't careless—ever. But there was no other explanation as to how they could have been found. Cal disconnected, and his feet pounded down the hall. He stretched his hand for the bedroom door, but it yanked open, and Lana's wild eyes searched his face.

"What is it?"

He grabbed her hand and towed her after him. Her fingers turned to ice in his palm and tugged on his hold. He didn't let go.

"Cal! Tell me—now!"

"They're after us. Stamos is coming with an army." They entered the kitchen, and Nate slapped a pair of keys in his hand. "Take my Chevy. It's parked in the pull-through garage that leads to the alley. I'll handle this."

Cal's feet rooted to the spot, his gaze searched Nate's. He couldn't leave him to fend for himself against a goddamn fleet of people.

"Ethan's not far behind them. We got this."

Lana's fingers wiggled in his. Headlights bounced through the window, and he accepted the keys.

"Go!" Nate growled.

Lana grabbed her shoes from by the door, and Nate ushered them to the garage door access. Cal clicked the key fob, and the doors unlocked. She slid into the passenger's seat, and Cal pressed the garage door opener.

Crack! Crack!

His shoulders tensed.

Lana's head whipped around. "They're shooting," she wheezed. The garage door rattled open, and he cringed as the sound echoed in the night. Return shots fired, splitting the air. He started the ignition. A dead calm seeped into his bones. "Get your seat belt on, and keep your head down."

He peeled out of the garage and down the narrow drive to the alleyway. At least they'd get a head start. The truck bounced over the gravel terrain and jerked when it slammed into a pothole. Bright headlights reflected in the rearview mirror. Lana craned her neck around.

"Cal, that vehicle is moving really fast." The headlights glared into their mirrors, making him squint. Lana breathed a curse as he whipped the truck out of the alley and onto the main road. The truck shot forward on the smooth pavement, but the vehicle behind them peeled after them.

Crack, crack!

Glass pelted the back of his neck. He shot his hand out and shoved Lana's head between her legs. "Dammit, stay down." He weaved through a column of cars, and the truck fell behind. Cal kept his gaze on the silver truck in the rearview mirror. He couldn't make out the bastard's faces, but there had to be at least three.

"We need to lose them. Where's your place?" Hysteria pitched her voice to a squeak. She parted her hair that had fallen like a dark curtain over her face.

"Just outside Baring."

"Alright, then we need to get on WA-522 going east. Take the next exit on your right."

"I'm not leading them to my place," he ground out.

"They don't know we have anywhere to go. We have lots of time to lose them." The turn approached, and his teeth sank into his tongue. In less than a second, they would miss it.

"Cal, turn!"

He whipped the vehicle, merging onto the on-ramp. But his fast move hadn't slipped past the assholes in the truck. They turned behind them, gaining speed swiftly behind the several cars that separated them. He slammed his foot on the gas, gunning them onto the interstate. He merged in front of a transport vehicle, cutting the driver off. His horn blared, but the silver truck had no choice but to merge behind the trailer.

"Good one." They traveled for nearly fifteen minutes, but with every lane change the silver truck flashed not far behind them. Lana straightened in her seat and unbuckled her seat belt. He grabbed her belt before she could release it. "What the hell are you doing? Stay buckled. As soon as they fall far enough behind, I'm going to lose them."

"You need to let me drive."

He did a double take, but her eyes were wide and determined. "Not happening, honey."

"It's only a matter of time before they get close enough to shoot out one of our tires. Unless you want *me* to shoot at them, you'd better let me drive. I'm better at navigating than you are, anyway."

He stiffened. "How do you figure?"

"Because you nearly missed our turn last time."

"I was trying to lose them."

"And I see that was successful. Now, seriously, stop being so damn macho."

He grunted. She was right. He'd have to take them out before more of their buddies showed up. "Fine. Come straddle my lap." She scrambled over the seats and settled her ass over his groin. His body tensed, and his blood heated. Her hands gripped the steering wheel above his, pulling him back to the moment.

"Put your foot on mine and I'll move out from under you."

Her dark head gave a sharp nod, and her small shoe rested on the toe of his. "Ready?"

"Yes, go! They're behind us now."

He moved his hands from the steering wheel to her hips, and eased out from underneath her body. She kept the truck steady and settled into the seat. He reached over her shoulder and pulled the seat belt across her chest, buckling her in.

"Stay low and do what I say." Shit, he must be crazy. All it would take would be one shot to her head, and—

He couldn't think about it. He pulled his Glock from the waistband of his pants and climbed onto the back seat where the back window was shot out. The truck's bumper loomed before him, closing in. He steadied his shoulders, aimed for their tire, and fired. The truck jerked, and the bullet hit the bumper. Cal ground out a curse. A large form hung out the passenger's side window.

Shit.

"Babe—" Shots fired, and the truck swerved into the next lane. He collided with the rear passenger door and righted himself. Lana had cut the vehicle in front of another semi. Two closed in behind them, shielding them from the truck. The vehicle jerked as she took an exit and the transport followed.

Yes, they just might lose them.

"Good one. I don't think they saw us turn." He climbed over the console and dropped into the passenger seat. Lana sat ramrod-straight, her knuckles white. He reached out his hand and grazed her arm with his fingertips.

"You okay?"

She nodded wildly. "Fine." Her eyes snapped up to the rearview mirror as she headed northeast toward the mountains. Trees began to crowd the sides of the road; they whipped past the long arms of the branches. A few minutes ticked by, and her shoulders relaxed. Cal ached to wrap her in his arms, but not yet. He couldn't let his guard down until she was safe. The wind whipped through the broken back window, sending a cool breeze through the truck. "Did we lose them?" Her voice was steady now and laced with hope. He glanced in the side-view mirror, but other than the transport's large headlights, there wasn't anyone else on the road.

"I think so," he said. He glanced back at her and took in the gentle creases around her eyes. "Do you want me to drive?"

Her eyes slid over to him, finally meeting his. Her blue orbs slammed into him, making his chest ache. If Ethan hadn't given them a head start... If one of the bullets had hit her...

"Yeah, I'll pull over at the next gas station." Her gaze narrowed on the rearview mirror. "Who's that? Passing the transport?"

He twisted in his seat and his body tensed.

Goddammit!

"It's them." He unbuckled his seat belt and climbed into the back.

"Are you sure? They're pretty far away." Her voice trembled.

"Positive. Keep it steady, I'm going to take out the driver when they get—" The truck shot forward, sending him barreling into the back seat. "Dammit, what are you doing? I have a loaded gun in my hand!"

"Sorry. I have an idea, but we have to hurry." They twisted around a bend, and their pursuers fell from view. The truck bounced as Lana pulled to the side of the road and turned the headlights off.

Irritation rippled through him. "Lana, we're sitting ducks right here. Get back on the road!"

She shifted the truck into reverse and cut the wheel sharply, sending the rear end of the Chevy back into a break in the trees. Branches scratched over the smooth paint as she edged them farther into the woods until dark foliage covered the hood.

Cal stared at her in the mirror. "Damn, you're smart."

She chuckled and pressed her back into the seat. "You're just realizing this now?"

He leaned forward between the seats, wrapped his hand around the base of her neck, and pressed his lips to her mouth. She melted into him, her mouth hot and wet on his. Desire stirred in his belly. He pulled away and pressed his forehead to hers.

"More of that later. Right now, I need to take these assholes out. Stay here, and if anything happens get back on the interstate and call Nate." He opened the door and slid out of the truck, leaving his phone on the passenger seat. He rattled off the code to his phone.

Her lips parted, and the rosy hue to her cheeks faded to pale white. "Cal, you can't be serious."

He winked at her. "I'll be back." The road lit up with long beams of yellow. He jogged to a tree, dropped down to one knee, and aimed his Glock at the road. Headlights grew wider until the lights touched the grass at his knees.

A silver truck filled his vision, racing across the pavement. He fired three shots. Two tires blew out, and the truck swerved back and forth over the pavement before flipping and rolling. He got to his feet and charged across the road. His heart rate slowed to a gentle hum in his eardrums. The passenger door creaked open, and a large form fell to the ground.

Cal grabbed him by the scruff of the neck and pulled him into a sitting position. The man howled in pain, and his hands grasped for his knee. A bone protruded through denim, blood coating his pants. A gun fell beside him, and Cal pocketed it. One glance inside the car showed the driver slumped over the steering wheel. Another passenger lay at the side of the road, the broken windshield evidence of his fate.

Cal dropped to his knee and shoved the barrel of his gun into the man's mouth. "Who the fuck are you?"

Brown eyes wide, with his dark hair plastered to his forehead, the man shook his head frantically. Cal removed the gun to let him speak, but kept it trained between his eyes.

"Stamos hired me! That's all I know. He was out for blood because you fucked up a job. If he doesn't kill you and the woman, they're going to kill him."

Rage coursed through his veins like a violent sea. He lowered the weapon to the man's thigh and fired. He screamed and curled into a tight ball, sweat pouring over his temples.

"Sorry 'bout that." His tone was dry. He got to his feet and checked the man sprawled on the pavement. He pressed his fingers to his neck; no pulse. Keeping his gun poised, he approached the driver's side door. Blood pooled out of the driver's mouth and onto his leg, his face battered from the airbag. Cal pressed his fingers to his throat. He had a pulse, but it was slow and wiry.

Even if he walked away alive, he wouldn't be in any shape to chase them. He pocketed the gun and stalked toward the truck. Lana's oval face stared back at him through the windshield. An iron fist formed in his stomach. He opened the driver's side door and snagged her cheeks in his hands. Her eyes darkened as he pressed his lips to her mouth. Damn, he hated that scared look in her eyes.

"Hop over. I'm driving."

She released her seat belt, climbed across the console, and dropped into the passenger seat. He pulled out of the trees and onto the road. Lana's silence hammered through him. She was shaken up, but as soon as they got to his place, he'd fix that. Darkness spread across the sky, turning the pavement to black ink. Fifteen minutes later, he pulled into the attached garage of the small, two-bedroom log cabin. He led her through the side door into the house and flicked on the lights of the small kitchen. His phone buzzed in his pocket, and he pulled it out as Lana sank onto one of the wooden bar stools. Relief washed over him as he read the text.

All good. Hope you made it safe, on our way.

"Nate and Ethan should be here within the hour. Can I get you a drink?"

"I'll have whatever you're having."

"I'm having tequila."

She made a face.

He laughed. "How about some wine?"

She nodded her approval. "Now you're talking."

He poured her a glass of pinot grigio and handed it to her. She brought the glass to her lips, sipped, and closed her eyes on a moan. "I needed that."

She wrinkled her nose as he fixed his drink. "How do you drink that?"

"It's tequila and water."

She stuck her tongue out. "Yuck. I'm pretty sure tequila is meant for margaritas and that's it."

"It's good for you. It lowers blood sugar and cholesterol. I drink it with water to avoid the sugar that comes with soda. It's clean, with no hangovers." He took a sip. "Tastes good, too. Want a sip?" He offered his glass.

She leaned away and clutched the wineglass to her chest. "I'm good with this, thanks."

He grinned. Her eyes lowered to her wineglass. She swirled the golden liquid. "Are you still leaving to find Will?"

Guilt twisted his gut. Christ. This was what it would be like. A future with Lana would only cause her disappointment. He would always have to see that sad and fearful look in her eyes, and he'd always feel like a piece of shit for doing it to her. Especially after what she'd been through the last hour. But he had to find Will. He could be the final link to ending this nightmare for good. The past few days had given him a glimpse of what life could be like with Lana. It could be happy. But how could he give everything up? All that he'd worked for? His career, his livelihood. Nothing else would amount to what he did now. But nothing—no one—else would amount to Lana.

He lifted her chin with his knuckle. "I won't be long, okay? I need to do this. We can't let this go on any longer. Are you all right?"

Eyes wide, her lips pressed together, she nodded. "I'm a little on edge, but I'll be fine. I'm sorry. I don't want you to feel torn."

"I'm not torn. I want to be here, and only here." He pressed his lips to hers. Her mouth was as smooth as silk, and her lips tasted of wine. "Wait up for me. There's something I want to show you later."

A blush tinted her cheeks. She lifted the glass to her lips. "I'm not promising I won't pass out."

He pointed a stern finger. "No more wine for you."

They hung out in the kitchen while Cal put some frozen pizzas in the oven. He always kept his place stocked with quick food in case of emergencies.

Ding-dong!

Cal stiffened. Lana's hands curled around the edge of the table as if ready to bolt. He placed a hand on hers. "It's only the guys. Wait here." He exited the kitchen and advanced on the front door. His hand hovered where his Glock sat at the small of his back. A glance out the side window showed Ethan and Nate. He opened the door.

Rufus came barreling in ahead of them, making a beeline for the kitchen.

"What the—"

"Thought you could use some extra security." Nate shut and locked the door behind them.

"That's a good idea, thanks." He'd never bothered to get a dog since he was rarely home. He loved animals, but it wouldn't be fair to leave one alone all the time. Rufus was a damn good dog and well behaved. It would be nice having him around for the night.

Lana squealed excitedly from the kitchen, greeting Rufus. "Oh, you're such a good boy!" She was on her knees, scratching his ears, when they walked in. "Hi, guys." She smiled.

Nate inhaled deeply. "What's in the oven?"

"Pizza. Make sure she eats." Cal nodded at Lana as she rose from her crouched position. A large gash split the skin above Ethan's temple. A butterfly bandage held it in place. Lana's gaze drifted to Ethan's wound, and her eyes grew soft and distant.

"You two all right?" she asked.

Nate nodded. "Yeah, it got a little crazy. They shot out my windows, and one idiot got inside and landed a lucky shot with the butt of his gun to Ethan's big head."

Ethan glowered at him. "There were five of them, and Stamos was shooting from the vehicle. We took out two of his men, and then they took off before the cops arrived. What happened to you guys?"

"One of the SUVs was hot on our ass from the moment we left your place. Lana did some quick thinking and hid the truck in the woods and I shot out their tires. One guy probably died from the crash, the other was nearly there. One was able to talk and only said that Stamos had hired him, but he knew nothing else. He had a broken leg, and I shot out his other one so he won't be a threat."

Ethan nodded, his expression somber. "We found an address for Will. Should we go?"

The sooner they left, the sooner he could get home to Lana. There was that word again, *home*. Lana was beginning to feel more like home than his house.

She lifted her chin, a shaky smile on her lips. "Go ahead, we'll be fine." Rufus sat next to her feet and gave him a big doggy grin.

"We won't be long." He pulled her tighter against him, not giving a damn what Ethan and Nate would say later, and pressed his lips to her forehead. Her arms came around his waist, her face buried in his chest.

"Where the hell you going, World War Three?" The corner of Nate's mouth lifted.

Ethan jabbed him in the ribs. "Shut up, you ass."

Cal turned and headed down the hallway to change into darker clothes. This time he was getting answers. The sooner they wrapped this up, the better.

* * * *

"Let's not kill anyone, alright? We'll collect the information and hand it off to Nate so he can do the FBI work." They sat in Ethan's truck, parked across the street from Stamos's apartment complex.

"I can't make any promises." He pulled black gloves over his hands. "We'll pop into Stamos's apartment first and then Shawn's. Just in case Will's there, he shouldn't have a clue we're after him, and I don't want Stamos tipping him off."

Ethan nodded his agreement. "We'll move quickly just in case and secure them both—if they're both there."

"Did you find any link between Will and Tanner?"

Ethan pulled his phone out of his pocket. "I hacked into both of their social media accounts, and it appears none of them are friends. However, they have numerous mutual friends, so my guess is there's a connection."

Cal shook his head. "We need to pay a visit to Tanner."

Ethan locked eyes with him. His jaw worked. "You think that's a good idea?"

"It would be cutting out the middle men."

"True, but he's not going to admit anything. It's best if we corner these idiots, get them to confess who hired them, and then take Tanner down with evidence. That guy has more money and influence than we can shake a stick at. If we don't have enough tallies stacked against him, there won't even be an investigation."

Cal nodded. It was a good thing Ethan, the levelheaded one, was here. He scratched his beard with his gloved thumb. Dammit, he'd forgotten to shave again. A picture of an aroused Lana squirming under him as he glided his bristled cheek across her naked body flashed through his mind. Shit. He did not need a hard-on while sitting next to Ethan.

"Alright, let's go."

They slipped out of the vehicle and crossed the dark street. A light flickered outside the building, casting strobe shadows. They entered the three-story walk-up and advanced up the stairs two at a time. The old, worn carpet on the stairs reeked like urine. The stench of BO and cigarettes breathed out of the grungy paint.

Ethan pressed his back against the wall beside Stamos's apartment, his gun pointing to the floor. Cal paused on the other side and pulled out his Glock.

Ethan nodded. It was go time.

Cal kicked his foot out, stomping near the handle. The door flew open and crashed against the wall. Wood splinters scattered the floor. They entered, their feet soundless on the carpet. Ethan closed the door softly behind him.

The heavy scent of cigarette smoke invaded his nose. "Come out, Stamos!" Cal barked. He stepped over a take-out box on the floor near the front door. Food-encrusted plates were rotting in the kitchen. The curdling smell of sour milk made Cal swallow over a lump of nausea.

Ethan strode toward the closed bedroom door at the back of the apartment. Cal scanned the living room and checked out the bathroom behind him. Ethan tried the knob.

"It's locked," he said gruffly as he took a wide step back and stomped his foot out. It connected with the wood, and the door sprang open, splinters and chunks of debris floating to Cal's feet as he charged into the bedroom behind Ethan.

He cursed.

It was empty. "Shit," he breathed.

Ethan lowered his gun. "I'm not surprised. He wouldn't come back here after coming after you."

Cal nodded. "Let's take a quick look around." He began opening the nightstand drawers, and Ethan moved into the living room. Hell, it was unlikely that he'd find anything remotely helpful. Stamos was stupid, but not dumb enough to leave a paper trail. The nightstand held a bag of weed and a bong, along with a small box of condoms.

"There's nothing here," Ethan called. Cal met him in the living room, and they left the apartment. They climbed into the truck and drove to the address Lana had given them. The difference between the two neighborhoods was staggering. Neatly groomed trees and shrubs lined the newly paved road to Shawn's address.

"Let's see if we can get through the back without drawing attention."

Ethan nodded his agreement, and they parked a street over. They moved swiftly down the quiet street and into someone's backyard. It wasn't as late as he preferred, but it was dark and quiet. They hopped the fence and landed in Shawn's yard. Cal pulled out his lock pick set, and Ethan held the flashlight steady. He inserted the tools and maneuvered the lock. It clicked softly. Ethan smiled and they pushed the door open. Silence greeted them.

Cal pulled out his Glock and Ethan stretched his gun out in front of him as they moved out of the laundry room and into the main area. The living room was lit up, and soft voices floated from the TV.

The metallic smell of blood hit them first. Cal's stomach churned. He knew that smell. Too damn well.

"Shit," Cal hissed.

"Goddammit." Ethan turned away from the sight. There, on the couch, was Will—or at least a body that appeared to be his—throat slit. Blood pooled on the brown leather couch beside him, a slow drip forming a puddle on the floor. Cal tucked his Glock into his pants and went for the man's pocket. He pulled his wallet out and opened it up.

William Anderson Lawson.

Ethan nudged him toward the door. "Let's get out of here."

Chapter 18

God, this was awkward. Nate was a nice guy, but having him babysit her in silence had her nerves on end. She cleared her throat for the second time, her brain grasping at conversation topics like straws. Nate tore his gaze away from the baseball game that filled the screen and snagged another handful of chips.

"Cal told me you two were in the military together?"

He settled back in the deep couch and nodded. "Yup, I've known him eleven years." He chomped into a chip and kept his gaze off of the TV. "Actually, I owe it to Cal for getting me out of there. He was the first to leave recon, and until he did that, another career never entered my mind. The night before he returned to the U.S. he sat me down and asked me if this was what I wanted to do for the rest of my life. The short answer was no."

"How do you guys remain so close when you have such different careers?"

Nate dusted the salt off his hands and rested his feet on the coffee table. He shrugged. "In some cases we get to work together, though not often. Cal is stealth, and very few people know who he is or what he does. That makes him indispensable to the FBI. He's done some undercover work, and has gone into places the FBI doesn't have jurisdiction."

Her eyebrows rose. Wow. Cal had told her his work was dangerous, but hearing the description from Nate made her palms sweat.

"That's impressive."

Nate nodded, scooped another handful of chips, then turned his hazel eyes on her. "So you really have no idea who could want you dead?"

Her mouth went dry, and a coil of guilt tightened in her stomach. These men, whom she barely knew, were sacrificing their lives for her…and she was clueless as to who even wanted to do her harm. She swallowed and reached her hand out to stroke Rufus's ears. He let out a snore and nudged his nose closer to her.

"It's been spinning through my mind nonstop. But I can't imagine anyone wanting to hurt me."

Nate's lips thinned. "Cal seems pretty dead-set on it being Tanner."

She rested her elbow on the arm of the chair and pressed her fingertips into her temples. Tanner. As Cal's primary suspect, he'd been at the forefront of her mind, too. But something didn't fit.

"Tanner is an ass, and I know everything stacks up against him right now...but it doesn't add up to me."

Nate leveled her with his stare. "How so?"

"Well, for starters, I don't see how he would benefit from my death. He has more money than he knows what to do with, so it's not an inheritance battle. Was he mad that I pushed him away and told Grace after he attacked me? Sure. But what would killing me do except leave him as a primary suspect?"

Nate held out the bowl of chips, and she shook her head. He dove in again. Geez, these guys could eat, she was still stuffed from the four pizza slices. Adrenaline sure worked up an appetite. "Thing is, men who commit murder don't think logically like we do. Unless you can think of anyone else, he's our strongest lead."

She let out a deep sigh, and a dull throb started across her forehead. Fatigue had settled in, and the last thing she wanted to do was spend one more minute talking about her possible enemies. She let the subject drop, and they chatted a bit more until she excused herself for bed. She wanted to be alone. She had a lot to think about. Before she scooted off to the bedroom, she refilled her glass of wine and said good night to Nate.

She climbed onto the neatly made bed and switched on the TV. A shower would feel heavenly. Goose bumps raced over her skin. No, she would wait for Cal. She took a swig of her glass and flicked through the channels. She settled on an old sitcom and got comfortable. Her father had loved this show. A pang of guilt formed in her chest. She hated that she couldn't call him, that she couldn't alleviate his and her mother's pain. God, they'd be frantic. Pain spread through her chest. They'd always been so protective of her...so fearful. For both of them, this would be a nightmare come true. It wasn't fair that she couldn't reach out to them. Even just a simple phone call would make a world of difference. They wouldn't understand what was happening, but if she could lift their terror even a little bit, it would be worth it.

She chewed her lip. Could she chance a phone call to her mother? Surely there would be no way to trace her here unless her mother was being watched. Her gaze shifted to the cordless phone on the nightstand. Her fingers itched to lift it up and make the call. No. Cal was risking his life for her. The least she could do was not make things worse. She'd suggest reaching out to them later, and maybe he could find a safe way to ease their minds.

She took a deep breath and let it out slowly. Maybe Cal would come home with good news and all this would be behind them tonight. The first thing she'd do would be to call her parents.

Her body warmed with each sip of wine. Its gentle effects took the edge off of her nerves. God, she hoped Cal was okay. A minute later, the slamming of a car door echoed outside the bedroom window. Then another.

That couldn't be Cal already. She looked at the clock. He'd been gone only a couple of hours. She scampered off the bed. Her foot snagged the blankets, sending her forward. She caught herself on the nightstand. Shit. Two and a half glasses of wine had done her in.

Rufus's ferocious bark and his nails scattering across the floor pierced the calm of the cabin.

She edged the curtain away from the window. It was Ethan's truck. Relief spread through her muscles. Cal *was* home. A thrill raced over her. She downed the last bit of wine and waited. Her palms grew damp.

The front door opened and closed. Cal and Ethan's voices reached her ears. She should go out to greet him. Two ideas tickled her thoughts. She could crawl under the covers and pretend she'd passed out—or she could be waiting for him, naked in the shower.

She'd opt for the latter.

A giggle rumbled in her throat. She tiptoed to the door and placed her ear to it. The guys were talking. She gnawed her lip. God, she hoped they weren't planning on chitchatting all night. Cal's voice echoed down the hall.

"I'm going to check on Lana."

She shot away from the door and scurried to the bathroom, leaving the door wide open. She pulled her shirt over her head, revealing her white lace bra. Her fingers hooked into the waistband of her pants just as he entered the bedroom.

"Lana?"

"In here," she said, her voice trembling. She moved her pants down her legs, exposing the matching panties. He rounded the corner.

"Jesus—" he breathed. His hands caught the door frame. She shimmied her pants down over her knees and stepped out of them, her eyes locked with his. A red tinge tinted his cheeks. Heat swarmed in her belly.

Her foot caught the edge of her pants. She pitched over, and a yelp squeaked out as she landed on the oak floor with a *thump*, her ankles still tangled in her pants.

"Shit, are you okay?" Cal crouched next to her. He helped her to a sitting position.

A laugh erupted from her throat. "That was sexy, wasn't it?" Her eyes watered, and her body shuddered on every chuckle. Cal smiled from ear to ear. His cheeks creased. He folded his arms over his chest, a sly glint in his eyes.

"You're wasted."

She covered her mouth, but the giggles leaked out. "No, I'm not."

"Liar. You have a habit of falling over when you drink, don't you? How much did you have?"

"Two glasses." She struggled to pull the tangled material off her ankles.

He lifted his eyes to the ceiling and shook his head. "Two glasses of wine and you're on your ass."

She narrowed her eyes at him. "What do you mean, I 'have a habit'?"

"You fell like that getting out of your friend's car on Saturday night. Or don't you remember?"

Her mouth opened on a silent "Oh." So he'd been watching her? "I tripped...both times." Her laughter settled to a gentle shake of her shoulders.

"I like this." His fingers traced the top of her bra, distracting her. "And this..." His hand coasted down to her panties, his voice growing hoarse.

Her giggles subsided. She swallowed.

"I'll be right back." He stood and disappeared. His footsteps sounded down the hall. "You guys need to go," she heard him say. "Now."

She got to her feet. He was right. She was drunk. She ran a hand through her hair. *Shoot, shoot, shoot.* She hoped it wouldn't ruin the mood.

Cal returned a few minutes later. He shed his shirt and tossed it to the floor. She clasped her hands in front of her waist, waiting. He came to her, his hand flattened on the small of her back, pressing her into him. Her hands rested on his shoulders, and her eyes found his.

Deep green pools devoured her. His other hand threaded through her hair, his lips hovering scant inches from hers. "It's insane how much I want you."

Her pulse beat against her throat. She licked her lips, but no words came to her mind. His thumb smoothed over the sensitive spot. He wanted her. That was obvious. But did he want more than just sex?

She rolled her lips in. Her eyes left his to trace the hard lines of his face, committing each edge to memory. She might not have him forever, but she had him for now.

Inching up to her tiptoes, she pressed her lips to his. His mouth opened on hers, and his tongue entered her mouth, probing her. He leaned her backward, arching her over his arm. A soft moan caught in her throat, and her fingertips dug into the bare muscles of his shoulder. Her hands trailed over the breadth of his chest, down the hard lines of his stomach. She found the snap on his jeans and loosened it.

He smiled against her mouth. "That ready, huh?"

She licked into his mouth, then pulled away. "Oh yeah."

He shucked his jeans down his legs and kicked them to the side, then did the same with his boxers. His member pulsed between them, the silkiness of his shaft resting against her belly. He backed her into the shower. Her hands locked around his waist. He reached behind him and turned the water on, then adjusted the temperature. Warm spray sprinkled over his shoulders to dampen her chest.

"This is what I wanted to show you." He nodded at the shower. "Have you ever showered in your bra and panties before?"

Her gaze flicked downward. She was still half-dressed. How had she not noticed that? Cal made her feel naked. Even fully dressed, he had that effect on her. Her tongue slid from one corner of her mouth to the other.

"No," she croaked.

Being partially dressed in the wake of his nakedness, combined with the steam of the shower, was erotic. Her body hummed with the side effects of the wine. Her head swarmed. Cal's face came into focus. The burning intensity of his eyes softened, and his lips parted. The pad of his thumb touched her cheek.

His lips molded to hers, and his hand coasted down her back, cupping her ass. A guttural groan vibrated from his throat.

Her eyes snapped open. She placed her hand on his chest, stopping him. He looked down at her, his eyes searching her face. "What's the matter, honey?"

She pushed him farther back so she could meet his gaze. "How many women have you had sex with in this shower?"

Humor sparked his eyes. A boyish grin lifted his mouth. He shifted his gaze away and lifted a shoulder. "You want a number?"

She pursed her lips. His hand still rested on her ass, gently moving over her skin.

"That many?" She hadn't expected to be the first. But she had hoped not to have been the hundredth.

All traces of teasing left his face. His eyes darkened. His jaw worked as if weighing his words. "I've never brought a woman here before. Only you." His voice was rough, barely above a whisper.

Her pulse stopped and started. The buzz ebbed away, and blood thundered through her ears. Her heart expanded in her chest. She took a deep breath through her nose. He wasn't professing his love. He was only saying she was different from the rest. But that was enough. She circled her hand around his neck and pulled his mouth back down to hers.

She let her hands roam his body, down, down, down, until she found his hard shaft. Her hand closed around him, circling him. She moved her hand, tightening, pulling, until his shoulders bunched. He crushed his mouth to hers, and a tremor shivered through him.

His hand snagged her wrist, stopping her. He dropped his forehead to hers, breaking the seal of their mouths. He spoke in a pant. "Slow down, babe."

She shook her head. "I want you." Slowly she lowered to her knees. Cal turned so the water was full-force on his back, blocking the spray from hitting her. Her hand moved again. At this angle, she could see every hard-worked line of his body. His thighs were stacked with muscle, his abs rock-hard. With her free hand, she toyed with his stomach muscles, admiring how they rippled. Then slowly, she took him into her mouth.

One of his hands grasped the back of her head, and the other grasped the wall, steadying him. "Jesus Christ," he breathed.

She smiled as she worked her tongue over him. His body jerked. He pulled himself away and helped her to her feet. "If you keep doing that, this is going to end very fast."

She giggled. "You like that?"

He turned her in his arms so her back rested against his front, the warm spray raining down over her body. "Hell, yeah," he mumbled against her ear, "but now it's your turn."

A quake ran through her. She sucked in her breath. His member throbbed against her tailbone, matching the pulsating need inside her. He unhooked her bra and peeled the wet material down her arms. It dropped to the wet tiles at their feet. He picked up the bar of soap from the dish and lathered his hands.

"Relax, Lana."

She rested her head back against his chest, water cascading over them. His soapy hands caressed her belly, leaving bubbles in their wake. He brought his palms to her breasts, cupping them. His thumbs moved back and forth over her nipples until they turned to hard nubs, demanding his attention. He opened his mouth on her throat, his tongue flicking over her skin. Her back arched, pressing her backside into his groin. A low growl sounded in his throat.

She kept her gaze on his hands as he moved over her, his fingers drifting down until they reached her panties. He pushed his fingers inside and worked them down over her legs.

"Mmm…much better."

Her body vibrated, waiting for his touch. He lathered his hands again and brought them back to her belly. The rough calluses of his palms softened by the soap bubbles, his hands glided over her skin effortlessly, from her nipples to the throbbing nub between her legs, then around to squeeze her ass.

Her breath came out in sharp, harsh rasps, and she panted with every stroke of his fingers. Her loins clenched and tightened, needing more.

"Cal, now, please." She turned in his arms, needing him inside her like she needed her next breath. He eased her back against the cool tiled wall. Steam swirled around them, dancing between their naked bodies. His eyes drank her in from head to toe. Her soaked hair stuck to her chest and back, and her skin glistened with moisture. A hard look came to his eyes. His carnal, masculine lust singed through her. He dropped to his knees in front of her, and his hands circled her waist as he brought one taut nipple at a time into his mouth. His tongue was rough and warm as he worked it over her nipple. Her head fell back against the wall, and her breath strangled in her throat. Just when she thought she would burst, he nudged her knees apart.

Her legs shook as she complied. He rested her hand on his head to help her steady herself. Her other hand clutched the soap dish as he trailed kisses from her breasts over her taut belly. The bristles of his beard rasped over her delicate flesh, and his tongue followed, soothing her. His mouth closed over her sex, hot and wet. She cried out. Electric currents shot fire through her veins.

"Cal," she breathed.

His thumbs spread her folds, gaining him access. When the tip of his tongue slipped inside her, a moan croaked from her throat. The world tilted on its axis as the steam spun around her. Her legs trembled on each wave of pleasure that washed over her. She arched her back, wanting more. He licked lazily until she cried out on each level of ecstasy. His mouth closed over her, savoring every pulse, gently coaxing with his tongue until her body convulsed on the surge of her orgasm.

Her body turned to mush. She drifted toward the floor until Cal caught her in the safety of his arms. With her legs drawn over his forearm, and her head resting on his shoulder, she closed her eyes. He turned her so the water washed over her body, insulating the warmth and bliss from her climax.

"You okay?" She opened her heavy eyelids. His mischievous grin, the one that made her tummy do flip-flops, greeted her.

"Oh God, yeah."

He laughed. "Let's finish this in the bed." He lowered her to her feet and reached for the towels on the hook, keeping a strong arm around her waist. She pulled the towel tightly around her body as Cal dried off with his own.

Once she exited the shower, she snagged another towel for her hair. She walked on shaky legs to sit at the edge of the bed and dry her wet strands. No way in hell could she stand any longer without falling over. An image caught her eye on the TV. She froze. Her breath caught. She grabbed the remote and turned the volume up, her finger branded on the button. Her blood turned cold.

"We're begging the public to please help in the search for our daughter. Lana, honey, if you're listening, I love you. Please come home." Her dad's voice broke on a sob. Her mom stood next to him, Grace on the other side, and Tanner next to her. Tears ran down her mother's cheeks. Her heart crumbled in her chest. Cal stood in the doorway, his eyes fixed on the TV. Tears burned her eyes, and he rushed to her side and pulled her in his arms. She buried her face in his chest.

"I have to let them know I'm okay, Cal." Tears leaked out of the corners of her eyes. Guilt formed an iron fist in her stomach.

He smoothed her hair back. "We will. I promise, baby."

Chapter 19

Damn, he was stupid. Lana's family—the ones who weren't involved in this—were crushed. He didn't have kids, but the thought of having a child go missing made his stomach churn. He pulled Lana closer to his chest. She wasn't asleep. Her hand knotted in a fist against his sternum, her breath erratic.

He was stuck between a rock and a hard place. As Ethan had said, they needed to tread carefully. Until they had evidence, it would be a huge risk approaching Tanner. Will's death complicated things even more. He'd informed Nate the minute they'd gotten in, and he had called in the murder. Someone had killed Will to keep him quiet. Tanner was the only plausible suspect. Nate had assured him that the FBI was investigating the man, but they hadn't brought him in for questioning yet. Cal wanted to talk to him first. He trusted Nate more than anyone, but Tanner had avoided conviction before. One thing was for sure, the law couldn't keep Cal from beating the truth out of him.

Tomorrow, he and Ethan would pay Tanner a visit.

"This feels like it's never going to end." She spoke slowly, her voice distant. He tightened his hold on her shoulders and pressed a kiss to her hair, inhaling her scent. Fuck, he hated that she was scared. Hated even more that she was hurting.

"It will. Very soon."

Her leg slid over his knee and up his bare thigh. Her silky satin skin was chilled.

"I feel so terrible." Her hand opened and closed on his chest, and a tear hit his shoulder and rolled down. She was crying. His throat constricted. He covered her hand with his.

"Please don't cry, baby. Everything's going to be okay. I promise."

"I'm not crying." Her voice hardened. Then she sniffled, completely undoing him. His heart expanded. He rested his cheek against her forehead.

"I love that you trust me with your body, babe. But you can trust me with your heart too."

A delicate shoulder rose and fell. His jaw worked. She was hurting, but she couldn't let go with him. He loved her strength and her ferocious independence, but why couldn't she let her guard down with him?

A pit formed in his stomach like a toxic black hole. It wasn't her fault. It was his. He'd kept her at arm's length, then turned around and had sex with her against the wall. How confusing was that? He'd warned her that he couldn't offer commitment, and he was now affronted that she'd only shared her body and not her heart. He shifted under her, then lifted her to lie across his chest. She pushed up on her arms to look down at him. Big, blue tear-rimmed eyes stared at him. The ends of her damp hair tickled his side. He scooped her hair back and over her shoulder. Her small pink tongue jutted out to wet her lips, still rosy from his kisses.

She shifted on him so her knees straddled either side of his hips.

"What are you thinking, babe?"

Her teeth pierced her bottom lip, and her gaze dropped to his chest, giving him an expansive view of her dark eyelashes against her porcelain skin.

"Can I ask you something?" Her voice was soft, tentative, her eyes still downcast.

"Of course."

Her finger smoothed over the shiny scar on his chest, beneath his shoulder. The one he'd seen her spot at the cabin.

"How did you get this?"

This was the ugly reality of his life. The danger. The shaky fear that rattled her voice was something that she'd always have if she was a part of his life. He couldn't lie to her.

"It's a bullet wound." His finger came up to touch the uneven skin, remembering the day. Had the bullet hit the opposite side of his chest, he'd have died instantly.

Her eyes met his, round and doubtful. "From the military?"

He shook his head.

"What happened?"

He tucked her hair behind her ear, then pinned his arm beneath his head so he could see her better. "Nate and I had been on a mission in Mexico. There was this organized ring of sex traffickers—a huge one. We went undercover and busted the operation." He took a deep breath, remembering the horrible day. "When the shit hit the fan and the FBI came charging in, the leader of the sex traffic ring and his group started firing. I was undercover, and one of the bastards shot me in the chest when they realized they'd been set up. We didn't get all the girls out in time. Three died."

Her eyes widened, and her face fell. She covered her mouth with her hand. "That's terrible."

He nodded. "It was terrible. That was one of the hardest moments of my career." He pushed the sordid memory from his mind. "We saved one hundred twenty-four young women and teens that day."

"That's incredible."

"It was. But that's one of the reasons I continue to do what I do. There are always situations like that, that I could prevent."

"You're a hero."

He smirked. "Hardly." He wouldn't tell her about the men he'd shot that night. How his anger had been so hot and violent that Nate had had to pull him back. Maybe another day he would share that with her.

"What else is on your mind?"

Her eyes wandered up to his exposed arm. "Your tattoos."

His eyes followed her gaze to his arm. He lowered it so she could see better. "These?"

"Yeah. What do they mean?" Her finger trailed the outline of the block lettering.

"It says *always vigilant*,' but the lettering is very unique. It's difficult to read."

The corner of her mouth tucked in. "'Always vigilant'? Why do you have that?"

He rested his arm back under his head. "It's a reminder for me to always be cautious and wary." He picked up a lock of her wet hair and wrapped it around his finger. "But also to withhold judgment whenever possible. That's a tough one to do."

Her eyes sparked with mischief. "I'll say. You judged me."

He opened his mouth to protest, then shut it. "You're right, I did. But mostly because I was stubborn and didn't want to admit how badly I had it."

She laughed. Her chin rested on her hands on his chest. Her eyes bore into his. "Do you still have it bad?"

"Hell, I have it worse now."

Her lips lifted into a gentle smile. "Good." Her eyes lowered to stare at his throat.

"Besides my scar and tattoos, there's something else making your wheels turn. C'mon, out with it."

Her eyes shifted, her lips rolled in. "You read me so well."

"I hate to break it to you, but you're an open book."

She didn't react to his comment. Her eyes stayed focused on his throat. "While my family was mourning my disappearance, I've been here, perfectly fine, having sex against walls and in showers." Her eyes dragged up to his, fiery orbs that torched him. God help him, all he'd heard in that confession was the part about the sex. Images flashed through his mind—the memory of her tight, warm body around his cock filled his head. He throbbed with the need for release. He would resist if it killed him. No way would he suggest they finish when she was feeling like this.

"Technically, we didn't have sex in the shower. But I'm not sure that makes you feel any better."

She didn't smile as he'd hoped. "I feel guilty," she continued, "for so blatantly ignoring what they've been going through."

"Lana, you've been through—"

"Shhh." She pressed her finger to his lips. "Aside from that, I don't regret it. I did all of that with you because I wanted to." Her eyes dropped again, and her finger left his lips to absently stroke the bristles he still hadn't had time to shave.

"I wanted to because it feels right with you, Cal. I don't expect anything. I know we can't be together, I get that—"

"Shhh." He silenced her with his index finger, mimicking her gesture. He couldn't take it anymore. The charade was up. He'd been fooling himself from the moment he'd laid eyes on her.

"I've been lying to you, Lana. And to myself." He stroked his finger over her cupid's bow, then down to the bottom lip she kept abusing. "What we have is different. It was wrong of me to tell you we could never have a relationship. Fuck, babe. I don't want to bring you into the danger of my life"—he cupped her satiny cheek—"but I can't imagine going back to what life was like without you." His lungs burned with the words he needed to say. He couldn't let her think she meant nothing to him and that he could just walk away after this. "We'll figure this out."

Her lips parted, and her breath sucked in through her lips. Tears glimmered in her lashes, and a shy smile revealed her even, white teeth. Relief let go like a dam breaking inside him. He cupped the back of her head and brought her lips to his. Her mouth moved over his, her tongue caressing his, mixing with her wetness.

"I can live with that." She laughed.

He hadn't planned on this. A relationship, he had thought, would never be in the cards for him. But he would make it work with Lana, or die trying.

That was the difference between her and every other relationship. He had the desire—no, the need—to make it work with her, whatever the cost. The further Lana moved into his heart, the further the devotion to his career moved out. It was time to settle down, to bring some joy into his life…to let someone—her—in. Images of the holidays flashed through his mind. No more lonely days spent drinking or going off on missions while others were at home, gathered with their families. He could have all that now.

He smoothed his thumb over her cheek. She dipped her head and turned her face into his hand, taking his index finger into her mouth.

Every muscle in his body tensed.

Her blue eyes burned with desire. She sucked on him, her tongue moving in gentle strokes over the rough skin of his finger. His dick throbbed, lying only inches away from the cleft between her legs. His skin sizzled with each lazy movement of her mouth, and her teeth nipped him as she settled herself closer to him.

"We never finished." Her voice was deep and husky. A rosy pink tinted her chest and cheeks. She was so damn beautiful and sexy that he lay paralyzed beneath her.

"You're upset—"

She nestled her crotch over him, and all words left his mouth. His brain turned to mush as his hands found the luscious curve of her ass. Her fingers closed around him as she guided him to her, sinking her body down. Her wetness surrounded him as she pressed deep. Her hands pressed into his chest, her eyes closed on a moan.

Feeling her, the wet, gentle cushion on his cock, was heaven. *She* was heaven. He groaned and moved her over him. Her breasts jiggled gently, her nipples pink and tight. He drank in the sight of her, her creamy skin and narrow waist, the soft and slight flare of her hips. Her sex, joined with his.

She moved steadily, her pleasure building with his. She drew him tighter, crushing him inside her as a moan shook her. He throbbed, and his body coiled tightly. A gasp broke in his throat. He held her breasts in his hands, his fingers gliding over her pebble-hard nipples, gently pinching as her orgasm rose. He hung on for the ride as her movements increased, her release frantic against him.

Needing to take over, to bring her over the edge, he grasped her waist and rolled her beneath him. Her legs locked around his hips as she gripped him. He ground deep inside her, holding his release at bay until her orgasm shook her. He pulled out on a slow stroke, and then drove deep, filling her. She cried out, her body jerking hard, begging for more. His release came next, a desperate need pulsating through him as he moved inside her, the friction taking him over the cusp until every muscle was ready to snap. He let go, falling into an oblivion of pleasure as he went limp over the top of her.

Cal woke hours later, stretched out on his side with Lana's face nestled into his chest. Her breath came out evenly, her lips lightly swollen, her cheeks pink and warm from his body heat.

Sonofabitch.

He'd slept with her without a condom. Being able to feel her softness and drown in her wetness was something he didn't regret. He hoped to hell she was on birth control or something. He was never careless with sex. But this was Lana, and everything had been different with her from the beginning. He was in it for the long run, whatever that meant.

He tiptoed to the bathroom and cleaned up, then pulled on a pair of sweatpants and a long-sleeved shirt. He grabbed his cell phone off the dresser and looked at the time: 4 a.m.

He'd slept longer than he had in months, and surely Lana needed more rest. His mind was already moving, planning his next step. He would talk to Nate before deciding if he would approach Tanner, but every instinct told him he needed to. Nate would be at his office today, so Cal would wait to call him until later. Ethan, he would call in an hour.

He made coffee, let Rufus out, gave him one of the dog cookies Nate had left him, and filled his dishes with food and water. He hadn't worked out in almost a week, and the lack of soreness in his muscles annoyed him. The cabin lacked the gym he had at home, but he kept weights and a skipping rope here. He had time for a light workout and then to make breakfast before Lana woke.

Slamming back his coffee, he made his way to the back of the cabin. One of the first things he'd done upon purchasing the place was to put on an addition. The thing that had attracted him most had been the lot size and view. He'd put in floor-to-ceiling windows, which gave the room the feel of a four-season porch. He closed the sliding door tightly, and turned some music on the sound system. It was still pitch-black out. He liked to get up early, and waiting for the sunrise was always a nice way to start the day. But today, for the first time, the bright reflection and inability to see through the window unnerved him.

This shit had to end. Today. He wasn't afraid, not exactly. But having someone to look after was new to him. That constant threat gnawed at the back of his mind. He hated being away from her at all, and leaving her side knowing someone wanted to kill her made his blood churn. They were safe here. But he wouldn't be at ease until this was over.

An hour later, drenched in sweat, he dropped the dumbbell. Man, it felt good to tear muscles. A lot of frustration had built up over the last week, some of which he'd released with Lana. The mind-numbing, muscle-burning workout had savaged the rest. He wiped the rivulets of sweat from his brow with the sleeve of his shirt and entered the house.

"Morning," Lana sang sweetly from the kitchen. Her hair was secured in a high ponytail at the crown of her head, and her dark locks tangled down her back. She wore one of his T-shirts that barely reached mid-thigh, and her legs were bare and her nipples visible through the thin gray material. The aroma of pancakes and coffee wafted to his nose. His stomach growled.

She flitted around the small kitchen and set two glasses of juice at the island. His heart pounded against his chest from the intense workout, and the near-glimpse of Lana's ass as she leaned forward to scratch Rufus's head. He caught her around the waist, drawing her back against his chest. He nuzzled his face into the crook of her neck, kissing her delicate flesh.

"Morning, sexy. You're up early."

She turned in his arms, her eyes shining with delight as she pressed her lips to his. She pulled away sharply and patted his chest. "Mmm-hmm. There wasn't much food in the fridge, so pancakes will have to do. You're all sweaty. Did you have a good workout?"

He slid into one of the chairs as she set a plate down in front of him. "This is perfect, thanks. It was great. I was hoping you would have slept longer, though. I didn't wake you, did I?"

She filled her plate, then took the chair next to him. "Not at all. I slept like a rock." She dipped her head. A shy smile spread across her face, as she took a bite of her breakfast.

"Glad to hear. Anytime you require assistance, you let me know."

She laughed and crossed her legs on the chair. He couldn't resist dropping his hand to feel the smooth skin of her sexy thigh. If she kept this up, he'd have to take her on the kitchen counter. That image danced across his mind. Definitely something to remember for later.

"Likewise." She winked at him and took a bite of her pancakes. "What's the plan for today?"

He finished chewing. "I have somewhere I need to go later, but nothing planned for this morning."

"Where are you going?"

He smiled. "I can't tell you."

Her eyes narrowed at him. He didn't relent. It was something he needed to do, something for her. He couldn't guarantee everything would end today and that the people behind her planned death would be held accountable, but he could damn well appease for it. The guilt over her family was something he had been stupid to ignore. Lana was sweet and sensitive, and something of that magnitude had surely weighed heavily on her slight shoulders. She'd hidden it well from him. Today, he would make up for the pain he'd seen in her eyes. Ethan would be more than happy to come by while he went out.

"Can I come?"

"Not this time, babe. But I won't be long, and I think you'll be pretty happy with what I bring back."

Her eyebrows rose. "It's a surprise?"

"Yup."

"Okay, you get brownie points for that one." A smile returned to her mouth, easing the frown lines on her forehead. She stood from the island, her plate not yet finished.

Her fingers clasped his, pulling him to his feet. He took a hasty bite of his pancakes before he let her drag him away. "I think I need a shower… and so do you."

The hunger in his belly died. His body went on alert. Good God, he loved her sexuality. He winked at her, sending her laughing and scampering to the master bedroom. He chased her into the bedroom and swooped her up and into his arms.

He could get used to this.

Chapter 20

They lazed around all morning until Ethan showed up. While Cal was gone, Lana put her sweats on and made use of the workout room. Her usually lithe and flexible muscles were as tight as a guitar string. The sun creeped over the mountains, lighting the sky with its pink and orange glow. She stretched out on a mat. Her hips—as well as other places—ached from sex. A delightful shiver raced through her. Amazing sex, but nonetheless, her body was sore.

Fuzzy warmth spread through her veins at the memory. The scar on his chest had been a harsh reminder of how different they were. But did it matter? Couldn't they try to make things work? It hadn't been an issue so far, but when she went back to her old life, it could be a problem. She would always worry about him. He was strong and capable, but he wasn't invincible. At the same time, she didn't want to come between him and his career.

Aside from that, there was her family to think about. Her mom had always been supportive, and if she knew Lana was happy, that would be enough for her. Her father, on the other hand… He cared about her happiness, undoubtedly. But to him, security and social standing were also important. Not just for her, but for his own image. As he'd told her a million times before, professionalism came first in order to be successful. That was why he'd always been so strict about her personal life.

She pushed herself up to a downward-facing dog pose, releasing the tension in her shoulders. She wasn't a child anymore. For God's sake, her mother had been twenty-two when she'd married Lana's father and twenty-three when she'd had Lana. Their marriage had lasted twelve years. Her mother had told her that they'd divorced because her father hadn't been able or willing to slow down. He'd been too busy growing his empire to spend time on his marriage. Eventually she'd had it, and she'd left.

At twenty-six, Lana didn't need his permission or approval regarding her personal life. Distaste filled her mouth. She didn't want to fight with him, but he would have to respect her decisions.

After her workout, she passed Ethan in the kitchen on his phone, talking to Cal. "She's right here, do you want to talk to her?" he said. Lana paused, waiting. Ethan nodded, then, "Sounds good, we'll see you in a bit." He hung up the phone.

She balanced her hand on her hip, her eyebrows lowered. "Cal didn't want to talk to me?"

He gave a slight shrug. The movement was awkward on his enormous frame. "He said he wouldn't be long."

That was odd. Why wouldn't he at least speak with her? She shrugged. Soon he would be home and she could ask him herself.

"All right. Can you tell him to come find me when he gets home? I'm going to shower."

Ethan's ears turned pink. He scratched his head, his gaze at the floor. "Ah, sure—"

"I mean…" Oh God. Her cheeks burned. How was she going to clarify that one?

He waved her off. She ducked her head and laughed as she exited the kitchen. In the shower, images of the night before branded her under the hot water. Cal's mouth on her wet body, her insides quaking as he brought her to climax. God, he knew his way around a woman's body.

She got dressed and applied her makeup. A glance at the clock showed her it was going on noon. He'd been gone almost two hours. What on earth was he doing that was so secretive?

Woof, woof!

She shoved the mascara wand back in the tube and straightened her shirt. Rufus's excited barks echoed down the hall. She frowned. It wasn't like him to carry on like that. Just as she approached the bedroom door, it opened. Cal's shoulders blocked the doorway.

"Come here, babe." He held his hand out to her. A wicked smile played over his mouth.

Her frown deepened. She curled her fingers into his palm. "What's going on?"

He chuckled. "Why so worried? Trust me."

Soft voices from the kitchen piqued her interest. "I'm not worried. Just nervous."

"You'll like this." He led her down the hall and to the kitchen. She rounded the corner.

Her breath caught. Tears filled her eyes before she could catch them. She covered her mouth with her hand and a small sob escaped her throat.

"Mom!" She threw her arms around her mother.

"My baby!" Her mother's soft voice eased the tremor in her body. Her arms locked around Lana, her lips pressed into her hair. "Oh, honey. I've been so worried."

"What are you doing here?" She pulled out of her arms far enough to spot Cal. A big, warm smile spread across his face. His eyes danced with pleasure. He shoved his hands in his pockets and winked at her. "How did you—"

"This man"—she gestured to Cal, her eyebrow raised with mock chastising—"cornered me on the street in front of my hotel. He told me that if I wanted to see you, I needed to come with him." She lifted a hand to her slight hip. Her cool blond hair was pulled back in a clip at the nape of her neck. "Scared the life out of me."

Cal grinned. "Sorry about that, ma'am. We're trying to be very careful."

"Please, call me Sonja." She waved at him. "Ma'am makes me feel old." She pulled Lana to her chest again. "Can we talk, sweetie? I want to know everything that's been going on."

"Of course."

"Would you like something to drink, Sonja?" Cal stepped away from the counter. "Water?" he offered.

Sonja accepted, and Cal poured her a glass from the fridge. Cal and her mother…in the same room. She looked from one to the other. Sonja was as gracious as always, but her eyes were sharp beneath her kindness. Her mother wasn't stupid. She would smell their attraction for each other a mile away. Aside from her daughter's disappearance, she would want to know every detail about Cal.

Wanting complete privacy from the men's ears, Lana brought her mother back to the master bedroom. The room she and Cal had had sex in.

Sonja set her glass down on a nearby table and situated herself on the edge of the bed. Lana folded her legs up next to her. Her face warmed at the still-rumpled sheets.

"What the hell is going on, honey?" Sonya's tone was gentle, yet demanding.

Lana rolled her lips in. Best not to beat around the bush. She breathed a sigh through her lips. "I'll tackle one topic at a time. First of all, someone hired some people—hired hit men—to kill me." She would not tell her mother that Cal had been one of those people. Of all the things to be disclosed, that was one that Sonja did not need to know.

Her mother's hand fluttered to her mouth like the wing of a broken bird. She closed her other hand around Lana's, and tears filled her eyes. Her brow snapped down, and fire shot from her eyes, which were the same hue of blue as her own.

"Who would do such a thing? How do you know this?"

She shifted on the bed. "We believe it was Tanner. He–he came on to me a few months ago, and it didn't go over well. I talked to Grace about it and I thought it had blown over." She toyed with the rumpled duvet cover. "One of Cal's friends is a special agent with the FBI. He did some digging on Tanner and found that as a minor he'd been charged with rape." She wet her lips. Sonja's eyes never left hers. "Then later, he was a person of interest in the murder of a different young woman. He was never convicted, nor did the suspicion cops had of him make it to the tabloids. That makes it look like he used money to protect his name."

Sonja pressed her fingers to her mouth. Her eyes clouded with worry. The faint lines that had begun to crease her face in recent years deepened. "Why would he do all of this? Why would he want to kill you over that?"

"If people were to find out about his assault on me—"

Her hand grabbed Lana's arm, her fingernails piercing the skin. "He hurt you?"

"No, Mom. He just behaved badly, and I had to throw him out with the threat to call the police. He left right after. But if people found out that happened, it could open up interest in the other cases he was a suspect in."

She released her hold. Her hand pressed against her chest. "Why didn't you tell me?"

She shrugged. "I handled it."

"You don't think it's all a misunderstanding? How do you know someone planned to have you killed?"

"Cal found the man who'd been hired."

Her lips pressed together, and her eyes narrowed. "How did Cal come into the picture? Who is he?"

Lana tucked her hair behind her ear. Shit. Nothing got past her mom. Ever. That was one of the reasons why, as a teenager, she'd chosen to live with her dad.

"He…he works in cases like this."

Sonja's brow furrowed.

She took a deep breath and continued, "He's a freelance security contractor."

If her mom's eyebrows could have flown off of her face, they would have taken flight. "He's a what?" she hissed.

"Mom, it's nothing like what you think." It was everything, and worse, that she would be thinking. "He was in the military and in recon. From there, he began doing freelance work, and now he's hired to help take down drug rings or find missing people."

Sonja's eyes widened. That was as PG as it was going to get. Her fingers dug into her palms, waiting for the backlash.

Her mom crossed and uncrossed her legs, then smoothed an invisible wrinkle from her dress pants. "I see. Well, you're a grown woman. You know what you're doing. I know something is going on between you two, I can see it."

Lana bit her lip. "Mom, you were around us for two minutes."

"That's all it took." Her hand closed around hers. "Just be careful, honey. It's easy to get fascinated by men like that." She waved her hand in the air as if she was shooing away a fly. "It's not real, though."

Lana straightened her spine. Certainty filled her veins. "I'm more sure of him than I am of anything in my life."

Sonja's eyes grew heavy with worry. She pursed her lips. "I suppose I'd better get to know him, then."

Gratitude warmed her chest. Years and distance had changed her mom. Lana was a grown woman and maybe her mother saw that now. A weight lifted from her chest, making her breathing easier.

One parent down, one to go.

She hugged her mom tightly. "Thanks, Mom. Can you tell Dad I'm okay?"

She patted her back. "Of course, honey. He's going to have a lot of questions, though. I don't know how I'm going to keep your location a secret. Your father's house looks like a beehive filled with men in suits. The phone lines are tapped, and he has private investigators scouring the streets. He's really bent out of shape."

Guilt lodged a painful rock in her throat. "Tell him that I love him and will be home soon. Just be sure he doesn't say anything to anyone."

She nodded. Together they made their way to the kitchen, where Cal and Ethan patiently waited.

"I hope Lana was able to cover everything you need to know and ease any concerns," Cal said as he led Sonja to the center island, where he'd set some chopped veggies, crackers, and cheese. Amusement rippled through her. He was trying to impress her mother.

Sonja accepted the small plate he handed her and sat. "So, tell me, Cal. What are your intentions with my daughter?"

"*Mom—*"

Cal scratched his head. Ethan whistled and filled his own plate.

"I don't suppose you intend to drag her around on all of these wild missions, and I sure hope you don't plan to leave her behind in a puddle of worry."

"'Missions'?" Cal's eyes found Lana's. She cringed and shrugged her shoulders.

"Lana told me what you do."

He cleared his throat. Lana kept her eyes down. Heat swirled up her face.

"So, what is your plan?" Sonja stabbed a cherry tomato and nibbled.

"Cal, you don't have to answer her." Then, to her mother, under her breath, "Mom, please. This is not the time."

Her chin lifted. "It's the perfect time."

Cal pushed away from the counter to stand behind Lana. He rested his warm, protective hands on her shoulders. "It's okay, babe. She has every right to ask these questions." He gently massaged her stiff muscles. Her mom watched them carefully as heat rushed to her face. Oh God, he was being intimate with her in front of her mother. She wished the floor would swallow her up. Cal must have sensed her unease, because he stepped to her side and drew her body tightly against his. She looked up at him, her heart in her throat.

He turned to Sonja. The lines of his face hardened, and his jaw worked. "You're absolutely right. I'm looking at other career options and will be ending that chapter of my life."

Lana's breath sucked in. Her mouth hung open.

Ethan, who had been engaged in an awkward conversation with Rufus, whirled on him. "Dude?"

Cal silenced him with a glare.

Sonja raised one self-satisfied eyebrow. A beat passed. She smiled at them. "Then I approve."

Lana's shoulders relaxed. The warmth from her face spread to her heart. Cal pressed a kiss to her temple.

Cal had held up under her mom's scrutiny like a true gentleman. Her mind whirled. He wanted to be with her and was willing to sacrifice his career to do so. A tremor of guilt shook her. Was he giving everything up because he felt he had no choice?

Later, she would question him. As much as she cared about him, she didn't want him to sacrifice his dream or his passion for her. If he wanted to continue his career, she would support him. Her parents would just have to deal with it.

Her mom approved. God, if only her dad would have the same reaction.

Chapter 21

"I'm coming with you," Lana said, her brows forming a stubborn line. Cal shook his head. Not happening.

"Sorry, babe. But I can't let you do that."

Her eyebrows rose an inch.

He crossed his arms in front of his chest in exasperation. Wrong choice of words. "It's not safe, and you know it."

She took a step closer to him, closing the gap between them in the small bedroom. She'd asked to speak to him alone seconds before he was to walk out the door with Nate. He couldn't blame her. Hell, he wouldn't want to be stuck in the house night after night while she went out hunting the streets. But there was no damn help for it. In order for life to return to normal, he had to leave her—for now.

"He's my stepbrother. I know you have good reason to suspect him, as do I, but I know him better than you do. I want to see the look on his face when we show up at his door, and I want to ask him myself if he had anything to do with this. I have a right, Cal."

He sighed and pinched the bridge of his nose with his thumb and forefinger. Why was he even fighting her? When Lana made up her mind about something, there was no changing it. If he wanted to get out of the house at any point tonight, he'd have to agree.

But dammit to hell and back, he didn't want her in any more danger. He'd finally gotten her in a safe spot, and with any luck, in a matter of hours this whole shit show would be over. Her slim fingers closed around his elbow, firm and insistent. He dropped his hand.

"I'm safer with you, anyway." Her voice was soft, and her fiery blue eyes seared through him, undoing his resolve.

"Alright, fine. But if we get there and I sense anything is off, you're leaving with Ethan. Got it?"

She raised her hands in surrender. "Got it." A small smile played at her lips. He released a breath through tight lips and snagged the back of her head, bringing her mouth to his. She moaned against his mouth, her warm lips moving against his. His body hardened against hers, and desire scorched his veins. He pulled away and pressed his forehead to hers. If he wasn't careful, he'd get carried away.

"You're going to be the death of me, you know that?" Her silky strands tangled over his knuckles.

She chuckled, and dammit, if that didn't melt him even more. "I know. Let's go, it's getting late." She winked and tugged him out of the room.

Nate and Ethan waited in the kitchen, their faces pinched in confusion as Lana barreled into the room.

"Change of plans. We're all going," Cal said.

Nate looked from him to Lana and his lips lifted. "You mean—"

"Yup. I'm coming."

"Uh…okay." Ethan rubbed his hand over his head and Cal shrugged. Lana led the way to the door and slipped her shoes on, and they followed. Ethan slanted his eyes at him. "You sure this is a good idea?"

"It's a terrible idea. But she has her reasons, and I respect that. If anything goes wrong, I'm leaving it up to you to get her out as quickly as possible."

Ethan nodded. "We'd better take two vehicles, then. We'll follow you guys." Ethan stopped on the front step. "Do you have an old pizza box lying around by chance?"

He frowned, remembering the recycling bin he'd forgotten to empty the last time he was there. "Yeah, why?"

"Grab it. It will be a good cover to get him to open the door without barging in."

He nodded. "Good call." Cal disappeared back into the cabin and dug the box out of the recycling bin. He jogged down the steps and climbed into the truck where Lana waited. Ethan and Nate pulled out of the drive and Cal followed. Lana sat ramrod-straight beside him, her knee bouncing up and down to the soft beat flowing from the radio. With every bounce, his regret expanded. She shouldn't be here. All it would take would be one fuckup…

He forced the thought from his mind. He wouldn't let her out of his sight.

Once they reached the city limits, Lana gave Cal directions toward the downtown district.

Tanner's town house was a large brick building, with three side-by-side units. His was the end unit, backing up to a park. A double garage completed the exterior. Steel-colored shades adorned the windows, blocking their view of the inside. A light clicked off upstairs, the warm glow replaced with black behind the dark window coverings. A few minutes later, more lights came on in the main area.

He parked down the street, and Ethan pulled in behind him. Lana hopped out of the truck, slamming the door behind her. Cal cursed and raced around the vehicle, snagging her arm.

"Would you slow down? Jesus." Her long hair caught the glare from the street lamp, illuminating the glossiness of her dark locks. Her hand slipped easily into his, and she slowed.

"Sorry, I'm just eager."

"I know, but he could have an army inside."

She scoffed. "I seriously doubt it."

He stopped her, his hold firm on her fingers. "Don't. Don't ever underestimate people. If you want to survive, you have to think to the extreme. It's saved my life more than once."

Her face paled, and her lips parted. Her dark lashes lowered, and she nodded. Shit. He wanted her scared enough to think—but not terrified.

"You guys coming?" Nate called from the sidewalk ahead. Cal nodded, grabbed the pizza box from the back seat, and circled his arm around Lana's shoulders. Her gaze dropped to the box as they moved swiftly toward the large town house. The street was dead quiet, so if he put up a scuffle, it shouldn't draw too much attention. Cal moved Lana behind him as they ascended the few steps of the front porch.

"Stay behind me until we're inside."

Her hand tightened on his shirt. "I think I should go to the door. I want to see the look on his face when he sees me."

"No, he'll see you through the peephole." He held his hand out in the air. "Just wait."

She folded her arms across her chest, and her lips pursed. He edged her farther against the wall, drew Nate back with them, and passed the pizza box to Ethan. "We'll wait off to the side, out of sight. I'll step out and hold him at gunpoint. That should prevent him from screaming down the neighborhood." Cal cracked his knuckles. "I hope his unit is soundproof. I have a feeling he'll try something."

Ethan snorted. "Don't worry, there's more of us than there is of him." Ethan jabbed the bell with his index finger. Cal scanned the quiet neighborhood. Everyone would be tucked inside avoiding the chilly wind.

The neighborhood was calmer than he'd expected for a bachelor's place. Then again, Tanner was a rich little prick who would prefer prestige over convenience.

Cal pulled his Glock from the waistband of his pants, keeping it poised low at his thigh. Footsteps sounded from inside. They stopped at the door, undoubtedly to look through the peephole.

The dead bolt clicked open.

"What the hell? I didn't order a pizza."

Ethan grinned. "You sure? It has extra douchebag toppings."

"You mother—"

Cal stepped in front of Ethan, shoving the barrel of his gun at Tanner's midsection. "Back up and let us in. Make one wrong move and I pull the trigger."

Tanner's body tensed. His cold brown eyes widened on Cal's. His lips parted, and all the color drained from his face. He raised his hands in front of him and backed up. They stepped inside, and Nate closed and locked the door behind them. Lana remained at the door, shielded behind the three of them.

"What's the matter? You can dish it out, but you can't take it?"

Tanner licked his lips. He glanced around him as Cal backed him up, as if he feared more people would jump out from behind him.

"What do you want? Money? Go ahead, take whatever you want. Just leave me the hell alone." His heel caught the foyer area rug. His arms flailed in the air, and he landed hard on his ass with a *thud*. Cal nudged his sock-covered foot.

"Get up."

When he didn't budge, Ethan approached. He hauled Tanner to his feet, twisting his arm behind his back.

He cried out. Ethan mumbled something to silence him and propelled him toward the kitchen at the back of the house. Cal grabbed a chair from the rustic eight-person dining room table and set it in the center of the kitchen. He motioned for Ethan to sit him down.

Ethan shoved him in the chair, grabbing the back of it before it toppled over. Tanner's eyebrows snapped down. Sparks flew from his eyes. His hands opened and closed on his lap. He shifted his eyes to Cal, his temper settling to a low simmer.

"What the hell do you want?" he ground out through clenched teeth.

A satisfying calm washed over Cal. He smiled. This was it. He'd waited weeks to get his hands on the sonofabitch who had hired him. The suffocating weight of that responsibility had bound his sanity. Now it was over. He wasn't leaving here until he got the answers he was looking for. He would tear Tanner limb from limb if it meant ending this shit for Lana, once and for all.

He nodded at Nate, and Lana stepped forward. Tanner's gaze left Cal's face and followed his line of vision. The muscles in his face went slack, and his green eyes grew as big as saucers.

"Lana! You're–you're okay? What the hell—"

Cal stepped closer to Tanner, his movements deliberate. He locked his eyes with Tanner's. "I want to know why you hired me to kill Lana." He spoke evenly, his voice barely over a whisper.

An insistent shove to his arm made him step to the side. Lana stood in front of Tanner, her fists on her hips and her dark hair billowing around her shoulders. Her lips moved into a tense frown, and her eyes sparked at Tanner.

"Tanner, you look like you've seen a ghost." Her words lashed through the air. Tanner didn't take his eyes off of her. His mouth snapped shut, and he nodded.

"I'm glad you're okay. Jesus, where have you been?" His eyes moved to Ethan and Nate. "And why the hell are you with these guys?"

Her hands lowered from her hips, and her eyes flicked to Cal before landing back on Tanner. "Someone hired Cal to kill me. Given our research into your background, it seems pretty likely that you had something to do with it."

Cal watched him carefully, examining every crease on his evenly tanned skin. The pleat in his brow deepened, and his hands fisted on his lap. He shook his head and wet his lips.

"Lana, I swear, I had nothing to do with it."

"Really? Because after you—"

Cal grabbed her arm, stopping her. Lana snapped her gaze to him, her eyes clouded with confusion. He eased her out of earshot and lowered his lips to her ears.

"You got to let me talk to him, babe. I don't want you to give too many of our cards away, alright?"

She narrowed her eyes at him. She'd wanted to confront Tanner, and she'd done that. But the real interrogation had to be from him. And she wasn't going to like his methods.

"Trust me," he said. When her pinched lips didn't waver, he added, "Please."

"Fine."

He nodded his appreciation and moved back in front of Tanner.

Tanner swallowed as Cal crouched in front of him, bringing him to eye level. "This is all really entertaining, Tanner. But it's time for you to start telling the truth." Cal unfolded his arms, revealing his Glock again.

Tanner's breath caught. "I told you, I had nothing to do with it! I wouldn't hurt her. She's my sister."

Ethan stepped behind him, placing his baseball glove–sized hands on Tanner's shoulders, stilling him. "If I were you, Tanner, I wouldn't lie. That's one."

Cal dropped his gun to Tanner's foot. A whimper broke Tanner's throat. "For every lie you tell, I will shoot you. Starting with your feet." Sweat rolled down Tanner's face. His hands clasped the arms of the chair, and his breath came out in a pant.

"Those hurt." Ethan shook his head. "Knees are a bitch, too. I can tell you that from experience."

"You're fucking crazy." Tanner wrestled against Ethan's hold. His efforts were futile.

"I'm going to ask you one more time, so listen up." Cal's voice raised an octave above a whisper. "You hired Will Anderson and Ian Stamos. Stamos gave me seventy-five grand of your money to kill Lana. I want to know why."

Tanner blew air through his lips. Spit dribbled down his chin. "I didn't hire them. I wouldn't hurt her."

Cal shook his head. "Wrong answer."

He pulled the trigger.

"Sonofabitch!" Tanner's scream echoed around the room. His body jolted, and sweat poured down his face. Ethan pinned him in the chair. Lana's cry of protest sounded from behind him. Her hand closed on Cal's shoulder, pulling him around to face her. She stood over him, her lips in a firm line.

"You didn't have to do that," she whispered. Slowly he rose to his feet, and her head tilted back to look up at him. Well, fuck.

"He's lying—"

Lana shoved past him and knelt in front of Tanner's folded-over form. Cal tensed. Dammit, why did she give a shit about this idiot? Sobs tore through Tanner's throat as he lifted his chin to face Lana. "Tanner, you need to tell us the truth." Then, in a hushed whisper, "These men are crazy. I have no idea what they're capable of, but if you don't start giving us some real answers, things could get ugly."

Tanner's lip quivered, and Lana squeezed his hand. Pride expanded in Cal's chest. She was playing good cop, trying to get Tanner's confession.

"You shouldn't be with these assholes." His eyes lifted to Cal. "They're fucking sick."

Cal shrugged and eased Lana aside. "You know what's sick? Rape. You know what else is sick? Murder. You know what else? Planning yet another murder."

"I told you I had nothing—"

"Don't make me shoot your other foot."

Tears poured out of Tanner's eyes. Blood pooled beneath his foot.

"Andrea Reid—does that name ring a bell?"

Tanner's mouth hung open. His eyes bulged in his head, either from pain or from fear.

"Ah, looks like I struck a nerve." He twisted his mouth. "I suppose you're going to tell me you didn't drug her and rape her at a frat party?"

Tanner's breath came out in short, sharp gasps.

"Come on, lie to me. I dare you." He lifted a shoulder, his tone cool.

"I didn't mean for anything to happen to her. Yes, I gave her a fucking roofie. But I didn't know what it was at the time or what would happen." His voice pitched like a pubescent teenager's. Tears leaked out of his eyes. "Please, man. Believe me."

A beat passed. Tanner was a little pussy. Cal had taken bullets to worse places in his body and had barely broken a sweat. The collar of Tanner's shirt was drenched, his face was an ashen gray, and his mouth twisted in a grimace. Cal looked up at Ethan. His eyes were steady, reflecting Cal's thoughts.

He could be telling the truth.

His jaw worked. He brought his gaze back to Tanner. Shivers racked his medium-sized frame. Cal smiled. "Do you know Ian Stamos or Will Anderson? And remember what happens when you lie." He shifted the gun to Tanner's other foot.

A whimper sounded from Tanner's throat. He nodded. His head was as unsteady as a toy bobblehead on the dash of a car. "Yes. Yes, I know them."

"How?"

"I went to college with Will's older brother, Shawn." His breath was shallow. He wiped the sweat off his face with his sleeve.

Cal pulled his phone out of his pocket. "What is your Facebook login information?"

Tanner told him. Cal kept the gun trained on his other foot while he scrolled through his friends until he found Will and Shawn Anderson. After more clicks, he confirmed they had gone to the same college.

He put his phone back in his pocket. "Do you still talk to Shawn?"

Tanner swallowed, his eyes watering.

"You answer this right, and we'll get you something for the pain, alright?"

He took a deep breath. "I talk to him. He works at my stepdad's office."

Cal nodded his approval. "Now we're talking." Then to Ethan, "Dude, go find him some Advil."

"He's going to need something more than that," Lana said as she moved past Nate and Ethan. She returned a moment later with a small glass of golden liquid and the bottle of Advil. Tanner took a big swig of the liquor, wiped his mouth on a pant, then downed several pills. The glass shook in his hand as he took another big gulp.

Cal took the glass from his hand and set it on the floor next to him. "Easy, we still have some questions for you."

Tanner straightened his shoulders. Color creeped back into his cheeks.

"Don't think that just because I gave you something for the pain, I won't still shoot your other foot if you lie. Got it?"

He nodded wildly.

"You have a thing for Lana, don't you?"

Tanner licked his lips. His eyes darted around the room and landed on Lana. Fear flashed across his face, and a new sheen of sweat coated his brow.

"Answer the question. One…two…"

Tanner's face flushed crimson. "Yes, okay?"

Ethan whistled. Cal pushed his tongue to the corner of his mouth and forced his temper down. At least the bastard was being honest. Cal focused on Tanner, and the muscles in his face tensed. "You were charged with rape as a minor, then you were a person of interest in a young woman's murder. You came on to Lana, assaulted her, and four months later someone hires me to kill her. You're telling me that's a coincidence?" His voice shook with the rage that pulsated through him. "For the record, I don't believe in coincidences."

He pressed the barrel of his Glock into the top of Tanner's uninjured foot.

Tanner gulped. His Adam's apple bobbed. "It's true." He shifted his eyes to Lana and then back to Cal, his eyes pleading.

"Are you aware that Will Anderson was found murdered in his apartment?"

Tanner's chin quivered. "W–will's dead?"

Cal ignored his question. "When was the last time you talked to him?"

Tanner's eyes shifted around the room, his face taking on a green hue. "A week ago…" He rubbed his hands over his face.

"I'm going to ask you one more thing, Tanner—pay attention."

Tanner's hands fell away from his face, his eyes sinking into his head, his breathing ragged.

"Who would want to silence Will? Someone killed him, Tanner. My instinct is telling me it wasn't you. Who would benefit from Lana's murder?"

He shook his head. "I don't know, man. I swear."

"What about Shawn?"

Tanner breathed through tight lips. "I don't know any reason why he would. Honest. If I knew someone wanted to hurt Lana, I would have told someone a long time ago. I had nothing to do with this."

Cal scratched at his five o'clock shadow. Goddammit, when was he going to get the chance to shave? He kept his gaze on Tanner. For the first time, a glimmer of doubt about Lana's stepbrother sparked inside him. Shawn was a new possibility. Could he have some kind of motive for getting Lana out of the way? Everything lined up for Tanner, though.

He always trusted his gut, and it had never failed him. Problem was, Lana was now clouding his judgment. Every atom in his body drew his focus to Tanner. Was that because he wanted it to be Tanner? It would be simpler that way.

No. That sliver of doubt was enough to make him inch back. He needed more information. He stood.

"If I were you, Tanner, I wouldn't breathe a word of our visit to anyone. You may have money, but you still can't hide."

Ethan sputtered. He pulled Cal aside. "We can't just leave him now. You shot him in the damn foot!"

Cal crossed his arms over his chest. "What's he going to do? Call the cops? That would only bring attention to him. Besides"—he glanced at Tanner's stiff form—"we've come to an understanding."

Ethan shook his head. "If you think it's okay…"

"He'll be quiet." Lana zeroed in on Tanner. "Right?"

Tanner nodded vigorously. "Yeah, I promise."

Cal stepped up to Tanner. "You should go get that checked out." He gestured to the injured foot. "I suggest you tell the hospital you were mugged—unless you want me to come back and take care of the other one."

Chapter 22

Lana peeled her clothes off and pulled her sweatpants from Cal's dresser. The TV droned on in the background, but her attention was far from the screen. Cal was in the shower, and she couldn't shake Tanner's reaction to their confrontation. Cal wanted him to be guilty, and he had a lot of reasons to go on, but her instinct told her he wasn't. Her chest expanded on a deep breath. She had needed to see her mom, to actually touch someone in her family. With Cal, she felt safe. But having her mom know she was safe lifted a tremendous weight from her chest. Guilt had swirled in her stomach since she had first placed her trust in Cal.

She stretched her neck from one side to the other, but the tension didn't ease. The water in the bathroom shut off, and she sat on the edge of the bed. The soft mattress called to her aching, tired muscles, but they had a lot to figure out before she could welcome sleep. He strode out of the bathroom a minute later, droplets of water dotting his chest and abdomen, a towel hanging loosely around his waist. His lips hitched up in a smile, as he sat down beside her and pulled her against him. Burrowed in his warmth, it was hard to believe all the shit that had happened was real. But it was.

"You okay?" he asked softly.

She let her shoulders relax and slipped her hand over his abdomen. His muscles flexed beneath the light trail of her fingers. Maybe after tonight this horror would be over and she could get back to normal life.

But what was "normal" life now? Could she go back to working with designers and creating buyers' dream homes? It seemed so distant now, so far from who she had become now. As much as she missed home, she needed to find a way to weave the old Lana into the new one. She and Cal needed to talk about how things would move forward. The last thing she wanted to do was put pressure on him, but she couldn't pick up where she'd left off, either, as if nothing had happened between them.

This felt like home now.

"I'm fine." She rested her hand against the stubble of his face. She loved him clean shaven, but the scruff was rugged and sexy, too.

"I know. I've needed to shave for days now." He ran his fingertips where her hand had vacated.

"I like it."

He grunted. "Good to know, but I don't feel very clean with all this hair. I should shave before we go to sleep."

A warm, fuzzy feeling spread over her skin. God, that sounded intimate… permanent. "Is that where we're going?" Her voice was rough and husky. Her fingers trailed over his collarbone and down to his erect nipple.

He chuckled softly, catching her wandering hand in his. "Oh yeah. But first, I need to ask you some things, babe." He rubbed his hand up and down her arm. "My mind keeps going back to Shawn—"

She sucked her breath in and shifted so she faced him. "Do you think Shawn had something to do with this?"

Seriousness settled into the lines of his face, turning the gentle curves into hard lines. His jaw clenched. "It looks like a possibility."

Like poison, his words sank in. Shawn. She barely knew him. What reason would he have to want her harmed? Her thoughts worked with rapid speed. "Do you still think Tanner is a suspect?"

Cal's thumbs moved the material of her shirt to find the bare skin of her back. A shiver raced over her. It was really hard to concentrate on serious stuff when he kept touching her.

"I'm still deciding whether or not I believe him."

Part of her wanted to cling to the hope that Tanner wasn't involved. After all, he was family. How could she have grown up with someone so sinister? How could she not have sensed his threat? Cal scratched his head, then returned his hand to her back.

"A lot of things point to him. I don't believe in coincidences, so I can't let that go. But I have enough doubt, too, that I believe something else might be going on. Something that involves Shawn."

"I can't fathom any reason Shawn would benefit from my…death." Her throat tightened on the word. The fact that Cal was the only reason she was alive right now restricted her airways. She couldn't think about what could have been. It hadn't been in the cards. Thank God for Cal. His jaw worked as his gaze combed over her face. His hold tightened on her.

She let her body relax in the safety of his arms. It was as if they had a constant invisible line of communication. He knew when she was hurting, when she was in need, or when she was putting up a tough front. No one in her life had ever taken that much notice, had ever been able to see her so clearly.

"Don't worry, baby. We're so close. Ethan and Nate will work on investigating Shawn."

She pulled out of his arms and frowned at him. "I don't want you going on another manhunt."

He ran the pad of his thumb over her cheek. "You don't need to worry about me."

"But I do. It's scary for me having you out pounding the streets and shooting people in the feet."

"It's a very reliable method." His eyes sparked with humor. She narrowed her eyes at him.

"You didn't have to shoot Tanner."

His smile faltered, and his gaze shifted. She pinched his pec and he laughed.

"Ouch. You have sharp little fingers."

"Cal." Her voice reverberated with warning.

"I had every reason to get the truth out of him."

She glared at him. It hadn't been easy watching someone close to her get hurt. But regardless, Tanner had a sordid past and had hurt a lot of people. She couldn't let that go.

"He's fine." Cal waved the air between them. "You don't understand my methods, babe. I could have done a lot worse, but the moment I realized he could be telling the truth, I backed off."

She lowered her gaze. A shot in the foot to Cal was as trifling as a punch to the face to anyone else. For someone like Tanner, it was next in line to death. But everything Cal was doing was to protect her and get this whole nightmare over with. What did she know about getting information out of people? And Tanner could be a self-righteous prick. If Cal had approached him in any other way, he would have been obnoxious and confrontational.

Tanner always got what he wanted, no matter the cost. If he hadn't seen to it himself, Grace or Marcel had gotten the results he had desired. As a result, Tanner had never failed at anything in his life. Her parents had raised her very differently. Her father had made sure she'd worked for every accomplishment. Money had always come easy, but he never let her forget the effort it took to make it and the value that it had.

"What's the matter, Lana?" Cal's knuckle lifted her chin.

She shook her head. "Nothing. I trust you, and I know you wouldn't set out to hurt someone for no reason." She combed her hair back with her fingers. "I just wish you didn't have to, that we weren't in this situation at all."

The corner of his mouth lifted salaciously. "I kinda like this situation." His fingers slipped into the waistband of her pants at the small of her back. Pleasure erupted in her belly. His mouth pressed a kiss to hers. Her lips prickled with the need for more. He groaned and pulled away.

"God, Lana. If you only knew what you do to me." His voice was haggard. "Just so you know, I'm very grateful fate brought you into my life."

Her cheeks tingled. She looped her arms around his neck and examined the gold flecks in his green eyes.

"Just so you know," she mimicked his playful words, "there's nowhere else I'd rather be than here with you."

His smile widened to spark his eyes with mischief. "Is that so?"

"Mmm-hmm…" She pressed her lips to his. His lips were warm and smooth against hers. His mouth inched open to welcome her, and his tongue came out to flick hers. Her insides tightened until her toes curled into the balls of her feet.

"Good to know." He breathed softly against her lips. His arm slid under her butt, lifting her over top of him and settling her legs around his hips. Rufus whined from his spot on the floor. Lana threw her head back and giggled.

"Rufus, you're killing the mood." His tone was playful, but he got up from the bed and ushered Rufus into the hall.

"Smooth."

"How much you wanna bet he waits right there?"

She squealed with laughter as he tumbled on top of her.

* * * *

Hours later, Lana lay sated and plastered against Cal's naked chest. After a delicious round of lovemaking, they had made some sandwiches, let out Rufus for the night, taken a shower, and crawled into bed. He'd shaved his beard, too, and she couldn't stop running her fingers over the satiny skin of his jaw. She drifted off to sleep to the soft sound of rain pattering against the windows and Cal's even, slumberous breathing.

Brrring, brrring!

The alarm system shrieked in warning. She bolted into a sitting position. "Cal!"

Her heart leapt into her throat. Cal was already off the bed, yanking on pants and a shirt. Rufus jumped from his spot on the floor, a deep, menacing growl sounding in his throat.

"What's going on?" She climbed off the bed. The chilly air in the room intensified the goose bumps on her skin. Her arms crossed over her chest. She was butt naked. Cal didn't turn on a light.

"Stay here." He stopped at the dresser against the wall by the door. "Sonofabitch," he ground out.

She scanned the floor. Goddammit, where were her clothes?

"What's wrong?" Her voice was barely louder than a whisper. She found a pair of sweatpants and sat on the edge of the bed to tug them on.

"My phone is in the kitchen. I wanted you to call Nate." He held his gun in front of his chest and advanced on the bedroom door. "Stay here and lock this behind me."

"How did they find us?" she hissed into the blackness that surrounded her face. She wrung her hands in front of her.

"I don't know. Don't leave this room. *Rufus, stay.*" Cal slipped out of the room on silent feet. Her pulse thundered wildly against her throat. Rufus paced the spot in front of the door. She stood on shaky legs and clicked the lock into place as softly as she could. She backed away from the door as if it blazed with fire. A stream of moonlight peeked through a slit in the blinds, illuminating the way to the bathroom. She took long steps across the cool hardwoods, her ice-cold hands clasped over her bare breasts.

Someone was here. In Cal's hideaway. Looking for her.

Her mouth went dry. Oh God, she had no way to call for help. She found one of Cal's oversized hooded sweatshirts and pulled it on. It did nothing to combat the chill that shook her. She found her way back to the bedroom door where Rufus waited. Her breath came in short puffs. A crash suddenly shook the silence that had fallen. It was close—in the kitchen. She swallowed over the lump in her throat and pulled Rufus against her legs.

"It's okay, boy." She smoothed his ears back. He kept his body positioned in front of hers. His slim and fit muscles bunched with tension, and he continued a low growl as if he knew they had to be quiet and that he had to protect her. Cal's ferocious voice boomed through the cabin. Her stomach dropped. Someone was in the house.

Crash! Bang!

And Cal was fighting whoever it was. She backed farther away from the door. Every muscle in her body was coiled as tight as a spring. Fear stung her mouth with its acrid taste. She was useless cooped up here in the bedroom—a sitting duck. Cal was capable...but what if he needed help?

She bit her lip. At the very least, Rufus could help to attack whoever had entered the house.

The hairs on the back of her neck stood on end. Sirens pierced the air. Rufus whined.

This was stupid. She had to do something.

But Cal would kill her if she left the bedroom. She raked her hand through her hair and searched the room for a weapon. She couldn't see a damn thing. Cal's angry voice shouted above the screech of the alarm. God, she hoped he had things under control. What if there was more than one intruder?

She inched away from Rufus's side and along the edge of the bed. She found Cal's nightstand and switched on the bedside lamp. A weapon, there had to be one. Something…anything. She opened the top drawer.

Condoms sat at the top. She breathed through tight lips. *That wouldn't help.* Aha! Brass knuckles. She slipped them on over her fingers. They hung heavily on her slight hands. Good Lord, that wouldn't help her. She moved on to the drawer beneath.

Her hand closed over the smooth, cool metal of a switchblade. She firmed her lips. Another crash and a yell sounded from the main area. She took a deep breath and clutched the metal. She'd never used a weapon before—much less a switchblade. She opened the knife. The sharp, shiny edge brought a sour taste to her mouth. If she had to use it to save Cal or herself, she would.

She gripped the handle and held it low, the edge pointed to the floor. Rufus spun in a circle at the door, sensing her exit.

Crash!

Something sharp pelted her legs. Lana let out a shriek and backed away from the shards. Her free hand clutched her throat. She whirled around. Glass scattered across the floor, as the window smashed in. A baseball bat swung at the window again, caving more glass. Rufus charged for the window. Her heart pumped wildly in her chest.

"Rufus!" She grabbed his collar with her free hand and dragged him back from the glass.

He stayed by her side. Her fingers fumbled madly on the door lock. Another crash sounded behind her. He was almost inside.

She tore the door open and charged out. Rufus raced into the hall, his ferocious bark enough to bring silence from the kitchen.

Her bare feet scuffed down the smooth hardwoods. Rufus's dark form rounded the corner to the kitchen. Her chest heaved violently. She sucked a deep breath into her nose.

It was silent.

She hesitated at the corner of the hall and the kitchen. Icicles prickled her spine.

A tall, black form rounded the corner of the kitchen. She screamed. Her back slammed against the wall behind her. She sliced the air with the knife.

"Lana!"

Cal.

She dropped the knife to the floor. It landed with a clatter and danced at their feet. She flung herself against his chest. He closed her in his arms.

"I told you to stay," he growled into her hair. Another crash sounded from the bedroom.

"Someone broke the bedroom window. He's almost inside." Her voice shook, and her body trembled like a leaf.

"Sonofabitch." His body bunched. He kept her close to his chest and led her into the kitchen with him. He snagged his phone off the counter and handed it to her. "Take this." He grabbed his keys from next to the spot that his phone had vacated. "Go in the garage, wait in my truck, and lock the doors. Don't unlock them until I come for you. Call Nate once you're safely in the truck."

She slipped the phone into the front pocket of the hooded sweatshirt she wore.

"The code is 1-1-2-7. His number is programmed in my phone." He turned her in the direction of the front of the house, where the garage access door was located. She nodded and started away.

"Cal, please be careful."

"Go. I won't be long." His voice was low, barely audible.

He crept to the edge of the kitchen and rounded the corner of the hallway. He moved as soundless as the wind. Rufus crept behind Cal.

She didn't look around for the attacker. Cal would surely have him restrained, unconscious…or worse. She made her way through the house. When she reached the garage access door, she shoved her feet in her shoes, unlocked it, and entered. The air was cool in the garage, sending a shiver over her skin. She took a deep breath and found the fob on his key chain. The door shut behind her with a soft *click*.

She depressed the unlock button. The truck's lights flashed in her eyes and beeped.

"Don't move."

Something hard and metallic pressed against the back of her head. Her breath sucked in sharply. Ice shot through her veins. Her body turned to lead, anchoring her to the spot. A scream caught in her throat. The cool metal kept it trapped in her chest.

The speaker snatched the keys from her hand. Another shape moved in the darkness. The rear passenger door opened.

"Get in," the cold, dead voice hissed. "Make a sound and I'll blow your head off."

Chapter 23

Cal motioned for Rufus to stay at the bedroom doorway. He inched his way into the room, his Glock poised in front of him. Someone else was trying to get in his damn house. Whoever it was was halfway through the window, his booted foot on the sill and gloved fingers on the side of the window frame. His head was down, shielded by a black baseball cap.

Anger rippled down his spine. He balled his hands into fists at his side. Hell, no.

He was done with this shit. Done with people terrorizing Lana, done with people thinking they could enter his property. The alarm company would have contacted the police already, but it would be a while before they arrived. He moved across the room on the balls of his feet. The intruder grunted as he tried to heave himself over the window ledge.

Cal's hands itched with the urge to jump him. Like the unconscious fuck in the kitchen, this sonofabitch was going to get a beatdown.

In one swift movement, he snagged the back of the man's jacket and flipped him through the window. His back slammed against the hardwood floors with a *thud.*

Air wheezed out of his lungs. He cursed over a groan.

Cal crushed the side of his foot into the man's throat. He choked and sputtered. Pleasure tickled his insides. They were going to pay…all of them. The guy's hands flew around like baby birds trying to pluck at Cal's sweatpants.

Light from the bedside lamp shone over his reddening face.

"You stupid little bitch," Cal snarled. The man's eyes rolled back. He eased enough pressure off of his throat for him to catch some air. Having him unconscious would do no good when the police got here.

"What the fuck do you think you're doing, Stamos?"

"I"—his breath rasped through his scrunched-up face—"had no choice."

Anger surged through him. He put more weight on his foot. Stamos's arms flailed in panic. Something popped beneath his foot. Stamos squinted in pain, and sweat rolled over his brows. He had a lot of balls coming here to Cal's hideaway, especially with an already bum shoulder.

"Why are you here?" Cal pointed the gun at his head, his hand unwavering.

Stamos's throat convulsed against his foot. His face flooded with purple, and each breath he fought to suck in stayed trapped at his lips.

"C'mon, Stamos, I don't have all night."

"P–please," he gasped between useless breaths.

Cal eased his foot off, but kept it placed against Stamos's windpipe. "Who sent you? Hurry up," he barked when Stamos sucked in another greedy breath of air.

"It was the old lady, man. She told me I would end up like Will if I didn't do what she said."

Cal's fingers flexed. His brain worked at rapid speed. "What 'old lady'? What's her name?"

"I don't know. I swear. She never told me." He pressed his lips together. Tears wet his lashes.

"How'd you find this place?" He'd kept his cabin discreet for three years, and he liked that he always had a backup plan. He'd been careful not to bring Lana here when he'd first taken her, but there hadn't been any help for it this time. And now it was fucking useless.

Stamos's eyes hardened in defiance. Stamos was pissed that Cal had fucked the job up for him, but he didn't give a shit. Cal aimed the gun at his injured shoulder.

"Alright! We hid a couple of guys along the road near where my other men crashed and followed you."

Anger rippled through him. No one had been on the road when he and Lana had returned from Tanner's. He was always careful about tails. But it had never crossed his mind that people could be waiting in the bushes to see what drive he pulled into. He reached down to grab Stamos's jacket and hauled him to his feet. He shoved him against the wall.

"Rufus, come." Rufus charged from the doorway. Stamos let out a squeal and cowered against the wall. Cal smiled. Had he known Stamos was afraid of dogs, he would have started with that first. Rufus paused, teeth bared, spit flying through his murderous snarl.

"You better think fast, before I let Rufus tear your balls off."

Stamos whined. "I'll tell you whatever you want to know. Just keep that mutt away from me."

"How did she contact you?"

Stamos licked his lips. His eyes never left Rufus. "Shawn called me and I met them somewhere."

"Give me your phone."

Stamos dug into his front pocket and handed it to him. Cal slipped the device into his back pocket. He would search through it later and find the source that way. Sirens screamed from the distance. The cops were on their way.

"You gotta let me go, man. There's a warrant out for me."

Cal snorted. "Why the hell would you think I'd give you a break?" He stashed his Glock at the small of his back and propelled Stamos out the door and down the hallway. He wound him through the dark halls and toward the front door.

Stamos was a dumb, snitchy sonofabitch. He wouldn't survive a week in prison. He paused in the foyer to enter the alarm password in the keypad. The blaring silenced. Stamos twisted in his hold, his efforts futile. Red and blue bubble lights flashed outside the cabin.

Bang, bang, bang!

"Police, open up!"

"Oh, look, someone's here for you," Cal said in a singsong voice.

Stamos groaned. "Fuck, man."

Cal shook his head. He unlocked the door, yanked it open, and welcomed the armed officers inside. One of the large officers took Stamos, cuffed him, and put him in the back of the patrol car. Cal gave a quick briefing of what had happened.

"There's another man restrained in my kitchen. If you'll excuse me for a moment, my girlfriend is in the garage."

The officers disappeared through the house. Cal opened the garage door, flicked on the light, and stepped in.

"Lan—" His breath sucked in. The force of it burned his lungs. His truck was gone. The garage was empty. The hairs on the back of his neck stood on end. He turned in a circle.

"Lana?"

No. It couldn't be. His hands fisted at his temples.

Fuck, fuck, fuck.

He dug his fingertips into his scalp and paced the garage. She was gone. While he'd been wasting time getting information from Stamos, someone had taken her. An iron fist gripped his heart. He had to get her back. God, how had it happened? He needed help. The police were here, but he needed someone with more resources. Someone who could act now.

He searched his pocket for his phone. He pulled it out and stared down at it. Lana had his phone…he had Stamos's. His fingers hovered on the buttons. His brain told him to call his own phone, but he couldn't. If it rang, it would alert whoever had her that she had a phone on her. And if they found it on her, they would destroy it and he would have no chance of finding her at all. It was a shot in the dark without it. He dialed Nate's number. It rang and rang.

Goddammit, answer the phone, you asshole.

On the fourth ring, a breathless Nate came to the phone. "What is it?"

"Lana's gone." His words came out rough and broken. Rage shot through his veins, and every syllable required effort.

"*What?*" Nate rasped. An annoyed woman's voice sounded in the background. Nate shushed her. The fucking guy was getting laid while all this shit was going down. A sharp pain pierced behind his eyes, the headache nearly blinding him. Cal pinched his temples together with his thumb and forefinger and willed it away. He had to find Lana.

"Stamos and some other guy came to the house. I told her to wait in my truck, and when I went to get her, she was gone. Along with my truck and my phone."

"She has your phone?" The sound of a belt buckle clanked.

"Yes. Please tell me you're getting dressed and not the other way around."

"Of course, you dipshit." Nate's muffled voice sounded in his ear. He whispered something appeasing to the woman, then came back on.

"I can trace your phone. I just have to get my equipment up and running. Call E, tell him to come to your place and call me when he gets there. By then I should have a location."

Dammit, he hoped to hell Ethan could get there fast. He never should have taken Lana so far from town.

"Done." Cal disconnected, placed a call to Ethan, and after he promised to be there as soon as possible, Cal raced back inside. One of the cops, a shorter one with close-cropped reddish hair, propelled the man from the kitchen toward the door.

Fear tightened its evil fingers around his soul. If someone had been waiting in the garage, she would have been grabbed the moment he'd sent her in there. Cal glanced at his watch. That had easily been twenty-five minutes ago. Christ. If they'd driven as fast as the cops, they could be anywhere by now.

He stepped in front of the red-haired cop and the sonofabitch with the broken nose and blackening eyes. Cal's fists bunched at his sides. The need to hit him again roared through his body.

"You," he spoke low, his voice even. "Who else was here?"

"Easy." The buff cop with short blond hair stepped in. His hand extended to part Cal from their prisoner.

Cal ignored him. He wasn't going to wait for a goddamn judge or some two-bit cop to question the stupid sonofabitch. Not while Lana could be anywhere—with anyone.

He didn't take his eyes off of his one good eye. "Who hired you?"

"Sir, you have to let us do our job."

Cal held his hand out. "One minute"—then, under his breath to the guy—"if I were you I'd answer the damn question, and fast."

He shrugged. The left side of his mouth lifted with indifference. "The old lady. S'all I know."

The redhead sidled past him, the other man in tow. Cal reached out for the other cop. "My girlfriend is missing. She was hiding in the garage when they broke into the house. Someone took her and my truck."

The cop scratched the beard on his face. His pale blue eyes watched Cal carefully. "Did she have access to your keys?"

Cal's brain crackled with frustration. "Of course she did."

"Could it be possible she just left? Maybe she was scared?"

He bit back the response that burned the tip of his tongue. "Can you at least report my truck stolen?"

He looked at his watch, nodded, and pulled out a pad and paper. At the very least, it wouldn't hurt to have more eyes out looking for his truck. He asked Cal a few more questions about the break-in, then left.

Cal couldn't bring himself to wait inside. Goddammit. He'd wanted to buy another vehicle many times to keep here, but he had been too busy. It had seemed pointless to buy a second truck when he barely had time to drive the first. But if he had indulged, he wouldn't be pacing the fucking driveway right now. Another fifteen minutes passed. He pulled Stamos's phone out of his pocket to dial Ethan. The battery flashed. Almost dead.

Headlights cut down the drive.

Thank God.

He jogged down the drive and met Ethan halfway. After climbing in the passenger seat, he dialed Nate on Ethan's phone.

"Don't worry, bro, we'll find her." Ethan peeled out of the driveway. Nate answered on the first ring. Cal put him on speaker.

"Take WA-203 South. They're moving, so that's a good sign." Nate's tone was even, his meaning unspoken. He didn't have to say the words. If they weren't moving, that meant they'd stopped. If they had stopped, they would be following through with their intent…to kill Lana.

Cal's throat clenched until pain shot through his chest. His hands opened and closed on his lap.

Ethan weaved in and out of traffic effortlessly. Minutes stretched, making them seem like hours. He couldn't take the silence. His heart thumped against his rib cage like a wild beast. When he got a hold of them, they would pay. He would be sure of it. Ethan pulled onto the interstate, thankfully clear of traffic at the hour.

"Are they still on 203?"

"Yup." Nate's breath came over the speakers. "Looks as though they're heading for Mount Teneriffe."

A beat passed. Images flashed through his mind. There were a million and one ways to dispose of a body in the deeply wooded trails and cliffs there. He massaged his temples.

"E, you have to go faster." His voice shook. He pinched the bridge of his nose. Every muscle in his body tensed.

A cold rivulet tickled his forehead. He wiped it with his sleeve. The inky liquid shone on the gray material of his shirt. Blood. From the bastard who had bashed him on the head with a solid stone candlestick holder. It should have hurt like a bitch, but was only an irritating throb.

Hang on, baby. I'm coming.

Ethan nodded. His foot slammed on the gas. Cal's head tilted back with the force of it.

After a few minutes, Nate spoke again. "You're gaining on them nicely." He took an audible, shuddering breath. "Not sure if this is a good time or not, but I thought I'd tell you guys that I met someone."

Ethan snorted. "You meet someone every night, dude."

"Yeah, but I think this is different. It feels different."

Cal's eyes rolled skyward. He appreciated Nate's efforts to distract him, but nothing and no one could intervene in his thoughts. Not now. Not until Lana was safe in his arms. He licked his lips. They were reaching the outskirts of the city, and with it came the raw, tinny taste of fear to his mouth. He never should have sent her to his truck. Never should have let her out of his sight. He'd been off his guard. Slipups like this didn't happen to him, and they sure as hell shouldn't have happened with Lana. She was his Achilles' heel.

He'd quit his career tonight if it meant getting Lana back safe and sound. He didn't need the money, he didn't need the rush, and he sure as hell didn't need anything but her as long as he lived.

"Nate, where are they?"

"Still moving. Looks as though they're coming up to the off-ramp to Mount Teneriffe. You need to hurry."

Ethan's knuckles turned white on the steering wheel. Horns blared around them. Cal's vision turned hazy. Clouds shielded the moon, and soft drops of rain landed on the windshield.

"Cal, buddy, you there?" Nate's voice was low, uneven. So out of character that it made Cal's skin prickle.

A barely audible response sounded in his throat. His Adam's apple pierced the thin skin of his neck. The muscles in his face pinched.

"It's going to be alright. I've texted the federal agents who are working on her case. They're hot on your heels."

"Stamos and the other thug mentioned an old lady. They said she'd hired them. I don't have much to go on here, but the only person that comes to mind is Grace Vanderpoel."

Ethan whistled. "No shit." Then to Nate, "Think you can get some agents to their house?"

"Just sent another text. Someone will go there now."

Ethan slapped his shoulder. "That's huge, bro. This is coming to an end. Everything's going to be okay."

Cal nodded. But it didn't feel okay. Nothing would be okay again if he didn't have Lana. A void in his chest opened, swallowing his heart. He couldn't survive a day without her—he took another breath.

"They've stopped moving."

Cal's stomach turned over. His heart stopped and started. This was it.

Chapter 24

The zip tie cut into the soft skin at her wrists. She twisted her hands. The sharp plastic only cut deeper. Panic beat its wild rhythm through her heart. She was going to die if she didn't get out of here. The interstate was empty, only the odd car littering the dark road. Her eyes darted around the floor of Cal's truck. She needed a weapon. Even if she could find something, though, it would be pointless with her wrists bound. There were two of them and only one of her. She took a slow, deep breath in through her nose. She had to stay calm. Stay calm and think.

By now, Cal would surely know she was missing. He would tear apart the city to find her. The awkward shape of Cal's phone lay against her abdomen in her front sweater pocket. If only she had use of her fingers…

Tears stung her eyes. She didn't want to die this way. She wasn't ready to leave this earth, her family, and especially Cal. A lump pressed against her throat. The reality was, she had very little chance at escape. They would shoot her without batting an eye. She shifted her gaze to the cool, shiny metal of the gun that rested on the lap next to her, its deadly mouth at level with her stomach. She couldn't use her hands, but she could use her words. Maybe, just maybe, she could talk her way out of this. At the very least, buy Cal some time.

"Please don't do this, Grace." She met the eyes of the older woman beside her. Eyes she had known for half her life. The once-kind, pale blue orbs now held enough ice to freeze hell.

Grace smiled. "Oh honey. Don't worry, this will be quick. You won't feel a thing." She smoothed her blond hair back and tucked it behind her ear. "Unlike what your friend did to Tanner. But he'll pay for that."

Anger simmered inside her, and she clenched her hands into fists. "How can you do this to me? To my father?" She blinked away the tears that threatened to fill her eyes. She wouldn't cry. If she was going to die tonight, she would die with dignity. "Why?" The word hissed through her lips.

Grace thinned her lips. "This was never my intention. I've always liked you, Lana. But I have to protect my son and my family's name at all costs."

"I don't understand." Her brows pinched together.

Grace shifted in her seat. Her thigh rubbed against Lana's. The corners of her mouth dipped. "You accused Tanner of sexual assault, my dear. Do you have any idea what that would do to him? To me?"

"You're doing this because of that?" Her voice dripped with disbelief. "I never told anyone about that—not even my father."

"It was only a matter of time. You don't know Tanner like I do. He doesn't take rejection lightly. He would have made another attempt, and you would have taken it further."

Grace knew. She knew all about Tanner's past and had covered it up. That was why she had always appeared hard on him. Because with every slipup he made, she'd had to come in and pay people off.

"Tanner should be sitting here. Not me. I know about the young woman he raped. And about Andrea Reid."

Grace's breath sucked in sharply. "How do you know about that?"

"I've been talking to the FBI." She raised her shoulder with indifference. "They know everything about Tanner." She was revealing her hand, but what did it matter?

Grace's eyes rounded. The lines on her face deepened, aging her before Lana's eyes. She shook her head. "No. You're lying. They couldn't possibly know about that."

Ignoring her, Lana continued. "The question is..." She spoke slowly, deliberately. "How have you been able to live with yourself? Tanner needs to be in prison...and so do you."

"I did what I had to do to protect my family. As for the FBI, I would know if they were investigating us. You're full of shit."

Lana scoffed. "You're wrong. They know everything. They know about Shawn, Will, and Stamos. If you kill me, that's one more felony tacked to the Normand and Theroux names."

Grace's cheeks tinted with red. She pressed her trembling lips together. Her eyes turned to gray stones.

"You're going to be sorry, Lana. If you think for one minute that the law is above my name, you're sadly mistaken."

"If you weren't so worried about conviction, you wouldn't be killing me to silence the secrets." She shook her head sadly. "You can't pay or kill people off anymore. Too many people know. It's hopeless. Your only chance is to turn yourself in."

The driver cursed. Grace's eyes flitted to him, then back to meet Lana's. "I don't believe you."

Lana lifted a shoulder. "Then don't. But the man you hired—you know, the man who was to kill me?" Disdain laced her voice. "He won't let this go. He will see to it that you pay for this."

Grace snorted. The sound rode from her immaculately made-up lips. "I'm sorry to break it to you, sweetheart, but I sent two men to his house to take care of him. He won't live to tell a soul."

Lana laughed. The sound rang out through the quiet truck. "You actually think you can hurt him? He had one unconscious in the kitchen and was taking care of the other one by the time I made it to the garage. Sorry to break it to you."

Grace's jaw worked. "If that's true, it doesn't matter. I have law enforcement on my payroll. I can have him framed and charged in a matter of hours. No one will listen to a damn word he has to say."

"What do you think the chances are those idiots you sent to Cal's house will remain loyal to you? And the FBI agents I mentioned? Those are Cal's friends."

Silence reverberated through the vehicle.

"I can't fucking believe this," the man in the front seat breathed. Lana leaned forward in her seat.

She gasped through parted lips. "Shawn?" She hadn't been able to see his face before. In the garage, Grace had ushered her into the back of the truck and tied her hands. It had been dark, but she'd recognized Grace's voice.

He met her gaze in the rearview mirror. His face hardened. A glint of remorse shone in his eyes. He shifted his attention back to the road.

"How can you do this to my father?" she whispered. Edward had always been kind and generous to him and Vanessa. His Christmas bonus alone rivaled an average person's annual income. Red-hot anger seized her. "You won't get away with this."

Shawn sighed. "I had no choice, Lana. Believe me. Tanner and I go way back…if he went down, he would take me with him."

Grace's icy fingers wrapped around Lana's bicep. She pulled her away from the edge of her seat. "Enough of that." Her voice trembled with warning.

Lana yanked out of her hold. She turned to the woman, the woman who had been at her graduation, whose vows she'd professed to her father on their wedding day years ago. Grace had been not just her stepmother, but someone Lana had cared for and respected.

Nausea rolled in her stomach like acid. She didn't know this woman. All this time she had been nothing but a façade. How could she have been so stupid? She had even snuck under Edward's sharp radar.

Lana narrowed her eyes and leaned in close to Grace. Her nose hovered inches away from her face. "If you follow through with this, you will be prosecuted. Everything is going to come to light, and your family name and history will be wiped of its pristine image." Grace's eyes never wavered from hers.

"But it doesn't end there. You're going to rot in hell, Grace. And your son will be right beside you."

Grace's mouth tightened. A vein beneath her eye twitched. She turned her attention to the road. "Take the next exit, Shawn. Let's get this over with."

Hope deflated in her chest like a burst balloon. Grace didn't give a damn. All those years, all the memories…nothing. A bright light cut through the darkness. Grace held her cell phone, her thumb gliding quickly over the keys.

Lana worked her hands again. Dammit. There was no give in the tight plastic. Thankfully, they hadn't wasted time tying her feet. She'd attacked Cal successfully with her hands bound. This time, though, her hands were secured at her back. She wouldn't be able to throw her fists. It didn't matter. She would find a way. She had to.

The soft *click* of the turn signal chimed. Shawn took the exit, and the vehicle slowed. Her pulse beat against her throat. She pressed her knees together to keep them from shaking. No. She wasn't going to die tonight. The headlights cut down the gravel drive, illuminating the thick foliage ahead.

She had to get away.

Shawn's resolve had wavered. He was her chance. Lana's eyes locked on the gun resting casually on Grace's lap. She had to disarm her. Without the use of her hands. She swallowed over the lump in her throat. What choice did she have? They were going to shoot her regardless. If she could divert them enough, maybe she could escape. She had Cal's phone. If she could get far enough away and hide, she might be able to work it out of the pocket and dial.

She had to try.

The vehicle slowed, and Shawn cut the engine. Rain fell in thick drops to splatter the windshield. They picked up with frequency as the seconds passed. The headlights switched off. Darkness closed around them. Grace opened her door first.

"Get the flashlights," she instructed Shawn as she climbed out. She stood at the door and waved the gun back and forth, gesturing for Lana to follow.

She gulped. The sound echoed in her ears.

"C'mon, I don't have all night."

Shawn slid out first. Lana shuffled across the seats. God, if only she had on running shoes. Flats would be a challenge to outrun them in. She kept her eyes down.

"Where'd you put the flashlights?" Shawn asked from the open driver's door.

Lana curled her toes. She shifted her weight to her hip on the seat.

Grace huffed. "They're under the back seat—"

She snapped her foot out with rapid speed. The top of her foot caught Grace's hand. The weapon careened through the air.

"You little bitch!" Grace barked into the wind. "Shawn, get the flashlight over here, I can't see."

Lana flung herself out of the vehicle. The balls of her feet landed on the gravel. Grace shot her hand out. Her fingers locked around her wrist. Lana twisted until her hold broke. She tore through the night, as if she was running on hot coals.

"Shawn, get her!"

Lana took flight. Her feet pounded through the stones. Dirt flung around her. She charged for the trees. Rain pelted her forehead and hair. Hurried feet crunched the ground behind her. Her breath came out in sharp pants. Her shoulders screamed for release. She tore through the bushes. The trees welcomed her into the shelter of their arms. The smell of rain and rotting vegetation settled in the air. Grace yelled something at Shawn behind her.

Her hair whipped in front of her face. She shook it free. The dirt was moist and slick from the rain earlier that evening. A tree root caught her toe. Her breath sucked in on a cry. She caught herself in a lunge and leapt back to her feet. Branches clawed at her face, nicking her skin. The soles of her feet caught a sharp rock. She bit her lip as pain shot through her toes.

God, please don't let them find me.

The violent beating of her heart pulsated through her body. Her lungs burned in her chest. She surged on. She threw a hasty glance over her shoulder. A bright yellow globe bobbed in the air...then another. They had flashlights.

No, no, no!

They were going to catch her.

She needed somewhere to hide. Needed to call for help. Tears stung her eyes. She fought them back. She wouldn't die out here. She ducked low, blending into the darkness. Thank God for her dark clothing and hair. The lights cut through the leaves to her right, but the beam was unsteady.

She weaved deeper between the thick tree trunks. Cold, wet mud sucked her feet into its hold. She tore her foot out and her shoe remained glued to the sludge. She took a wide step out of the muck, and lost her footing. A cry caught in her throat, but she silenced it as she went down. Her knees sank deep.

She squeezed her eyes shut. The bouncing yellow circles grew to the size of tennis balls. They were getting closer. She squinted through the darkness. All she needed was cover. Her eyes zeroed in on the darkness. A few feet in front of her, the land dropped off.

A ravine.

Hope soared through her. She kept her head low and crawled out of the mud on her knees. She inched her way to the edge of the ravine. The flashlights whipped around the trees, but not in her direction. Their hushed voices carried through the wind. If they reached the deeper mud of the trail, they would see her footprints.

This was her only shot. She scooted on her butt down the slippery slope of the ravine. Without the use of her hands, she struggled to stay upright. She made it down the leaf-covered slide. Six inches of ice-cold water covered her ankles and her one bare foot slipped along the stones at the bottom. Her teeth chattered. The moon shone through the canopy of trees, illuminating her way. About a hundred feet away, the ravine twisted around a bend. If she could make it that far, she could try to get the phone out and alert Cal.

She lifted her feet gingerly, one after the other, being careful not to splash. The sound would carry. She took long strides. Something slimy crawled into her pants leg.

Her teeth pierced her tongue to stifle the scream. She shook her leg wildly. *It's okay. It's just a bug. Keep moving.*

Her teeth chattered in her face. The small pinch of tiny legs was gone. She took a deep breath. She craned her neck back to see the top of the ravine where she'd come down. No dancing orbs yet.

She just might make it.

Crack! Crack!

Gunshots rang through the night. The sound of critters scattering through the bushes followed. Birds squawked, torn from their slumber. She rounded the edge of the bend and dropped to her knees.

Her breath rasped out through her teeth.

A beam of light hit her in the face. Her heart slammed against her breastbone. Terror ripped through her. She threw herself to the ground, shielded by the curve in the ravine.

They had found her.

Bullets split the night. Their deadly shapes whizzed past her. She searched the darkness for another way out. She wouldn't be able to climb the ravine—not without the use of her hands. She was a sitting duck.

Tears leaked out of her eyes and ran down her cheeks. The taste of mud and salt ran over her lips. Bugs buzzed around her. They weren't far now. The crunch of branches reached her ears.

Cal's phone.

She leaned on her side and bucked her hips. It slid out of her pocket and into the mud. She wriggled in front of it, her hands searching through the wet sludge behind her to pick up the device.

She licked her lips with new hope.

With the phone in her hand, her finger swiped over the screen. All she had to do was tap the call icon and it would dial the last number he'd called. Her hands fumbled awkwardly. The mud was too thick, and her fingers were caked in it. The phone slipped out of her grasp...and landed in the shallow water beneath her feet.

No!

Her head hung. She closed her eyes as tears leaked from the corners. She was doomed.

Chapter 25

Cal's knee bounced up and down. One hand gripped the door handle; he was ready to bolt when they stopped. The other held his seat belt buckle. The hair on the back of his neck stood on end like metal antennae. They were almost there. He blew his breath through his lips. Ethan guided the truck to the off-ramp at Mount Tenerife.

Hang on, baby. I'm coming.

Ethan didn't slow down. They bumped over the gravel road. The headlights caught his truck in their glow. *Shit, shit, shit.*

"There." His fingers left the door handle to point ahead. Ethan nodded. Of course, he'd seen it. Three of the truck's doors hung open. The interior light's glow beamed through the night. A gunshot rang out, echoing in the still woods.

"Sonofabitch," he rasped. Air expelled from his lungs.

Ethan screeched the truck to a halt. Cal flung the door open, and bits of gravel swarmed the air and pelted his legs. His feet hit the ground, and he ran as if the hounds of hell were on his heels.

"Go! I'll get the flashlights and be right behind you," Nate called.

He pounded the short distance to the forest. Sirens sounded behind him. Branches whipped his body. He ducked a low-lying branch and leapt over a scatter of tree roots. His heart raced in his chest. Sweat rolled over his brow. He wiped it away with his sleeve. Every muscle in his body flexed.

Crack, crack!

More gunshots. He swore. He was too late. No. It couldn't end this way. He pulled his Glock out from the small of his back. Aiming at the trees overhead, he pulled the trigger. Once. Twice.

I'm here, baby. Hang on.

A bug hit him in the face. He slapped it away. The forest closed in around them. He had no idea where they were. The gunshots had been close. They couldn't be far.

He cupped his hand around his mouth. "Lana!" His voice boomed through the trees. The sound echoed and bounced around him. He waited. His breath puffed quickly around him in little white clouds.

God, please don't let me be too late.

"Cal!" Her voice split the air. His heart leapt into his throat. She was alive. He took off in a dead run in the direction her words had come from. Voices sounded behind him, and the glow of flashlights bobbed the night around him. He didn't slow. His booted feet crunched over twigs and leaves. His arms ruthlessly slapped the branches out of his path. Lights moved into his line of vision—their flashlights. Rage slowed his pulse to a flatline. He couldn't think about them. He needed to get to Lana, make sure she was safe…then he would let loose the beast inside him that needed to kill these motherfuckers.

"Cal!" Her voice trembled through the night. Her fear was raw and ragged. Ahead, the land pitched downward into a ravine. The lights from the flashlights moved quickly along the top of the slope. He charged at them.

One form grabbed the other. "Get her. I'll take him," a woman hissed. A tall form hedged down the slope—toward Lana. The woman's other hand extended. The glow from the moon caught a metallic sheen. She pulled the trigger. He dove for her. His arms closed around her waist. The bullet whistled over his shoulder, missing his head by inches.

The woman screamed. The gun fell from her fingers as her fists collided with his shoulder. They tumbled down the ravine and landed with a splash, her beneath him. His fists clenched. He wanted to finish her. Every atom in his body pulsated with the need to destroy.

Lana's scream tore through him. He shot to his feet. His boots splashed in the shallow water. The man stood about fifty feet away, but a small body hunched on the ground at his feet caught Cal's attention.

Panic turned his veins solid. His chest ached with every breath. Cal pulled out his Glock and pointed it at his target. His steps slowed as he got closer. The man stood just feet away from Lana. Her face turned up to him, the porcelain of her skin reflected in the moon's light.

"Let her go," he breathed.

The man shook his head and looked down at Lana. "I'm sorry." His hand trembled. Cal's jaw locked. He held his hand steady, directed at the man's head.

"Drop your weapon. This is your last warning."

The man grunted. He turned the gun to his temple…and pulled the trigger. The man's head snapped to the side, and Cal fired a second too late. Cal's bullet connected with his chest, and he dropped to the ground like a bag of bricks. Without wasting a second, Cal rushed for Lana. His hands closed around her shoulders.

"Are you okay?"

Tremors racked her body. Her teeth chattered, and her lips shook. She nodded wildly. "I'm fine." He pulled her against him. He ran his hands over her body, everywhere he could feel, searching for an injury. She was frozen. The sweater she wore was heavy and soaking wet. Her hair hung in damp tendrils down her back. He pressed his face into her neck. His heart pumped in his chest. The steady rhythm reminded him he was here. She was alive. They were going to be okay. Her body convulsed in his arms.

"I can't believe you're here. You found me," she said against his shoulder. Her voice was small, unrecognizable. He smoothed his hands quickly over her back, trying to warm her. She pulled far enough out of his arms to look into his eyes. "How did you do it?" she whispered into the night. He wiped a streak of mud from her cheek.

He smiled. "You have my phone. Nate was able to trace it." His lips quivered. "I was out of my mind, Lana. Losing you was the scariest thing that has ever happened to me." Tension ebbed through his chest as he took a deep breath. "Lana, I love you so damn much." He ran his thumb over her bottom lip.

Her eyes filled with tears, and a soft laugh bubbled through her lips. "You have great timing." Her lips spread into a slow smile. "I love you, too, Cal." She rested her head against him, and he cradled her neck in his palm. "I thought I was going to die here." She spoke slowly, as if it took great effort to form the words.

"Shhh. Don't think about it, okay?"

She nodded and pulled away. Her shoulders wriggled uncomfortably. "My wrists are tied."

He pulled the switchblade from his pocket, found the plastic zip tie at her wrists, and cut them free. She moved her hands to rub the area. He rubbed his thumbs over the cut on her delicate skin, then traced his own hands over her thighs and up under the sweater. "You're freezing. Take that sweater off. I'll give you my shirt." He pulled at the hem of his shirt, but her hands stopped him.

"No, it's okay. Let's just get out of here…please."

He nodded. His hand closed around hers. "You're sure you're okay? I heard shots."

Her tongue came out to wet her lips. "I'm fine. Just cold. They did shoot, but they missed." Her gaze shifted over his shoulder to the man's body. "Is he…"

Cal nodded. "Yeah, babe. He shot himself."

"You shot him, too?"

"Hell, yeah. I couldn't take the chance of him turning that gun around on you."

"And Grace?"

"I'm right here." The chilly, self-satisfied voice sounded behind him. Cal whipped his head around. His senses tingled. There, before him, stood the woman he'd just rolled down the hill with. She held a gun trained on them. Lana gasped in his ear. Her body tensed in his arms. He pulled her tighter against him, shielding her.

Shouts sounded from above them. "FBI! Drop your weapons!"

A hard glint crossed Grace's face. Her finger moved on the trigger. Cal threw Lana to the ground and came down on top of her. A shot rang out.

Voices screamed around them.

* * * *

"Cal, are you okay?" Lana's sobs filled his consciousness. Her hands ran over him. He pushed himself up to look down at her. The shot hadn't hit him—or her. Flashing lights filled the night. Bustling people came down the slope. Grace sat on the ground beside Shawn, a bullet in her shoulder.

Cal grabbed Lana's face, forcing her to look at him. "Are *you* hurt?"

"No. Are you?" Tears streamed down her cheeks.

A hand grabbed his shoulder. Ethan pulled him off Lana. "Are you guys okay? Anyone hurt?"

"You shot Grace?" Cal looked up at his friend.

"Fuck, yeah. She was going to shoot you, man. I just hit her enough to disarm her. That bitch is going to rot in jail."

Lana threw herself into Cal's arms. He lifted her against his chest and got to his feet. He followed Ethan out of the ravine.

When they finally reached the parking lot, Cal weaved through the squad cars that surrounded the two trucks. A police officer approached them.

"Miss Vanderpoel?"

In his arms, Lana nodded.

"We need to get a statement from you, please." The officer was tall, almost Cal's height, with dark curly hair. Lana's big, tired eyes locked with Cal's. She needed to rest. Or at least get out of her wet clothes.

"Can I have a word with you?"

The officer nodded. Cal lowered her to her feet. "Honey, go wait in Ethan's truck and turn the heat on." He didn't have his damn keys, otherwise he'd have put her in his own vehicle.

He turned to the burly officer. "She's had a hell of a night and is soaked to the skin. Can someone meet us at my house so she can at least get warm and changed first?"

He nodded slowly. "I can understand that. Let me check with someone, but I don't see a problem."

He disappeared to approach another officer, then came back. "Sure, let me get your address." Cal gave him the needed information and waited for Ethan.

Cal opened the passenger side door where Lana sat. "You holding up okay?" She held her hands splayed out in front of the vents. Her cheeks and nose were still tinted pink from the cold.

"I'm fine." Her tone was even, strong. In her eyes, he read another story. Dark circles surrounded them, and her face was pale and ashen. His lips thinned. She kept saying she was fine, probably to keep from falling apart. He needed to get her home and let her have the space she needed.

"Do they need to ask me questions right now?" Her gaze wavered from his to land on the light sprinkle of rain that littered the gravel beneath his feet.

"They're going to meet us at the cabin in a bit. Let's get you home and cleaned up, okay?" Her shoulders dropped, and relief washed the tension from the lines in her face.

"Thank you."

"No need. Let me find Ethan and we'll be on our way."

She nodded, and he closed the door to lock in the heat. Ethan stepped out of the woods; Grace, her hands cuffed behind her back, followed.

His fingernails dug into his palms with the need to take the bitch out. His chest tightened. He couldn't do that. Not with all the uniforms here. Grace would be prosecuted. And he wanted her to live through the scandal and shame.

Ethan approached him. Cal dug his hands in his pockets. "They're going to question Lana at my house. I need to get her home and changed. She's freezing. I haven't been able to find my keys, so can you give us a lift?"

Ethan pulled his keys from his pocket. "Here, you take my truck. I'll go look for your keys. I bet either Grace or the guy in the ravine has them. If I don't find them, I'll get a ride from one of the cops."

"Sure, thanks." Cal accepted the keys and jogged the short distance to the truck. He climbed in. Lana's attention was riveted to Grace being put in the back of the cop car.

He reached over, pulled the seat belt across her chest, and buckled it. He turned the truck around and drove down the mouth of the gravel drive toward the interstate. Lana tucked her knees in close to her chest and stared straight ahead.

He didn't know what to say.

Her whole life had come crashing down around her ears. All he wanted to do was comfort her. He reached over and took her hand. Her fingers were as cold as icicles. His heart twisted at the memory of her sitting in the cold ravine, soaking wet, waiting for the bullet that would kill her.

He'd almost been too late. Another minute or two and things would have ended completely differently. Lana let loose a shaky sigh, jarring him from his dark thoughts.

"You were right about Shawn. That was him in the ravine."

He squeezed her hand. "He got what he deserved."

She cleared her throat. "I don't feel sorry for him." She threaded her fingers with his. "I can't believe I lived among all those people. Grace, Tanner, Shawn… How could I have been so oblivious?"

Fire spurred in his guts. "You weren't, Lana. They were stupid. Take a look at the outcome."

She snorted. "I suppose you're right." She turned her head to look out the passenger window. "I really miss my dad."

He lifted her hand to his mouth. "Do you want to call him?"

She nodded. "Yeah, as soon as I get out of these clothes."

A little while later, they pulled into the garage. He came around the truck and lifted her out. "Cal, I can walk." She swatted at his shoulder. He held her tighter against him.

"I don't want you to."

Her head rested against his shoulder in defeat. A small sigh sounded in her throat. He entered the cabin through the garage access, greeted by a very excited Rufus. Without pausing for a beat, he made a beeline for the bedroom and flicked the lights on along the way. Rufus danced at their heels, but Cal shooed him out of the room until he could clean the glass up. He set Lana down on her feet in the bathroom. Under the bright lights, he grimaced inwardly.

Leaves and twigs littered her hair. Streaks of mud and blood from small scratches smeared her face. Her cheeks were hollowed out, and her eyes dark and red-rimmed. Jesus Christ.

"Am I a mess?" She stretched the hem of his sweater out and looked down at herself. Instead of answering, he took the hem from her hands and pulled it over her head. Dirt and debris clung to the damp skin on her bare chest. He reached behind her and turned the water on. She shimmied her sweatpants down her legs and tossed them to the floor. His eyes raked over her. She was so slight and delicate, her body in such sharp contrast to her strength.

"Will you come in with me?"

"You really think you have to ask?" He yanked his shirt off and tossed it to the floor, then chucked his pants. She smiled.

"What about the officers? Aren't they coming to talk to me?"

"They can wait." He pulled her under the spray. She rested her cheek against his chest. The hot water beat down on her back. A shiver shook her body against him. "Still cold?" He rubbed his hands up and down her back.

"No, just can't shake the chill." He lifted her mass of hair in his hands and washed the debris out. She leaned her weight against him as if her bones had turned to spaghetti. He filled his hand with shampoo and began to work it through her strands.

"You don't have to do that."

"Shhh. Just rest, okay?" He continued to wash her hair. When he finished, he grabbed the bar of soap and ran it over her skin. Her trembles slowed down until they stopped. A yawn broke through her lips, and she stifled it with the back of her hand.

Shit. "I wish you could go straight to bed."

She shook her head. "I'm okay. I wouldn't mind something hot to drink, though, and I'm actually kind of hungry."

The corners of his mouth lifted. Anyone else would be a mess right now. He might be taking care of her, but only because he'd insisted. Lana was a force to reckon with. Admiration for her swelled in his chest.

He pressed his lips to her head. She smiled up at him. They got out together, and Cal passed her a towel. Once they were dressed, he led her out to the kitchen. She stayed close to his side, her hand curled into his.

"Sit." He directed her to the island. "I'll fix you a tea and something to eat."

"Do you mind if I call my dad first? I know it's late, but I need to talk to him."

He plucked the cordless phone linked to his landline up from the counter and handed it to her. He would need to replace his cell phone tomorrow. "Of course, babe. Take all the time you need."

She gave him a tight smile and took a seat in the living room. Rufus followed and kept her company. Part of him wanted to go to her and hold her hand, but he knew this was something she wanted to do on her own.

He filled the kettle and took some tea bags out for her. Shit, he was in need of groceries. All he had was enough for a couple of sandwiches. By the time he had the sandwiches on plates and her tea poured, she was off the phone. She set it down on the counter. Her eyes misted with tears. He pulled her against him and held her tight. She was so damn small, it made his heart ache that she was hurting.

She smiled up at him, then eased out of his arms. "Thanks."

"Do you want to talk about it? If you're tired, it can wait till tomorrow." Before she could answer, the doorbell rang. Rufus charged for the front door. "Let's get this statement over with and head to bed. You can tell me everything later."

She slid on the bar chair, her chin resting on her palm, and his oversized sweater pooling at her elbow. "That sounds good."

Chapter 26

Lana stretched. Every muscle in her body screamed in protest. She groaned and rubbed her eyes. God, she felt like death. The bed was cool beside her, telling her that Cal had gotten up long ago. She hated sleeping in. Especially today. Her family would be frantic to see her.

It had been after 2 a.m. when they had finally fallen into bed. The statement had taken longer than she'd expected, but considering the circumstances, they'd had to be thorough.

The memory of her dad's tired voice sounded in her head. Her stomach flipped over. She could count on one hand the number of times she'd seen her father cry. Last night, she'd been able to hear the tears in his voice. She had suggested going to see him after the statement, but he had insisted she get some rest.

His last words before hanging up echoed in her ears: *"I'll see you tomorrow, honey. And be sure to bring your friend."*

They had gone to bed right after the police had left, so she hadn't mentioned it to Cal.

Oh God. Would Cal be up for meeting her dad? Was that something he even wanted to do? She unraveled the sheets from around her and made her way to the kitchen. Only one way to find out.

Cal greeted her with a steaming mug of coffee. His arm circled her shoulders. "You're finally up. Did you sleep well?"

She nodded. "What time did you get up?"

"A few hours ago. I've already worked out and eaten. Ethan just left, he brought my truck over and picked up his. Can I get you something to eat?" After her late snack last night and thinking about her chat with her father, she had lost her appetite.

"Not right now." She leaned back against the counter and took a sip of the warm liquid, letting it awaken her soul. Cal crossed his arms and leaned back against the opposite counter. He smiled at her. The lines around his face crinkled.

"How are you feeling?"

She lifted a shoulder. "Like hell."

He chuckled. "Well, you don't look like it. But I can tell something is on your mind. What's the matter, babe?"

Her insides tightened. He might not want to meet her father yet. If that was the case, she would have to accept it.

"Last night I told my dad I would go see him today."

Cal's eyes focused on hers. The light and laughter left like a cloud blocking out the sun.

"I'm sure he can't wait to see you. We can leave whenever you want."

"Actually, I told him I would be there this morning. I hope that works for you."

He shrugged. "I don't have any plans. We can go as soon as you're ready."

"There's something else." She wet her lips and tucked her hair behind her ear. This was stupid. She shouldn't be nervous. "He wants to meet you."

Cal's eyebrows rose. Other than that small hint of surprise, his expression didn't change. He straightened away from the counter and filled his mug with what she assumed to be at least his third cup of coffee.

"Sure. I was hoping to meet him today."

Her shoulders relaxed. "Are you sure? I don't want you to feel uncomfortable. He can be...intense."

He glanced at her over his shoulder. His lips lifted in a smirk. "I can handle it."

"But do you want to? I mean—"

He chuckled, turned around, and bent to press a kiss to her lips. "Stop making a big deal out of it, okay? Now, go get ready." He swatted her butt, and she scurried in the direction of the bedroom, coffee in hand.

Her chest inflated with delight. He wasn't scared or unwilling. Should she have expected anything less? Cal was the type of man to take on any situation. Why should meeting her father rattle him? In the bedroom, she grabbed a fresh towel and hung it beside the shower. She undressed and took the last gulp of her coffee. Her love and appreciation for Cal had just grown astronomically.

Less than an hour later, she was showered and dressed. She'd had a piece of toast before they left. Now, sitting in the truck, her stomach coiled in knots. She would have to explain everything to her father. The

FBI knew all the details, so surely Edward knew, too. It wasn't going to sit well with him.

Cal's hand grabbed hers. "Would you relax? You're acting like I'm being sentenced to the electric chair."

She chewed her lip. "It's going to be hard to explain what you do, and even harder for him to understand."

"I'm sure your mom filled him in on some things. Don't worry about it. I will handle the questions. He has every right to be leery and cautious. I would be, too. What's the worst that could happen?"

"He could hate you." She laughed. The brittle sound echoed in the truck. The sun beat through the window, warming the inside of the car. Cal slid his sunglasses on.

"You're right, he could. But that's the worst-case scenario. I can't change my past, or who I am. But I love you, and the sooner he knows that, the sooner we can come to an understanding and set aside our differences."

Her heart hung on the only words it cared to hear. Satisfaction settled in her belly. "I love you, too." His thumb brushed over her knuckles. "It's just weird for me. I haven't brought any men home since college, and that didn't go too well."

"It will be fine." Cal pulled off the interstate. They were minutes away from her house. Cal's hand rested calmly on the steering wheel, his legs stretched out in front of him. He was so at ease. Seeing his calm demeanor lessened the tension in her body.

He pulled up to the gate, Lana gave him the code, and it swung open. He parked in the circle drive and turned off the ignition.

"Ready?"

She took a slow, steadying breath, nodded, and climbed out of the truck. Cal rounded the vehicle, his hand extended to her. Together they walked up the front steps. Her hand lifted to open the door. She hesitated. For the first time in her life, she had the urge to knock. Her hand closed over the cool metal. A breeze kicked up and rustled leaves across the stamped concrete steps.

Cal's hand smoothed over her back. "You okay?"

She was being ridiculous. This was as much her home as it had always been. She nodded and swung the door open.

"Dad? I'm home." She kicked her shoes off. The rustic beaten hardwood floors were rough beneath her sock-covered feet. Cal slid his shoes off and shut the door. A moment later, Edward emerged from his office off of the foyer.

The temples of his raven-dark hair sported gray streaks that hadn't been there a week before. Dark bags shadowed his vibrant blue eyes. He'd always looked much younger than his sixty-one years. She couldn't say the same now. His face softened on her. Tears shone in his eyes. Without hesitation, she raced to him and threw her arms around his neck. He'd lost weight. A choke sounded in his throat.

"I'm so happy you're home, honey."

She stepped out of his embrace and wiped the tears from the corners of her eyes. "I missed you, Dad. It's been a hell of a week."

He snorted. "You can say that again."

Lana turned back to Cal, her hand looping around her dad's arm. "Daddy, I want you to meet Cal Hart." Introducing him as her "boyfriend" seemed too insignificant. Edward's shoulders straightened, and he extended his hand. Cal stepped forward, his eyes sparking with interest. He shook his hand.

"It's a pleasure to meet you, sir."

"Likewise." Her father's clipped tone made her cringe. "Let's have a seat in the family room." He gestured for Lana to lead the way. Her hand dropped from her father's arm, and instinctively she reached for Cal. His hand closed around hers reassuringly. Her spine stiffened. Edward's hot gaze burned a hole through the back of her head.

Best he understood their relationship right off the bat. She led Cal down the hall and to the back of the house. The family room was one of three large sitting areas on the main level. Often they preferred this room, as it was off the kitchen and had a stunning view of the manicured backyard. A large pool and hot tub carved up the landscaping. Hidden from the main house's view behind the pool house lay her private suite.

She sat on the oversized white leather couch, Cal took a seat next to her, and Edward sat in the wing-back suede chair adjacent to them.

Edward broke the silence. "First of all, I would like to apologize." He tented his fingers in front of his chest. His tone was grave, his eyes heavy and dark. "Lana, honey, I never in a million years thought Grace was anything but who she had seemed. I loved her very much, and I suppose that made me blind—"

"No, Dad. It's not your fault. I didn't see that coming, either."

His lips thinned. He nodded slowly. "Why didn't you tell me about the encounter with Tanner?" She shifted awkwardly in her seat. Cal squeezed her fingers.

"I didn't want to upset you, and I thought I had handled it." Her lips rolled in. "Did he know about Grace's plan?" She shifted her gaze to include Cal.

Edward looked to Cal for the answer.

He cleared his throat. "The FBI is still trying to determine that, but it looks as though he didn't have much to do with it." Cal leaned forward.

"I'm unclear as to your role," Edward directed to Cal. "Sonja told me you're a 'freelance security contractor,' but I don't quite understand what that is or how you got involved in this situation." His tone was cool and professional. Her teeth bit into her lip. He was getting right to the guts of everything.

"To be honest with you, I was hired to kill Lana."

Lana closed her eyes on an exhale. Good God, was he out of his mind? Her father's face hardened. His eyes turned to slate.

"Let me make it clear that that is not my line of work. The person who came to me with the job had very little knowledge of my profession"—he paused—"for which I'm grateful. I couldn't stand back and let it happen, though. At the same time, it was obvious there was a lot at stake, and not knowing who was involved, I concluded that the best decision was to take her out of the situation and keep her safe until we figured out who was behind it." His tone was calm and cool. Lana watched her father carefully. He stared at Cal, his gaze unwavering.

"But you two had never met before. Didn't it occur to you how terrified she would be?" Edward's voice was steady, but Lana recognized the tempered anger beneath the calm.

Cal cleared his throat. "Of course that crossed my mind. But there weren't any other options. In my experience, going to the police is not a safeguard. And as it turns out, Grace admitted to Lana that she has many police officers on her payroll. Had I filed a report, it would have blown up in my face, and someone else eventually would have been sent to do the job—and would have succeeded."

Edward lifted an eyebrow. "I see." He crossed his arms over his chest. "Sonja mentioned something about you having connections with the FBI?"

"That's correct. A good friend of mine is an agent with the FBI. He assisted us through the process and did a lot of investigating to help."

Edward's silence cut through her like a knife. When he was quiet, his mind was working. Not a good sign.

"Cal saved my life, Daddy. On more than one occasion. Some of the men Grace had hired found us at a hotel we were staying at. They set the fire alarms off, and two men attacked us. One held a gun to my head. Cal shot him before he could shoot me."

His hand squeezed hers. He smiled at her. Still, no sign of worry etched his eyes.

The blood drained from Edward's face. His eyes shifted between her and Cal. "How is it you got into this line of work?"

Cal let go of her hand to lace his fingers together at his knees. "I was in the military and worked recon for several years. That's where I met Ethan and Nate. Both of them helped to keep Lana safe and work on this investigation. After a while I realized I had a knack for contract work, and I began to freelance."

Edward raised an eyebrow. "That's dangerous work."

Cal nodded. "It is. But I want you to know that I have Lana's best interests at heart." His fingers reached over to squeeze her knee. He turned his attention back to her father. "I will be retiring from my career." He looked over at Lana and smiled. "I've always wanted to open a mixed martial arts training gym. I have a significant amount of experience and several belts in various arts of fighting."

Edward nodded slowly. Lana bit her lip to hide her smile. Something like mixed martial arts was so foreign to her father. He turned his eyes to Lana and held her gaze. A small, tight smile hinted at the corners of his mouth. "I suppose you're here to tell me that you're moving out."

She took a deep breath through her nose. Shit. She and Cal hadn't really discussed their living arrangements. Cal's hand reached for hers again. Its warmth gave her strength. Cal loved her. That was all that mattered.

She lifted her chin and squared her shoulders. "Yes, Dad. I'm moving out." She looked at Cal as heat crept into her cheeks. He grinned at her. "I love him."

Edward's mouth opened and snapped shut. He scratched his jaw with the back of his knuckles. "Well, then. I suppose that's settled." He pressed his hands to his knees and stood. "Coffee, anyone?"

Cal stood and followed him to the kitchen. She massaged her temples. What just happened? A weight lifted from her chest. She peered over her shoulder. As Edward fixed their coffees, Cal was answering something he'd asked about his time in the military.

Happiness flooded through her. All this time, she'd been so worried about Cal fitting into her world and being accepted. And she had been wrong. Her parents hadn't judged him. Relief washed over her like a warm shower. She didn't need to hide or pretend to be someone she wasn't. She didn't have to choose between her family and the man she loved. It was over. The pain and fear of the past week wouldn't disappear overnight. But she was on the mend, and excitement sent a flurry of warmth through her body. She was ready to start her new life with Cal.

He winked at her when she finally made her way to the kitchen. They enjoyed a coffee with her father, and then Cal walked her out to her suite to grab some of her belongings.

She sank the key her dad had given her into the lock and swung the door open. Cal looked around the small space as she flicked the lights on.

"I won't be long."

"Take your time."

It was eerie being home. All her things remained untouched, unaffected by the changes that had shaken up her world. Cal took a seat on the floral-patterned couch. She disappeared into her room. Had it really been a week ago that Cal had kidnapped her? A smile touched her lips as she pulled her gym bag from the closet and began to fill it. She had put up such a fight in the beginning—and now she was moving in with him.

She opened her panty drawer. A thrill raced over her. She held up her sexiest pair of mauve panties. Cal would like these. And the matching bra. Having her own things, her own style, back was such a luxury.

She packed as many clothes as she could fit, then grabbed her personal items from the bathroom. She half-dragged the bag to the living room. Cal switched the TV off.

"All set?" He stood and took the bag from her hand. "Jesus, what did you pack—bricks?"

She giggled. "No. Just a few things to get me by for a while." Slowly, she stepped closer to him. Her fingers twined with his T-shirt. "Are you sure you want me to move in?"

He laughed. His eyes twinkled at her mischievously. He circled his hands around her waist and pulled her against him. "Now you decided to ask?"

Her mouth hung open. "I—"

He tweaked her nose. "I'm teasing." His eyes turned serious, but his grin remained. "I'm glad you knew that's what I wanted. Your dad took everything really well."

She rested her head against his chest. He pressed a kiss to her forehead. "I feel bad that he'll be here all alone."

Cal stiffened. "You want to stay?"

She lifted her chin to look at him. "No."

He brushed her hair over her shoulder. "We'll visit often, okay? We're not far away at all."

"I know. I'd like to see my mom today, too."

"Absolutely."

She pinched his abs. "Okay, let's go."

"Wait a minute." His arm circled her waist, and he pulled her back in place. His fingers threaded into her hair as he pressed his lips to her mouth. She tightened her grip on his waist. His tongue parted her teeth, and her toes curled. The world tilted. He lifted her in his arms, and her ankles locked at the small of his back.

Lana laughed. "Cal, we can't do this here."

He nuzzled her neck. "Let's get home, then."

She grinned down at him. Her teeth nipped her bottom lip. "That has a nice ring to it." He lowered her to her feet. He lifted her bag, and she clung to his free hand. Together, they left her suite and got into his truck.

The excitement of their future rippled through her. She was going home.

Epilogue

Her breath caught in her throat. Her hand clamped over her mouth. Oh God.

Tears stung her eyes. She took a deep, steadying breath and stared at the tiny screen on the pregnancy test.

Two pink lines.

She was pregnant.

She sat down on the closed toilet seat lid and tried to slow the rapid beating of her heart. It had been more than six months since the whole fiasco had been over with. It wasn't until yesterday that she realized her period hadn't come. She'd checked her calendar, and sure enough, it was two weeks late.

She was pregnant...with Cal's baby. Happiness flooded through her. She bit her lip. A dark fire took over her. What if Cal wasn't happy? Before, he'd said that one day he wanted a wife and kids. That didn't mean today. She loved living here with Cal; it felt more like home to her than her father's ostentatious mansion ever had. She loved waking up to the warmth of his body.

Everything had fallen into place. With the persistence of Nate, Andrea Reid's case had been reopened, and Tanner was now being charged. Shawn had turned out to have an even darker past, which explained his suicide that fateful night. Grace, too, had confessed her plan to murder Lana. She was looking at a long prison sentence. After taking some time out to cope, Lana had gone back to work, and now Cal's MMA training gym was under construction. In a few months, it would be open, and already he had a growing list of athletes waiting to join. Nate and Ethan had been a big help in recruiting members, and several were FBI agents.

After she finished work last night, she'd stopped at the drugstore to pick up a pregnancy test. She hadn't wanted to worry Cal, so she didn't mention it. Now it was Saturday morning and he lay in bed asleep. She had to tell him. It couldn't wait.

She clutched the test in her hand and exited the bathroom. Maggie, their new pitbull rescue dog, lifted her head from her bed near the window. Her chocolate eyes scanned Lana with sleepy disinterest before dropping back down.

She tiptoed over the cool floor and climbed into bed. Cal's arm draped over his eyes, his chest bare like the rest of him beneath the blankets. She tucked the test under her pillow and cuddled next to him. He stirred, and his arms stretched above his head before he closed her into his warmth.

"Morning, babe." His voice was deep and husky with sleep. Her hand rubbed against his stubble.

She forced a smile. "Good morning."

He looked at the clock beside him; it read just after 7 a.m. "Geez, I slept in today." He smiled down at her. "I blame you for that."

She giggled. "Blame yourself. You're insatiable."

He rolled on his side so he faced her. "'Insatiable'? No way. You satisfy me every time."

"I'm grateful for the review."

He tweaked her nose. Her gaze fell to his chest.

"Hey, what's the matter?"

She kept her gaze down. Tears stung her eyes. Dammit, she didn't want to cry. Her hand moved under the blanket to rest on her tummy. A fierce love for the tiny baby growing inside her flooded her chest. If Cal was anything less than happy, she wouldn't be able to handle it. No way in hell would she let her baby feel anything but acceptance.

Cal rolled onto his stomach to look down at her. "Lana, you're scaring me. What's the matter?"

She met his warm green eyes. Love poured from his soul, and concern etched the lines of his face. If he loved her at all, he would love their baby without hesitation. She sniffed and wiped her eyes. She swallowed over the constriction in her throat.

"I have something to tell you."

She pushed herself into a sitting position. Cal sat erect next to her. His hand closed over hers. She pulled the blankets up to cover her nakedness and wet her lips.

"Baby, whatever it is, you can tell me."

She nodded. Her throat tightened. Her mouth opened and closed. His hand squeezed hers impatiently, urging her. She had to tell him. She turned, reached under the pillow, then handed him the pregnancy test.

His eyes fell to her hand. His face froze. Slowly, as if it was made of fine china, he accepted the stick. He let her fingers go and held the test in both of his hands. His eyes searched the screen over and over, as hers had.

He swallowed. His Adam's apple bobbed. The stick lowered to the bed. "You're pregnant?"

Tears spilled over her lids to roll down her cheeks, but she didn't wipe them away. She nodded.

"We're going to have a baby?" His eyes fell to her covered tummy. "Now?"

Lana laughed. The sound shook out of her tangle of nerves. "Well, not today. In about eight months or so."

"Jesus," he breathed. His hands raked over his shaved head. "Holy shit." His lips lifted. His smile froze. "Honey, you're not happy?"

She couldn't stop the tears. Cal pulled her onto his lap; his hands caressed her bare spine as he pressed her face to his throat. "Baby, tell me why you're upset." His body tensed. "You don't want to have a baby?"

She tore herself away from him. Her hand still held her flat tummy. "I do. More than anything. I just—I don't want you to feel trapped. I was so scared that you wouldn't be happy."

He tucked her hair behind her ear. "Are you crazy? Why wouldn't I be happy?" His hand came around to rest on her belly, replacing hers. "I love you. And I love our baby."

Relief washed over her with the force of a tidal wave. Her arms closed around his neck. She breathed in his musky scent. God, she loved him. "You're amazing."

He laughed. "You know, I had something I wanted to talk to you about before you so rudely broke this news to me."

She pulled away. Her eyes narrowed at him. "What?"

He reached under his pillow and pulled out a small black box. Her breath caught. Her eyes met his. They sparked with mischief. His thumb moved to the lid of the box, prying it open.

"Lana, will you marry me?"

Her hands closed over her mouth. She stared down at the sparkling diamond ring. A wave of giddiness vibrated through her. Cal was proposing…and they were having a baby. Fresh tears sprang to her eyes, happy ones. She nodded wildly. He chuckled, pulled the ring from the box, and took her left hand. He slid it over her ring finger.

"Still worried you're trapping me?"

She laughed and dashed her tears away. "Not anymore."

His hand slid to her bare shoulder and cupped the back of her neck. "You make me so damn happy, honey. The only thing that would excite me more is if we found out we were having twins."

Her eyes widened. She shook her head. "I don't know about that." He laughed and tumbled over her onto the bed.

"Maybe we can make it happen if we hurry."

She laughed. Giggles racked her body—until Cal moved over her, his lips hot with need on hers. Her chest expanded, and every void she'd every carried her entire life had closed up. Everything she'd ever wanted in her life had come together over the last few minutes. He was everything to her...and now, their baby was, too.

Up next in the Dangerous Distractions series

BAIT

Former military and ex–FBI agent Ethan Worth is searching for a new way to serve and protect. On a break in Beaufort, North Carolina, he may have just found it. It starts with saving a tipsy damsel in distress from a shady troublemaker. But it ends with the surprisingly sober beauty outraged by his rescue. That's all Ethan needs for his expert instincts to kick into high gear . . .

Riley Jones is back in Beaufort for one reason only: to find her missing best friend, Hanna. If that means using herself as bait for the kind of guy who'd prey on a vulnerable young woman, so be it. She doesn't need a rugged knight in shining armor like Ethan distracting her, and she doesn't want his help. But it turns out she needs it. And together, as the heat between them rises, so does the danger. Until both their lives are on the line . . .

About the Author

Photo credit: Daunine McLauchlin/Sol Tree Studios

Samantha Keith resides in Saskatchewan, Canada, with her husband and brilliant daughter, who share her love of literature. Teddy, the family multi-poo, completes her family. Samantha writes steamy, fast-paced, romantic suspense novels in the rare moments she has uninterrupted—even interrupted, she manages to apply words to paper. Aside from her love of writing, her other interests include cooking vegan meals and creating recipes. *Abducted* came in first place in the romantic suspense category for the Heartland Romance Authors' Show Me the Spark Contest. Connect with Samantha online at:

AuthorSamanthaKeith.com
Facebook.com/AuthorSamanthaKeith
Twitter.com/AuthorSamantha

Printed in the United States
by Baker & Taylor Publisher Services